MELANIE YOUNG

WITH FOREWORDS BY MAF
AND ELIZABETH CHABNER THO

getting
Thi f
my
Chest

A SURVIVOR'S GUIDE

to **STAYING**
FEARLESS & **FABULOUS**
IN THE FACE
of **BREAST CANCER**

PLAIN SIGHT PUBLISHING
AN IMPRINT OF CEDAR FORT, INC.
SPRINGVILLE, UT

In Memory

Melvin Asher Young
Julie Gandle

ISBN 13: 978-1-4621-1323-1

Published by Plain Sight Publishing, an imprint of Cedar Fort, Inc.
2373 W. 700 S., Springville, UT 84663
Distributed by Cedar Fort, Inc., www.cedarfort.com

Cover design by Angela D. Olsen
Cover design © 2013 by Lyle Mortimer
Edited and typeset by Whitney Lindsley

Printed in the United States of America

10 9 8 7 6 5 4 3 2 1

THE INFORMATION AND RESOURCES PROVIDED IN THIS BOOK are intended to be used as helpful information based on the author's experience and interviews with other breast cancer survivors and experts on the topics discussed. This book is not intended to serve as a medical reference or medical advice regarding any reader's diagnosis and treatment. Patients should consult with their own physician(s) on all matters related to diagnosis, medical condition, treatment, and side effects, including any allergies, side effects, or other conditions experienced before, during, or after treatment.

Medical advancements and legal issues in cancer testing, diagnosis, treatment, and medication continue to evolve. Patients should discuss any and all updates and new developments with their physician to stay up-to-date.

Neither the author nor publisher is responsible for any damages resulting from any health risk, side effect, action, or consequence to any person who reads this book. Resources provided at the end of this book are intended as helpful information and not as endorsements. Information contained may be subject to change.

Every cancer patient's condition and treatment is unique to that person. Readers should not compare their condition and reactions to treatment to the author. Always seek professional medical advice from your physician.

PRAISE FOR

Getting Things Off My Chest

"Melanie's frank depiction of her personal journey will empower other women facing breast cancer to feel more in control of their lives during this difficult time. Readers will find helpful advice to make personal decisions, get better organized, and improve how they look and feel as they manage treatment."

Jacqueline Reinhard, executive director, SHARE: Self-Help for
Women with Breast or Ovarian Cancer

"Melanie Young's approach to facing the challenges of a breast cancer diagnosis is an inspiration for any woman dealing with her own diagnosis. Her humor, strength, and professionalism in the face of such personal adversity is a lesson that every woman can apply to her own life."

Lynnette Marrero and *Ivy Mix*, cofounders, Speed-Rack

"I watched Melanie expertly handle her own diagnosis, treatment, and now survivorship with grace and humor. Her book offered hard-earned wisdom and practical advice for living a fuller life throughout the cancer journey and coming out on the other side a stronger and healthier person. While medical treatment is essential for combating cancer, so too, is a positive 'can do,' take-control attitude, Melanie provides a road map on how it's done."

Susan Bratton, founder, Meals to Heal

"Melanie Young has been a force in the food and beverage industry, and she is now using her abundant energy to focus on helping women with breast cancer to make smart, confident choices and to take better care of themselves. This book will be a tremendous resource for the newly diagnosed and for their caregivers."

Marc Murphy, chef and owner, Benchmarc Restaurants

"Melanie's book, *Getting Things Off My Chest*, based on Melanie's firsthand experience facing cancer, is an invaluable primer to help newly diagnosed women."

Anita Lo, chef/owner, Annisa restaurant, and *Iron Chef* champion

Contents

Section 3

Section 4

Acknowledgments

I T TOOK LOSING MY BREASTS TO FIND MY VOICE. I ALWAYS had a voice, but working as a communications specialist meant that it was usually busy putting words into other individuals' mouths. A year after I completed my treatment for breast cancer, having kept my diagnosis under wraps during that time, I began writing for therapy and speaking out as an advocate for the empowerment of women. I continue to write to inspire women to face challenges head-on and to be fearless and fabulous no matter what is placed in front of them. There are no road-blocks to getting somewhere—just annoying detours to navigate around. Whatever you do and wherever you go, just try to enjoy the ride.

I'd like to thank the following people who joined the ride and helped me navigate my own journey:

- My husband and loving caregiver, David Ransom

- My mother, Sonia Young, a.k.a. The Purple Lady, who taught me to be fabulous

- My late father, Melvin Asher Young, who taught me to be fearless

- My agent and friend, Bonnie Tandy Leblang

- My breast cancer mentor, Melanie Grisanti

- The talented doctors at Memorial Sloan-Kettering Cancer Center, who treated me and made me listen (for once!)

ACKNOWLEDGMENTS

- The survivors who reached out to share their wisdom
- The experts who shared their time and knowledge for this book
- My friends and family members, who formed my support network
- The editors at Cedar Fort, Inc., who heard my voice and responded
- Photographers Jennifer Mitchell and Charise Isis, who documented my transformation

Forewords

ELIZABETH CHABNER THOMPSON, MD, MPH
FOUNDER/CEO, BFFL CO

I CAN USUALLY TELL WITHIN MINUTES OF MEETING SOMEONE if they have passion for what they do. "What they do" is often a tricky thing to figure out. For the lucky among us, it's our work, family, sport, or craft. When I met Susan Bratton, I knew right away that she and I were both lucky enough to work in our passions. Then Susan introduced me to Melanie, whose energy instantly shouted "passionate, hardworking, and completely devoted" to her mission—helping women with the difficult mental and physical challenges of breast cancer. Melanie met me in my office, and we discussed our paths and got things "off our chest." We even discussed our very different reconstructions. Her 410s were hard and never moved; my Mentor rounds looked like grapefruits. Neither of us were 100 percent satisfied with what we had in place of our natural breasts, but who cared? The risk was no longer there, we hoped.

I spend some of my days as a radiation oncologist trying to cure women with breast cancer. But my passion is helping women recover after surgery. I was up and running twelve days after my prophylactic mastectomies. I told only my mother and one friend about my decision because back when I had the surgery in 2006 it was considered "barbaric self-mutilation."

"You mean you don't have the 'gene' but you had your breasts chopped off?" That was the question I heard when I finally opened up about my decision. People couldn't really wrap their heads around it. So I stopped talking about it. I had nobody except my mother and my dear friend Julie to confide in. During my recovery, my husband took care of the kids and worked. I kept it all "on my chest." Nobody could really tell that I had undergone surgery. I kept myself covered and kept my decision to myself until I decided to share my passion for recovery with BFFL (Best Friends for Life) Co. And that's when I met Melanie.

In 2011 Melanie had not gotten everything off her chest. But she had an idea to write a book about her experience and to help women. Then Christina Applegate, Guiliana Rancic, Allyn Rose, and many other brave women discussed their plight on morning television. Well, that certainly fueled Melanie's passion and her fearlessness to "get things off her chest." It's amazing how far we've come in such a short time. Thank you, Melanie, for writing this book for others, and thank you for including me in your passion for helping women.

MARIA THEODOULOU, MD
MEMORIAL SLOAN-KETTERING CANCER CENTER

Melanie has successfully managed her career with an attention to detail, correcting any errors to perfect her presentation. But how do you correct the error of cancer and erase it from the presentation of who you are? Melanie's reluctance to speak openly and directly about her cancer diagnosis was a self-induced silence, but this silence was short-lived.

During this quiet time, she listened. She found a way to integrate information given to her, move forward with what sounded right, and research what may have been in question. She listened to the information she received from her doctors, coming into the consultations after her due diligence, and leaving, knowing her homework was not over. She listened to the fears and strengths of others who had been diagnosed with, treated for, and survived breast cancer. By listening to these women who were or had been patients, Melanie developed her own tools to deal with the day-to-day ordeal she was now going through, finding the way back to her own strengths. She never lost her own quiet voice. This voice told her inner self that there was still humor, hope, love, and life in her every moment.

As she navigated her way through her surgeries, chemotherapy, menopause, and endocrine therapy, Melanie found her voice in her blog. She wrote with insight and humor and with an honest practicality. This book is the successful outcome of a smart, funny, sensitive, and sensible woman, and a testimony of a woman who lost and found her voice and decided to share it with all her fellow human beings. How lucky for the women diagnosed with breast cancer, their family and friends, and the clinicians who care for these patients. We are now listening to Melanie and finding our own better voice. Bravo, Melanie!

Overview

ONE IN EIGHT WOMEN WILL BE DIAGNOSED WITH BREAST cancer. Think about it: you could be having lunch with seven other women, and one of you could be diagnosed with breast cancer in her lifetime. According to the American Cancer Society, an estimated 232,340 new cases of invasive breast cancer are expected to occur among women in the United States in 2013; and 39,620 women will die from it, making it the second-leading cause of cancer death in women. Breast cancer is the most frequently diagnosed cancer in women, and there are nearly three million breast cancer survivors in the United States, including women who are in treatment or have completed it.[1]

In August 2009 I became "one in eight." I found myself offering advice and encouragement to the newly diagnosed, who, like me and so many others, started out confused and overwhelmed and not entirely sure what to ask or expect. You can visit doctors for medical advice, but it takes a real survivor to provide the *life essentials* for getting you through a breast cancer diagnosis, or any cancer diagnosis.

I am a passionate traveler and a pragmatic businesswoman. And, like many newly diagnosed women, I had a full life of family, work, friends, and community. When I received my diagnosis, my first thoughts and questions were these:

- But my last mammogram nine months ago was fine. How did this happen so fast?

- But I'm not sick! I feel fine right now!

- How is this going to impact my overall health?

- How am I going to fit cancer into my life and my already busy schedule?

- Will I lose my hair? Am I going to shrivel up and age?

- Am I going to be buried in bills, lose all my business, and go broke?

- How long will this take? When will I have my life back to normal?

The thought of losing my life was not at the top of my list; I was more concerned about how the *quality* of my life would be impacted. And I worried about becoming incapacitated from illness and buried in medical debt. Throughout my treatment, I focused hard on maintaining the best quality and balance I could muster.

LET THIS BOOK BE YOUR BREAST CANCER MENTOR

While conducting research for this book, I asked other survivors to share what they learned from their experiences. Almost everyone said, "I wish someone had told me what to expect," "My doctors were helpful with my treatment, but I learned how to deal with day-to-day challenges on my own," or "It was my cancer mentor who really helped me deal."

I had a great breast cancer mentor—my friend, another Melanie, diagnosed a year before me. She brought me a list of questions to ask my surgeon and taught me how to hang in there. And I hung on to every piece of advice she shared with me. What I learned is that unless you know what questions to ask, you can't be sure you have all the right answers. Your medical doctors and surgeons will treat your cancer and rebuild your body. But there is so much more to it! Looking back, I wish I would have known a lot more ahead of time.

Getting Things Off My Chest combines practical and manageable survivor's tips for challenging cancer head-on and managing your diagnosis and treatment. It's a book for women who do not want their cancer to control them. It's a primer for dealing with a health setback without letting your quality of life take a back seat. If you are buying this book, you may be newly diagnosed or have a loved one who just received the news and is facing tough decisions about her health. Or you might have a friend who is in treatment and needs a pick-me-up of a survivor's wit and wisdom and helpful tips and resources for taking better care of herself.

My hope is that this book will help groom the trails for your journey through Cancer Land so you can be informed, empowered, fearless, and fabulous!

NOTE

1. American Cancer Society, "What Are the Key Statistics about Breast Cancer?" www.cancer.org/cancer/breastcancer/detailedguide/breast-cancer-key-statistics. Last modified February 26, 2013.

My Experts

EVERY INDIVIDUAL'S CANCER EXPERIENCE IS DIFFERENT. This book is intended to empower you to make more informed decisions and help you keep your life in check as you navigate your own cancer journey. It is important that you do not compare your experience to mine or to anyone else's. The only thing you could not control was your cancer diagnosis. The rest is up to you.

While the intention of this book is to be a "survivor's guide," I reached out to my doctors and to other experts to provide their insights and to review the chapters I wrote for accuracy and professional perspective.

PHYSICIANS, SURGEONS, ONCOLOGISTS

- Margaret Chen, MD, FACS, attending breast surgeon, New York-Presbyterian, Columbia University Medical Center
- Joseph J. Disa, MD, FACS, Plastic and Reconstructive Surgical Service, Memorial Sloan-Kettering Cancer Center
- Sheldon Marc Feldman MD, FACS, chief, Division of Breast Surgery, and Vivian L. Milstein, associate professor of clinical surgery, Columbia University College of Physicians and Surgeons
- Jeffrey Hartog, MD, The Bougainvillea Clinique, Winter Park, FL

- Alexandra Heerdt, MD, MPH, FACS, breast surgeon, Memorial Sloan-Kettering Cancer Center

- Melanie Marin, MD, OB-GYN, New York Physicians, assistant clinical professor of obstetrics and gynecology, New York-Presbyterian, Columbia University Medical Center

- Maria Theodoulou, MD, Breast Cancer Medicine Service, Memorial Sloan-Kettering Cancer Center

- Elizabeth Chabner Thomson, MD, MPH, founder/CEO of BFFLCo

NATUROPATHIC ONCOLOGY

- Lise Alschuler, ND, FABNO, coauthor of *The Definitive Guide to Cancer: An Integrative Approach to Prevention, Treatment and Healing* and *Five to Thrive: Your Cutting Edge Cancer Prevention Plan*

ONCOLOGY NUTRITION

- Susan Bratton, founder/CEO, Meals to Heal

- Jessica Iannotta, RD, CNO, CSO, chief clinical officer, Meals to Heal

- Holly Mills, MS, RD, CNO, CSO, cofounder, FreshView Nutrition

SKIN, NAIL, HAIR, AND DENTAL CARE

- Kate Conn, program coordinator, The Wig Exchange, Westchester County, NY

- Mario E. Lacouture, MD, Memorial Sloan-Kettering Cancer Center, author, *Dr. Lacouture's Skin Care Guide for People Living with Cancer*

- Thomas Magnani, DDS, assistant clinical professor, Columbia Dental School

- Kattia Solano, founder, Butterfly Studio Salon, New York, NY

- Karol Young Moses, I. C. Artistry, makeup artist, breast cancer Survivor

PHYSIOLOGY AND MOVEMENT

- Martha Eddy, CMA, RSMT, founder, Moving for Life, New York, NY

- Brian Nathanson, physiology, New England Physical Care, Norwalk, CT

PSYCHOLOGY AND SEXUALITY

- Carla Marie Greco, PhD, clinical psychologist, Lifespan Psychological Services
- Barbara Musser, sex educator-counselor, author, *Sexy After Cancer: Meeting Your Inner Aphrodite on the Breast Cancer Journey*

HEALTH INSURANCE AND WORKERS RIGHTS

- Howard Goldstein, LUTCF
- Adam Paskoff, esq., founding member, Paskoff & Tamber, LLP, and former editor in chief of the *NYLS Journal of Human Rights*

PEER SUPPORT, EDUCATION AND PROGRAMS FOR PATIENTS

- Christine Benjamin, breast cancer program director, SHARE
- Rosalie Canosa, LCSW-R, program division director, Cancer*Care*
- Jane Levy, LCSW-R, director of Patient Assistance Programs, Cancer*Care*
- Helen Miller, executive director, Cancer*Care*
- Jacqueline Reinhard, executive director, SHARE
- Linda Tantwai, CEO, Susan G. Komen New York

PROSTHESES

- Kate Rubien, certified mastectomy fitter (CMF), Underneath It All, New York

LYMPHEDEMA

- Holly Miller, National Lymphedema Network

Numerous studies on breast cancer research, risk, treatment and health management exist, and since my own diagnosis in 2009, a number of interesting reports have been released. I cite several in this book. At the end, I list several useful resources to help you stay informed.

Introduction

DON'T **BE** PUSHED
BY **YOUR** PROBLEMS.
BE **LED** BY YOUR
DREAMS.

TUSCANY, NEW YORK, CHATTANOOGA, HONG KONG, HAWAII, Provence, and Bordeaux. These places come to mind when people ask me about my breast cancer experience. I own a wine and food marketing and special events business and work with many international clients, so one of the pleasures and perks of my profession is the opportunity to travel to beautiful places to learn and taste. As a passionate traveler and planner who likes to savor my experiences and drink in every moment, I research and pack for each trip with eager anticipation. I also document each journey with an assortment of diaries that comprise the story of my life: where I went, what I ate and drank, who I was with, and what I experienced and felt.

During 2009 and 2010 I took an extended and unexpected journey to a destination that had been visited by many before me. It was my first—and I hope last—visit to Cancer Land.

I felt the lump in my left breast on a business trip to Tuscany with my husband. Nine months earlier my mammogram had shown no issues.

When I came home to New York, and after I got the lump examined, my OB-GYN delivered the news on August 9, 2009. At that time, I also adopted a new family: the oncology specialists at Memorial Sloan-Kettering Cancer Center.

Friends turned my tears into laughter at their home in Provence shortly after I was diagnosed. No, I did not cancel my trip. I used it to calm my nerves and dubbed it my breasts' "farewell tour."

Before my double mastectomy, I flew home to Chattanooga, Tennessee, where I grew up, to see and say good-bye to my father, Mel Young. He had been moved into hospice with advanced prostate cancer and renal failure shortly after my diagnosis. I don't know what was harder: hearing that I had cancer or looking into his eyes for the last time. We buried him just after my second surgery and, thankfully, before he had to watch his only daughter undergo chemotherapy. My heartbreak at letting him go was a third wound to my chest, and the last to heal after my double mastectomy.

I turned in many hard-earned frequent flier miles that were intended for a trip to Hong Kong and Thailand to ring in the New Year and celebrate my January 1 birthday and instead booked a stay at the chemotherapy suites at the Evelyn Lauder Breast Cancer Center (the Four Seasons of breast cancer centers, in my opinion).

Midway through chemotherapy, I went to Hawaii to restore my body and celebrate my wedding anniversary. Juicy Hawaiian pineapples were one of my go-to comfort foods during chemo.

A year later, back with my friends in Provence and Bordeaux, I celebrated the end of treatment and tossed off my wig to unveil my spiky new platinum-blonde hair. It felt so good to toast to my health in France, a place that always lifts my spirits.

When I was feeling a bit low or prepping for chemotherapy, I mentally escaped to these beautiful places and others that I dreamed of visiting when I was well again. I maintained an ever-expanding bucket list in my cancer journal.

I always receive the best advice about traveling to a destination from people who have been there before me, so I've decided to share my advice to you on your journey to Cancer Land—including tips on how to prepare, organize and navigate your journey. It's an adventure trip of sorts that involves a huge adrenaline rush, lots of endurance tests, many highs and lows, bumpy rides, a few bouts of (e)motion sickness, dietary challenges, and, I hope, smoother sailing with a great companion and skilled medical captains to guide you. You can hang on for dear life, or you can gear up and prep yourself to ride it out and deftly navigate the obstacles. My hope is that when you reflect on your journey, you can say, "Been there. Done that. And I'm not going back. I'm moving on to the next adventure, and I'm choosing my destination this time."

MY DIAGNOSIS

I SEEM TO HAVE STEPPED ONTO THE WRONG STAGE

In 2006 my then-boyfriend David Ransom proposed to me in front of 2000 people. We were onstage at the annual James Beard Foundation Awards, the Oscars of the food and beverage industry, which I produced at the time. The surprise of his proposal and the hiccup of emotion took my breath away. A few seconds later, I gathered my thoughts and accepted. "I am starting a new stage of my life," I announced to the cheering audience.

I just didn't think that new stage would be Stage IIA breast cancer. "How did I get here?" I wondered. Granted, I was overworked, overstressed, and carrying a few extra pounds. And I had a lot of things weighing on my chest. My dad's prostate cancer had advanced, and he was given only a year to live. My public relations business was facing more competition than ever. The economy had tanked, and clients were not paying their bills on time. One of my closest friends died from metastasized breast cancer. My body was bloated, and my skin kept developing strange rashes. A tipping point was when a business colleague came up to me at an event, patted my stomach, and asked when my baby was due. I wasn't expecting that question or a baby. I knew something was off and consulted a nutritionist. But cancer never crossed my mind, and my mammogram in October 2008 was fine.

On a business trip to Italy over the summer, I felt the lump in my left breast and had it immediately checked out upon my return. My OB-GYN said, "I don't like this." Neither did I!

The core biopsy that she scheduled felt like someone was biting my left breast repeatedly. Gritting my teeth, I got up from the table, dressed and prepared to leave the Lenox Hill Radiology clinic as fast as I could. I was just about to walk out of the examination room when the lab technician said, "Wait a minute! We need to biopsy the other tumor."

"What other tumor?" I asked. I only knew about the one in my left breast. That's when I knew there was trouble. After I left the building, I called my husband and broke down in tears right in the middle of Madison Avenue. Then I gathered myself together took a long walk through Central Park to clear my head, and called two friends, both cancer survivors. We met at a French bistro, and they cheered me up over some glasses of chilled rosé.

WRAPPING MY HEAD AROUND IT

- As a traveler, I study guidebooks and plan routes to ensure that I take the scenic roads, learn insider tips, acclimate to the local culture, and memorize useful words and phrases.

- As an event planner, I make tactical lists and time lines to ensure all questions are asked and all details are addressed.

- As a communications professional, I carefully craft each message and image I want to convey.

- As a businesswoman, I look at the bottom line and decide when to invest to stay competitive and when to cut or save to be practical and stay healthy.

- As a human being, I know when to be strong, when to be gracious, when to realize my limits, and when to ask for help.

I used each of these skills to face my cancer diagnosis.

Diagnosis:

CONGRATULATIONS!
YOU ARE NOW
A CANCER CARDHOLDER

"We don't see things as they are; we see things as we are."

—*Anais Nin*

Digesting Your Diagnosis

"You don't know any more now about your life expectancy than you did six months ago. You were just reminded that it might not be as long as you like."

—*Elizabeth*, diagnosed 2010

MY DAD ALWAYS TOLD ME TO "STAY POSITIVE" WHEN things were tough in the business world. But *positive* has dual meaning in cancer lingo.

"You have a *positive* carcinoma" is med-speak for "You have cancer." It's the one of the few times in your life when the word *negative* would have been music to your ears. And from the point of diagnosis onward, it seems like anyone you tell will remind you to "keep a positive attitude."

Nearly everyone I spoke with who shared their story with me said the same thing: "The diagnosis took my breath away!" or "It was like a hard punch to the chest." It's numbing and frightening, and it puts you in a suspended state of disbelief and denial. You have the right to mourn and cry and scream and feel really sorry for yourself . . . in the beginning. After that, put on your best armor and get ready to fight the invader with all you've got. You have to hold on tight to your wits and your wit. You will want both close at hand.

FOCUS ON ASKING THE RIGHT QUESTIONS AND DON'T WASTE YOUR ENERGY ASKING THE WRONG QUESTIONS

QUESTIONS YOU WILL WANT TO ASK BUT SHOULDN'T BOTHER

Did I Do Something Wrong?

Try not to dwell on "Why me?" or "What did I do to myself to get cancer?" You will be tempted. Here is the list of reasons I was convinced my lifestyle was a contributing factor: excessive stress, a rich diet too much alcohol, weight gain, not having children, twenty years of taking birth control, drinking water from plastic bottles left sitting in my car all summer, a demanding work schedule.

Yes, many factors may contribute to breast cancer; in fact, you can read an entire list of them online at www.cancer.org and on many other websites. Looking back may give you insight and hindsight and the foresight you need to change any negative lifestyle habits down the road. Now is the time to use your energy positively to focus on fighting the cancer, getting through the treatment, and living the rest of your life in a way that reduces the risk of recurrence.

Will I Ever Feel Sexy and Desirable Again If I Lose My Breasts and Have Scars on My Body?

Maintaining a positive (there's that word again!) body image is one of the most important self-treatments you need to embrace to feel better about yourself as your body heals. Use this time to focus on beating the cancer and taking the best possible care of yourself inside and out. The tips I provide in this book will help you. Stick on your mirror a huge card to yourself that says, "Hello, Gorgeous!" and never think differently. In truth, if you didn't feel you were beautiful and desirable before you were diagnosed, you may not feel any different afterward. But it has nothing to do with having cancer; it has to do with how you view yourself.

Am I Going to Die?

Focus on living. Enough said.

Survivor Wisdom

It is not worth it to dwell on the path that led you to cancer. Don't play the blame game. Now is your chance to take control of the situation.

Ask the right questions, get the right facts, and decide, along with your team of medical advisors, how to keep yourself healthy.

- Having cancer does not mean you are contagious or untouchable.

- Having cancer is nothing to be ashamed about.

- Having cancer means that you need to be more pragmatic, have more patience, and be more positive.

- As a patient, you have the right to be informed and empowered.

- Cancer may be bad, but you are fabulous.

Getting Organized

FIVE CANCER COMMANDMENTS TO FOLLOW

IF YOU HAVE EVER PLANNED A WEDDING, PREPARED FOR THE birth of baby, or scheduled an extensive trip, you know the importance of conducting research, hiring the right specialists, organizing information, and preparing for the road ahead. Getting ready for your journey to Cancer Land is no different. By making a plan to manage your cancer diagnosis, you can help put cancer in its place in your life.

Here are my five commandments for immediately dealing with your diagnosis:

COMMANDMENT 1: MAKE A "HEALTH MANAGEMENT PLAN"

Contact the team of advisors responsible for your health and well-being. Tell them you have been diagnosed with cancer and discuss the best precautions and preparations. Here are examples:

OB-GYN: Your OB-GYN needs to be made aware of your diagnosis and you will want to continue seeing him or her for annual tests (see chapter 22).

Internist: If you have not had a full checkup in the past year or have delayed getting a flu shot, schedule these before you start any treatment. Prior to your surgeries you will undergo separate presurgical testing. Ask your internist if you should undergo additional tests prior to starting treatment, such as a bone density scan or a colonoscopy.

Dermatologist: Discuss topical treatments you can use for rashes and scars related to your surgeries and treatment. Schedule any other skin treatments before surgery or radiation/chemotherapy.

Ophthalmologist: Get an eye exam. Chemotherapy can toy with your vision. After treatment, have another eye exam. If you need a pair of glasses, get them fitted. Treatment can dry out your eyes and make wearing contact lenses uncomfortable.

Dentist: Ask, "What can I take or do to make sure my teeth and gums stay healthy during cancer treatment?" Later in this book I include advice from a dentist.

Pharmacist: Set up a relationship with a nearby pharmacist. Get the pharmacist's phone, email, and fax information so your doctors can easily call in prescriptions. Make sure your pharmacist has all your health insurance information, including co-pay amounts. Confirm whether your pharmacy is open twenty-four hours or can deliver medications, and be sure your pharmacist knows who is allowed to pick up your medication if you cannot.

Financial Advisor or CPA: Having cancer will result in a lot of medical bills. Ask your tax advisor if any of the medical expenses you incur may be tax deductible.

Survivor Wisdom: DECIDE HOW TO HANDLE PAYING THE BILLS

- Check with your credit card companies to confirm your spending limits and interest rates. This may be a good time to ask for a review to increase your spending limit to cover medical costs. If you do not have credit cards, look into CareCredit, which provides a line of credit for emergencies (www.carecredit.com).

- Ask your medical facility and health care providers what forms of payment they accept and if they expect you to pay at the time of treatment.

- Make a list of every bank account and credit card you have in case you are incapacitated and need to rely on someone to pay your bills.

COMMANDMENT 2: KNOW HOW YOUR HEALTH INSURANCE COVERAGE WORKS AND HOW YOU WILL PAY FOR YOUR TREATMENT

You may wonder why I am addressing insurance and finances at the start of this book. Here's why:

- Medical debt is one of the leading causes of bankruptcy in this country. Stay on top of bills as diligently as you stay on top of your cancer treatment. If you find you cannot manage your finances while you are undergoing treatment, ask someone you trust to help you organize and pay your bills.

- Cancer is a disease, but it is also part of an industry called *health care*. You need to understand the ins and outs of both sides of cancer, as they apply to your physical and financial health.

- One of the first questions you will be asked when you register at a hospital or doctor's office is "Do you have health insurance?" Bring your health insurance card and, if required, a referral from your primary care physician.

One of my first calls after I hopped out of the stirrups at my OB-GYN's office was to Howard Goldstein, my longtime insurance agent. I was an independent small business owner with a group insurance plan. I realized I didn't really understand how the plan worked in terms of a catastrophic or long-term illness. I wanted it spelled out for me: "How does my health insurance work?" "How is a cancer diagnosis going to affect my husband and me financially?" I asked Howard to provide me the details of my policy and a list of questions to ask the doctors I would be interviewing.

If you don't know what to ask about your health insurance, it can *really* turn to into a $64,000 question, because the costs for treatment and care run up quickly. Know how the system works.

QUESTIONS TO ASK YOUR INSURANCE AGENT OR
HEALTH INSURANCE COMPANY

- What are my deductible, coinsurance, and co-payments?

- What is and is not covered within my situation, and for what percentage of cost? Examples: breast reconstruction, physical therapy, specialized tests, medications, and so on.

- Do I need a primary care physician referral? If yes, do I need a paper referral in hand, or are these recorded electronically and made accessible to the specialist on the insurance company web portal?

- How many medical opinions are required for a treatment, and does my coverage include reimbursement for co-payment or other cost for the additional opinions?

- What are the co-pays for office visits, consultations, surgery, and medications (both brand name and generic)?

- Does my insurance cover a "full cranial prosthesis" (wig), and how many are covered in a one-year period?

- Will my health insurance cover a medical breast prosthesis and mastectomy bra, and how many are covered in a year?

- Does my plan cover naturopathic medical treatment or alternative medicine and for what conditions? (Plans and coverage can vary by state.)

- Does my plan cover experimental drugs or treatments? Often the costs for experimental treatments are covered by the sponsoring companies or organizations, since health insurance companies may shy away from anything "experimental."

- Is my coverage limited to my region, or can I seek treatment out of state? This will vary by policy and the kind of coverage you're seeking. Get it in writing. Check your insurance card to see if there is an "out-of-state" code or symbol. BlueCross BlueShield, for example, has a little suitcase on the card.

- Do I have an out-of-network plan? If so, how does it work?

OUT-OF-NETWORK PLANS = WATCH THAT OUT-OF-POCKET!

"The key health insurance pitfalls people face when dealing with a health crisis include not understanding their out-of-pocket responsibilities and not understanding how out-of-network charges apply to them," says Howard. The following are some questions to ask if you think you may want or need to go out of network for a doctor or treatment:

- What services and costs are covered out of network versus in network, and what are the differences in costs between going in and out of network? Often out-of-network benefits have substantially higher costs, higher deductibles, lower coinsurance, lower reimbursements, and higher out-of-pocket limits.

- What is the "usual and customary" reimbursement arrangement for your plan?

For out-of-network services you can have a "usual and customary" plan that can be in the seventieth, eightieth, or ninetieth percentile. This means that the insurance company will calculate the *allowable charge* for a particular service based on what 70, 80, or 90 percent of doctors charge in a certain region. (The eightieth or ninetieth percentile is best; at the seventieth percentile, the allowed charges may come up short. *Do not confuse the "usual and customary" percentage, which applies to out-of-network costs, with your coinsurance, which is your actual share of the allowed charge cost you will need to pay.*

- You may have a plan that reimburses out-of-network physicians on a maximum allowable coverage (MAC). If you have one of these plans, you may not be reimbursed for anything close to what you actually paid. As my insurance agent, Howard suggests you may not want to use the out-of-network benefits on a MAC plan. After your insurance provider applies your "eligible expense," deductible, and co-pay, you will be responsible for the difference. This gap could be significant.

- When facing a costly procedure, ask your physician for both the procedure or treatment code and the cost beforehand. Check with your insurance company to see if the "allowed amount" is in line with the charges. If they do not match up, contact your physician's office and ask if they will accept the amount that your plan will allow. If not, you'll need to cover the difference.

READ THE FINE PRINT

If you do any significant reading regarding your condition, make sure it includes your medical statements. Keep all your financial and insurance paperwork. Howard says this is important for several reasons, and his professional tips are listed here:

MAKE SURE ALL PROCEDURES ARE DOCUMENTED
AND THE NUMBERS MATCH UP

The insurance provider should generate a written "Explanation of Benefits" (EOB) for every medical claim. If you have a chronic illness, you need to save all of your EOBs because they will document how each claim was processed: the total bill sent to the insurance carrier, what they paid, and your total "patient's responsibility." These documents need to be compared to the actual invoice (not statement) from the physician or hospital to make sure you were not charged the wrong amount. This includes every test and every procedure. If your provider does not pay for something, it will be stated under an EOB code. Make sure you understand the codes. Most insurance companies have an online portal where you can sign up to access this information.

IF YOU SEE SOMETHING, SAY SOMETHING
SOONER RATHER THAN LATER

If you see something amiss on either the bill or on the EOB, contact your insurance company immediately to inquire. Most insurance carriers allow 90 to 180 days for patients to address and dispute claims. It is your right to appeal any claim. It is best to address the matter when it is fresh in your mind and before the insurance company decides you waited too long and will not entertain an appeal.

IF YOU DON'T UNDERSTAND, ASK SOMEONE TO EXPLAIN

If you see something confusing on your paperwork, contact your insurance agent to explain it. Some carriers will assign you a caseworker if you let them know that you are facing a major health challenge, and he or she can be your point of contact for any questions or concerns.

KEEP A FILE FOR TAX RECORDS

Being the daughter of certified public accountant (CPA), I ask a lot of questions about taxes and tax deductions. According to my current CPA, a person has to incur a considerably high number of non-reimbursed medical expenses to claim a tax deduction. At the time of this book's publication, these expenses must be in excess of 7.5 percent of your adjusted gross income. After December 31, 2016, it will change to 10 percent. Keep and log every receipt, including any out-of-pocket expenses for traveling to and from treatments and doctors' appointments.

A PRESCRIPTION FOR MINDING YOUR DRUGS

Depending on the kind of treatment you receive, cancer drugs can be costly. Here are five tips from Howard on how to save money:

- Know your drug plan, what it covers, and what the co-pays are for generic versus preferred-brand or specialty drugs.

- Does your policy allow you to choose generic in place of brand-name drugs? Ask what constitutes a "specialty drug."

- When your physician prescribes a medication, ask its generic name and if there is a less-expensive drug option that will work.

- Ask if medications from a mail-order pharmacy are covered and if the co-pay is different.

- If ordering medications from a mail-order pharmacy, ask if you can order a ninety-day supply versus a thirty-day supply. Ordering a ninety-day supply can save you money on co-pays and shipping.

LET YOUR FORMULARY BE YOUR GUIDE

The National Formulary (NF) is the official guide for drug standards in the United States. Many health insurance portals allow you to access and print company-specific formularies that you can review with your doctor to see if there are less-expensive options for the drugs you need to take. Most hospitals and pharmacists keep a copy of the Formulary in their offices.

THE AFFORDABLE CARE ACT: WHAT DOES IT MEAN TO YOU?

The US government's Affordable Care Act, which was signed on March 23, 2010, resulted in comprehensive health insurance reforms. The complete law and how it affects individuals and businesses can be found at www.healthcare.gov/law. While the outcome of the new legislation is still evolving, you should understand how the following things relate to your diagnosis:

- You cannot be turned down for health insurance based on a prior (preexisting) illness or condition, and there is no longer a preexisting condition waiting period.

- Everyone is required to have health insurance (or pay a penalty for not having it).

- Companies with fifty or more employees are required to offer a group insurance plan (or pay a penalty for not offering it).

- If you are self-employed, both the federal and state government will offer regulated plans. Review plan options carefully to decide what kind of coverage you need and what you can afford.

- There are no lifetime caps on coverage.

- Health coverage now includes preventive care.

- Young adults can be covered on their parents' insurance until age twenty-six.

Another helpful website that explains how health reform legislation works for both currently insured and uninsured cancer patients is that of the American Association of Clinical Oncology, www.cancer.net. This website also offers information and resources for managing the cost of cancer care and finding financial assistance in your community.

WHAT IF I CANNOT AFFORD TO PAY FOR MY COVERAGE?

If you cannot afford to pay for health insurance and need financial assistance, here are some steps you can take and resources to contact:

- Contact your city and state's Department of Social Services to ask what programs or types of financial aid are offered by the state you live in? This includes Medicaid if you qualify financially.

- Discuss financial assistance or payment plans with your health care facility.

- Contact your local American Cancer Society (www.cancer.org) or United Way (www.unitedway.org) office to ask about resources.

If You Need Help

I already mentioned www.cancer.net earlier, and the following are other helpful resources.

Cancer*Care* (www.cancercare.org) helps individuals who find themselves financially challenged while facing treatment. Cancer*Care* provides information on finding resources in your local community, and individuals who qualify can receive limited financial assistance for incurred costs such as transportation to and from treatment, childcare, home health care, and hospice services. The Cancer*Care* Co-payment Assistance Foundation can provide financial support for drug co-payments for qualifying individuals or can refer you to a list of organizations for financial help. See www.cancercareco-pay.org or call (866)-55-COPAY for more details.

The Cancer Financial Assistance Coalition (CFAC) offers a database of national and regional organizations that provide financial assistance and other services to people with cancer (www.cancerfac.org).

Living Beyond Breast Cancer publishes an online "Guide to Understanding Financial Concerns" (www.lbbc.org).

Survivor Wisdom

Stay current with your health insurance payments. If you stop paying your insurance bill, the carrier may cancel after sixty-three days of non-payment. It may help to arrange for an automatic payment plan. You do not want your insurance to lapse.

If you are a member of a professional or trade organization, inquire if there is a group health insurance plan for members.

COMMANDMENT 3: ORGANIZE YOUR RECORDS

Managing your cancer treatment is not too different from managing your household or business. First, get a loose-leaf binder to collect and organize your information. While keeping data online is convenient, you will receive a lot of paperwork from your doctors, hospitals, pharmacies, and insurance companies documenting your diagnosis, tests, treatments, and costs that you need to keep on file for your permanent medical and, possibly, tax records. You will need to maintain these things in your binder:

SECTION ONE: YOUR MEDICAL HISTORY AND PROFILE

- Full legal name (e.g., on driver's license or passport)
- Your contact information and an emergency contact
- Your age and date of birth
- Your blood type
- List of your doctors' primary and emergency phone numbers and the names of their assistants
- Identification numbers for health insurance and hospital patient accounts

- Calendar to log appointments
- Date of last physical exam and primary care physician's name and contact information
- Date of last OB-GYN exam and physician's name and contact information
- Date of last menstrual period—if you are in menopause, confirm for how long
- Current and prior medical conditions and dates treated—you will want to discuss each condition with your doctors to make sure your treatments and medications work together and not against you
- Prior surgeries (including all elective or cosmetic surgeries) and dates
- List of all medications you currently take and their dosage amounts and frequencies—this includes over-the-counter medications
- Vitamins and supplements you currently take—some vitamins and supplements interfere with certain medications, so be very thorough and honest about this
- List of any known food or contact allergies, including latex
- Family history of cancer, including great-grandparents and all blood relatives, and what kind of cancer they had
- History of smoking, drinking, and recreational drugs (and frequency)
- Sexual history and STDs
- Any sensitivities, irregularities, or recent changes in your body

SECTION TWO: CANCER TREATMENT RECORDS

- All doctors' contact information, including those who provided second opinions
- Lab tests and pathology reports
- Reports from each doctor for each visit
- Pre- and post-surgery and treatment paperwork and prep tips

- List of all medications (and any side effects) and foods to avoid
- List of side effects you experienced and how treated
- Calendar for appointments and note pad

This is your personal medical dossier. Bring this information to every doctor's appointment and update it as you start new treatments and medications. Arrange for your most recent mammogram, lab, and radiology tests, and slides to be sent to your breast surgeon's office in advance to allow him or her enough time to review them. Request a second set to take with you since you may need to leave the first set with your doctor. You will want to have a set available for the doctor who gives you a second or third opinion.

YOUR FINANCIAL ORGANIZER

Have separate files for other receipts such as out-of-pocket expenses related to your treatment. I have provided a list of examples below. Discuss with your CPA which of these expenses may be tax deductible if not covered by health insurance. I suggest keeping both hard files and scanned files. If you are inclined to use an accounting system like Quicken, set up a cancer management file. Listed below are the receipts and records you will want to file by category:

A. Treatment

- Medical and treatment bills
- Pharmacy bills and co-pay records
- Filed claims
- Processed and paid claims
- Your patient account number and, if you are paying bills online, your log-in name and password
- Contact and phone number for patient accounts at the facility where you are being treated

B. Out-Of-Pocket Expenses (Document What Expense or Portion Is and Is Not Covered by Your Insurance)

- Receipts for breast prostheses, mastectomy bras, wigs, and wig care

- Receipts for post-surgery medical supplies
- Receipt for transportation to and from doctors' appointments and treatment

Survivor Wisdom

Start your cancer battle armed with the right questions and plan to be as informed as possible. Keep your cancer clutter-free and organized.

COMMANDMENT 4: ESTABLISH A COMMUNICATIONS PLAN

"I joined a support group and realized that so many women of all ages, races, and backgrounds were affected by this disease and that perhaps I did nothing wrong in my years prior to deserve this diagnosis."

—Corina, diagnosed 2006

We have come a long way from the days when the words "breast cancer" were only whispered, but saying "I have breast cancer" out loud to people you love or work with is still difficult. Thanks to ever-increasing education and advocacy initiatives by major breast cancer awareness organizations, the whisper has turned into a roar.

"Susan G. Komen for the Cure completely changed the conversation about breast cancer," says Linda Tantawi, CEO of the Greater New York City Affiliate of Susan G. Komen for the Cure. The organization raises funds to support local breast health education, outreach, service, screening, and treatment programs for underserved and uninsured cancer patients. "Today, with the spread of awareness that started with Komen for the Cure, the stigma associated with breast cancer is gone, and more women are speaking out and becoming advocates. Now there are more community-based programs to help women who, for socioeconomic, cultural, or religious reasons may still be uncomfortable speaking up and reaching out for help."

Many women said it took several days or longer to say the words "breast cancer" without breaking down. I practiced saying it in the mirror. Still, I held my diagnosis and treatment close to my chest out of concern that people in my professional life would look at me as "incapacitated" or "incapable" and would turn away. It was not until well over a year after my treatment ended that I truly "got things off my chest" to my professional community. It took me nearly two years after my treatment ended to be able to say the words "I had cancer" out loud and publicly without choking up and with confidence, knowing that I had nothing to fear and everything to share to help other women face their own fears.

But I had a communications plan from the get-go! What's important is that *you* control your communications and decide when and what you want to tell people and who you want to tell. Early in your diagnosis, take out a piece of paper and address these questions:

- Who will I share the news with? (Break this into specific groups: immediate family, extended family, close friends, and acquaintances.)

- What do I tell my children?

- What do I say to my work colleagues?

- How do I handle dating (if single)?

- How will I juggle my treatment around my personal and professional commitments and explain any absences?

- What do I want my message to each of these groups to be?

I divided my groups into the following:

Caregiver: This person accompanies you to doctors' appointments as a crucial "second pair of ears," cleans your drains, administers medications, holds your head when you throw up, wipes away the snot and tears, props up your pillows, and makes sure that you are covered up at night and that you are properly nourished. This person is your physical and emotional rock to lean against and is in it to win it with you for the long haul. Usually this is a spouse, a parent, a sibling, or another close family member, but not always, so discuss it carefully with the person you have in mind. Your caregiver must be coolheaded enough not to become queasy or shrink at the sight of blood, needles, or strange liquids or smells. Sometimes even those closest to you cannot deal with this. Sadly, some women shared stories with me about their husbands leaving them during their treatment. It's harsh, but it happens. But, if people can't take it, you don't want them around anyway. You only want people who care about you by your side.

Share-givers: These people are your support network and safety net. They share their time to make your life more manageable. They run errands, bring meals and gifts, accompany you to treatments, organize fun outings to distract you, make you laugh, and take your calls at all hours when you want to talk. A share-giver respects your time and your confidentiality and understands that you may have ups and downs. These are usually close friends and trusted advisors.

Family Members: Family members may or may not fall into one of the above categories and you should be prepared for this. Also, some family members live far away and cannot be there for you day in and out. Some family members will handle your cancer diagnosis better than others. Some react with a positive "We're going to beat this!" attitude and become part of your core team of upbeat supporters. But others may have trouble processing what you are going through. Do not allow their negative emotions (denial, anger, fear) to cloud your outlook. If you sense that this is happening, ask your caregiver to intercede with the family member.

Your Children: If you have children or other dependents, be age-specific when you discuss your condition with them. Older children may want to take a protective role. Younger children may not understand why Mommy is too tired to play. You may want to notify your child's school counselor or principal so they can be sensitive to any changes in your child's behavior.

Your children can be the most wonderful support network of all simply by being your companions. Play board games, curl up and watch movies, ask them how their day is going, listen to their jokes, and so on. Think back on all the times before breast cancer that you may have been too busy for your kids and take advantage of any downtime to relax with them and enjoy their company.

CONTROL YOUR MESSAGE

Be prepared to answer questions in a way that is reassuring and reveals exactly what you want to say. Here is a sample statement if you want to keep things simple: "I was recently diagnosed with breast cancer. It was caught early. I have a great medical team in place to help me through it and will be undergoing treatment. I ask you to respect my privacy at this time, and I appreciate your concern and support."

People will ask you all kinds of questions. They will want to suggest "the best cancer doctor in the world." They will stare at your chest when they ask, "How you are doing?" They will mean well but sometimes will just drive you nuts. Realize that everyone will want to call or email you to check in. Unless you want to spend your time telling the same story over and over and answering a lot of emails, I recommend that you designate someone—be it your husband, your sister, or a close friend--to be your communications gatekeeper. That way, you can rest, regroup, and focus on making decisions about who is going to treat you and what treatments you will be undergoing. My husband, David, wrote eloquent status reports regularly to friends and family. Another survivor I spoke with said her husband made forty to fifty calls a day to update loved ones. My own time management tactic for responding to calls and emails from friends and family was to handle it all on one day. I called it "Cancer Fridays." Everyone was told I would take personal calls on Fridays to chat; the rest of the time I relied on my husband to handle the inquiries and keep loved ones updated.

You also have the option of sharing your progress within your network on password-protected community websites. Two websites to check out are www.mycancercircle.net and www.thepatientpartnerproject.org.

Survivor Wisdom

Control your message and try to control your time so you do not get overwhelmed.

DON'T TAKE THINGS TOO PERSONALLY

You will find that some people close to you may become distant because the C-word makes them uncomfortable or it brings back memories of a bad experience in their lives. I was lucky; all of my friends and family rallied around me closely. But one survivor told me her husband simply could not take it and left her. I watched my best friend succumb to breast cancer. One of her last wishes was to make amends with her estranged ninety-year-old grandfather. I telephoned him at his home in Florida and begged him to call his granddaughter. He refused, saying to me, "That's too bad." Then he hung up! Discussing my cancer with my mother was hard since she was dealing with a dying husband at the time. How much more did she need on her plate? And I don't think she really shared the details of my father's end-of-life struggle with me out of concern that I was under enough stress.

But you will also discover friends who become like family to you and acquaintances who step up to do amazing things. My friend Laura flew in from Hong Kong to host a belated birthday dinner for me since I had to cancel my birthday trip to visit her. My friends Dawn and Carol took the Acela train up to New York for the day to take me to lunch and shopping. My sister-in-law Julia sent me a note of encouragement before each chemotherapy session. My friend Melanie sat with me during the hours before my surgery. A business colleague, now a breast cancer survivor herself, sent me a beautiful survivor bracelet once she heard my story.

DON'T HOLD IT ALL IN

"I was diagnosed the day Barack Obama was first elected president of the United States. I was in Philadelphia campaigning with a group of volunteers when I received the call from my doctor with my diagnosis. I didn't say anything to anyone other than my husband or sister for days. I didn't want to burst the bubble of euphoria everyone was feeling. Looking back, I would have shared my diagnosis earlier rather than keeping it wrapped up inside my head."

—Melanie, diagnosed 2008

You may want to take a little time to digest the information internally, but don't let it percolate for too long. It is healthier to reach out, and those who care about you will appreciate that you did.

Most hospitals will provide a social worker to meet with if you so desire. There are also a number of organizations like Cancer*Care* that provide free one-on-one counseling with a professional oncology social worker who is experienced in working with cancer patients and caregivers. "When you call our helpline, you are connected directly to a caring professional who has expertise and training working with cancer patients. Through counseling, a social worker can help you make a plan to understand and deal with the challenges you are facing," says Rosalie Canosa, LCSW-R, program division director.

Peer Support

Many of the women I contacted said that mentors and other breast cancer survivors helped them get through their own experience. The wisdom of someone who has been down the road before you is something you cannot pick up at a clinic. A cancer mentor is different from a cancer support group or online breast cancer community. Each option provides support and insight but operates differently. You need to decide which option will work for you and fit into your busy life.

A Cancer Mentor is someone who has had a similar experience to yours. Your breast cancer mentor will be with you throughout your journey, providing insights, answering questions, and encouraging you. It's like having a personal trainer for dealing with your cancer. I was fortunate to turn to a dear friend to guide me. Organizations like SHARE, Living Beyond Breast Cancer, and Young Survivors Coalition are great organizations for meeting women facing similar challenges to you.

Cancer Support Groups are divided into two types. The first is led by a certified specialist, and the second is led by a trained cancer survivor. Groups may meet on a regular schedule, or they can be one-off sessions on a specific topic pertaining to diagnosis, treatment, or living with cancer. There are different support groups for women in different stages of cancer, age ranges, or cultural backgrounds. The sessions are about learning and sharing with each other.

An Online Cancer Community is where women with breast cancer can connect. Two that I have participated in are www.mybcteam.com, which is specifically for women with breast cancer, and the cancer survivor site www.IHadCancer.com, started by my friend and fellow breast cancer survivor, Mailet Lopez. Some of the sites provide online experts and all offer the chance to share stories. Like most social media, staying connected to the community and sharing your updates take time, and you may want to adjust your computer settings so your inbox is not overloaded with participants' comments. Also, online communities represent a wide range of socioeconomic, ethnic, age, and cultural backgrounds. It can be overwhelming getting caught up in the "conversation," and there can be a lot of emotional unloading. *Also, you should never measure your experience to anyone else's. You can listen and share but do not compare*!

To get insight on peer support, I turned to Jacqueline Reinhard, executive director, and Christine Benjamin, director of Breast Cancer Programs, for SHARE: Self-Help for Women with Breast or Ovarian Cancer (www.sharecancersupport.org*)*. Reinhard and Benjamin are both breast cancer survivors, as are all of SHARE's volunteers, who help you face the emotional and practical issues of your cancer diagnosis. SHARE provides a free telephone helpline, support groups, webinars, and educational workshops in English and ten other languages for women and men of all ages and ethnicities.

Benjamin says, "Breast cancer is not discriminatory. It affects women of all ages, cultures, and religions anywhere in the world. For all women a cancer diagnosis is life-changing. But among some cultures or religious groups, it can be devastating. A woman may no longer be considered marriage material if she can no longer conceive [due to ovarian cancer].

Some cultures teach women that it is wrong to touch their bodies (or private parts). Other women worry they will no longer be attractive to their spouses. Many are fearful to talk to anyone other than our volunteers. At SHARE, we will match you with a volunteer mentor who will stay with you throughout your journey and will check in with you to make sure you are okay."

To find support in your area, inquire through your hospital or through organizations like SHARE or Susan G. Komen for the Cure. Support groups tailored to different ethnic groups and religions are also available. I have provided a list of some of them in the "Resources" section at the end of this book.

> My husband and my dear friends were a wonderful source of support for me. However, when my business partner, Sandy Samberg, who founded SoleRyeders, a cancer support organization (in Westchester County, NY), put me in touch with at least five women who had just gone through what I was about to, my stress level dropped. These women could speak to me as no one who has not had cancer could. They made me feel like I could really get through this and gave me great advice about treatment options as well. The ability to speak to someone who has been through it before was a big part of why I wanted to create The Wig Exchange. (Kate Conn, program coordinator, The Wig Exchange, New York)

CANCER AND YOUR CAREER

For women in the workplace, the decision on how and when to tell your employer about your diagnosis is difficult. I ran my own business and faced the tough decision of whether to inform my clients and business associates. I feared I would lose business and have no means of income. I chose to keep things close to my chest and put my best face forward, plugging away at emails with an IV strapped to me and propping myself up at my desk to face the computer after chemo. I even had a new business presentation meeting four hours before I went in for my first chemotherapy session. I tried to be cool as a cucumber even though I was burning up inside.

Looking back, I think it was good for me to feel that I was conducting "business as usual." Fortunately I had a small staff that respected my confidentiality and a fiercely protective husband who worked with me. I worked from home and could adjust my hours and responsibilities to my energy level. My company also had a good health insurance program, and I have short and long-term disability insurance coverage, thanks to my astute father who helped manage my company taxes and benefits.

If you are salaried employee at a business, you are protected by certain legal workers' rights. For more information, I turned to Adam Paskoff, Esq. a founding member of Paskoff & Tamber, LLP, and a practicing attorney licensed in New York and New Jersey for over twenty years. Adam is the former editor in chief of the *NYLS Journal of Human Rights*, and maintains his law practice in mid-town Manhattan.

When Should You Tell Your Employer You Have Cancer? (e.g., Once You Are Diagnosed, Prior to Treatment, Only If You Think You May Need Time Off, etc.)

"Decisions about disclosure and other employment matters will be unique to each patient. You do not have to disclose any information about your health status to your employer if you do not require any accommodations for your job. However, unless you have disclosed your health condition to the employer, you are not protected by the Americans with Disabilities Act (ADA) and do not have the right to request accommodations. If you do decide to tell your employer about your cancer diagnosis in order to use benefits or request a reasonable accommodation, your employer has the right to ask for documentation of your condition, such as a letter from your doctor or a completed medical certification form.

"However, once you tell your employer about your health condition, your disability cannot be used against you. The law requires that any health information you give to your employer must be treated as confidential (private) with limited exceptions. One of the exceptions is that the employer can provide information to supervisors and managers if it is necessary for creating an accommodation. Remember, any information that you share with your coworkers is not protected. Generally, you should tell your employer after you have discussed with your doctor your treatment plan, necessary time off from work, and accommodations that can be made at work to allow you to continue to perform the job."

What Laws Protect You against Discrimination, or Being Fired, Replaced, or Demoted?

"The Family and Medical Leave Act (FMLA) provides eligible employees with the right to take unpaid family and medical leave under certain circumstances for up to twelve work weeks. The FMLA is enforced by the United States Department of Labor (DOL) and applies to employers with fifty or more employees. Basic requirements for eligibility include (1) working for the employer for at least twelve months, (2) working at least 1,250 hours in the twelve months prior to requesting the leave, and (3) a work site where the employer employs at least fifty employees within a fifty-mile radius.

"The FMLA can also be used for a reduced work schedule. When the need for leave is foreseeable, it is advisable to give thirty days' notice of the leave and to give your employer an estimate of its duration. The FMLA requires employers to place non-key employees in the same or a substantially equivalent position with equivalent pay, benefits, and other terms and conditions of employment upon their return. However, being restored to your job is not a certainty if the job was eliminated or if you refuse to return to your job after the leave.

"The American with Disabilities Act (ADA): Employers may not discriminate against qualified individuals with a disability (including cancer) from current or prospective employment. The ADA applies to employers with fifteen or more employees and is enforced by the US Equal Employment Opportunity Commission (EEOC). An employee must first be determined to be disabled before he or she can qualify for benefits. Cancer may be a disability when it, or its side effects, substantially limit one or more major life activities. Disability generally requires a medical determination and is made on a case-by-case basis depending on (1) the nature and severity of the impairment, (2) its duration or expected duration, and (3) its permanent or long-term impact. A covered employer is required to provide reasonable accommodations for the limitations of an otherwise qualified individual with the disability, unless the employer can demonstrate that the accommodation would impose an undue hardship. An employee needs to provide sufficient information to put the employer on notice that an accommodation is needed to address a disability. Once the request is made, an employer has the right to verify the disability, and usually an ongoing dialogue begins between the employer and employee concerning the need for and scope of a reasonable accommodation. Reasonable accommodations can include (1) job restructuring, (2) providing time off or a modified schedule for medical treatment, (3) modifying a workplace policy, (4) reassigning nonessential job functions to other employees, or (5) transferring an employee to a different position.

Union workers may have additional rights contained in the collective bargaining agreement. There may be additional remedies under state laws. Employers must comply with state laws that may provide more protection. A few states may permit paid family and medical leave."

Does the Size of the Company You Work for Matter?

"The FMLA applies to companies with fifty or more employees. The ADA applies to companies with fifteen or more employees. State laws may vary."

If You Believe You Are Being Treated Unfairly or Discriminated Against, How Should You Document and Address the Situation?

"Under the FMLA you would file a complaint with the Wage and Hour Division of the Department of Labor (DOL). A complaint can be filed in person, by telephone at 1-866-4USWAGE (1-866-487-9243), or by letter with any district office (www.dol.gov/whd/america2.htm). The DOL will investigate the complaint and issue a ruling. If you are in a union you can report suspected violations to your union representative. Employees also have the right to sue the employer directly for FMLA violations in state or federal court and an employee may be entitled to double whatever monetary damages were sustained. It is important to document all contact between you and your employer regarding your request for FMLA leave. Always keep copies of all of correspondence, including letters and emails. Request that your employer explain any FMLA denial in writing.

"The procedure for violations of the ADA is similar, except that violations are reported to the EEOC. Claims for a suspected violation should be filed as early as possible to allow for prompt investigation and resolution. Make sure to write down the facts involving the violation while fresh in your mind, including who you spoke with, when, and who else was present. You can call the ADA Information Line at (800) 514-0301 for more information or visit the ADA website to file a report. The EEOC will investigate and issue a ruling. Also, many states have created state agencies to investigate claims of family and medical leave and disability violations."

At What Point Can You File for Disability If You Cannot Carry Your Workload?

"If you cannot work at all and you do not have private disability insurance, the government offers Social Security Disability Income (SSD) and Supplemental Security Income (SSI) benefits. If you have paid into social security and are unable to work due to a disability, you may qualify for SSD benefits. You must first, however, meet the Social Security Administration's strict definition of disabled. Often applicants are denied benefits at first and must appeal the denials. SSD benefits are payable after six months of disability. After twenty-four months of receiving SSD benefits, you may qualify for Medicare. Cancer may qualify you for Social Security's compassionate allowance, which can speed up the processing of disability claims.

"SSI is designed to supplement the income of an individual or of a family in which there is a disabled person. SSI is available to families with a low income and limited assets. Like SSD, certain illnesses qualify for faster processing under compassionate care. The amount you qualify for varies from state to state, and from year to year."

What If I Am Self-Employed?

"Currently there are no alternatives for self-employed individuals with cancer other than disability insurance or job placement assistance (if the individual is well enough to work). There are general job placement programs through federal and state Department of Labor offices."[1]

As a both a self-employed business owner and a primary income provider, I was grateful that my astute father insisted I carry disability insurance even though I complained bitterly about the additional expense in my already tight budget. I did not need to file for disability during my treatment, but I learned a lesson about the importance of having it. I encourage self-employed individuals to think hard about the "what ifs" in their lives when it comes to choosing whether to have disability coverage and to do your homework on coverage options.

Survivor Wisdom

Don't pity me for having cancer. Respect me for being strong.

I finally came out of the cancer closet over a year after I completed my treatment. I told my story to my clients. Some were amazed and proud of me. Two said, "I wish you had told me. I feel badly for giving you a hard time while we worked together." My response was, "Don't feel bad for me. You should never give people you work with a hard time anyway."

COMMANDMENT 5: GET INFORMED AND
ASK MORE QUESTIONS

"Get the facts as they apply to you and ignore everything else."

—Elizabeth, diagnosed 2010

From the second you get your diagnosis, your mind is filled with both questions and anxiety. As you take your first steps into Cancer Land, there are a few essential steps that will prepare you for the trip to meet your new extended family—the doctors.

Here are a few important tips for your doctors' appointments:

- Plan on getting at least two medical opinions to make sure you are confident with your final choices.

- Arrive at least fifteen to twenty minutes early for each appointment to fill out paperwork, and then be prepared to wait.

- Bring a photo ID and be prepared to give your birth date over and over again.

- Bring your health insurance card and know your co-pay amount in advance.

- Bring your medical history profile to help you fill in the multiple forms you will need to complete.

- Bring your radiology and pathology films, slides, and reports to your doctors' appointments. This includes mammograms, CAT scans, PET scans, and anything else that may have photographed your insides. Also bring the written reports or arrange to have them sent in advance.

- Do not leave your slides with the doctor unless you have a second set. You will be meeting with different doctors to get multiple opinions. Once you select the doctor you want to handle your case, you can leave the slides with him or her.

- It is important to ask what health insurance programs the doctor *participates* in when you are booking your appointment. My insurance agent stressed using the word *participate* (as in "is part of") versus *accept*, which can be open ended. Write down your doctor's answers. If you have any questions about this, double check with your health insurance provider to confirm whether the physician is within the plan's network of health care providers.

- If a primary care physician's referral is required to see a specialist, get the medical code from the specialist and give it to your primary care physician. You do not want to get trapped in health insurance red tape. Allow plenty of time to get the referral; this is not a "day of" request.

- Be prepared to take a blood test. If you have a "better" arm (one at less risk for swelling, infection, or bruising) let the nurses know ahead of time. Do not sign any documents at the doctor's office that make you uncomfortable or commit you financially without talking to an advisor or your health insurance provider. This happened to me over one of my chemotherapy treatments, and I was fortunate to have a caseworker at my health insurance company to intercede on my behalf.

- If you are uncomfortable with anyone feeling your breasts or staring at them, get over it now. Your mammary mamas will be the center of attention. I found it helpful to wear easy-to-slip-on-and-off tops with comfortable pants to make the examinations go more smoothly. The hospital gowns—whether they are pink, blue, or cutesy seersucker—do not keep you warm and do not cover you up. Bring a sweater, scarf, or shawl for extra warmth.

- Bring bottled water or herbal teas and plenty of distractions for your wait. Ask if the clinic has free Wi-Fi so you can access the Internet and answer emails while waiting.

- Avoid talking on cell phones. Don't bring messy or smelly food to eat. Don't wear perfume. Be considerate of other patients in the waiting room who may be sensitive to smells and who also have a lot on their minds.

- If you have a cough or a cold, consider rescheduling. Cover your mouth and nose if you decide to go to the appointment. No one should be catching anything in a waiting room. Hospitals are contagious enough.

Survivor Wisdom

When you fill out your paperwork, you will be asked about assigning a health care proxy who can make decisions on your behalf if you are still in surgery or incapacitated. This person's name and contact information will need to be included on your paperwork. This individual should also have a copy of your health files. I created a list of important files (health information, insurance policies, bank accounts) and passwords for my husband in case of emergencies. Create a secure online file as well as a paper one. It will be easier to email documents to your doctors when you don't feel like going out and will be helpful for your caregiver to have a hard copy.

NOTE

1. These questions were answered by Adam Paskoff though personal communication.

Learning the Language

"Hello, I am female, age 50. Date of birth: January 1, 1959. I am DCIS/ ILC/ER-positive and HER2/neu-negative. There was no breast cancer in my family, but they say I am one in eight—pretty special, right? I am looking for a breast surgeon who is compassionate, tender, brilliant, well educated, and skilled with his hands. And I'd like to connect with women like me for peer support."

WHEN YOU VISIT A FOREIGN COUNTRY, YOU NEED TO LEARN the language, or at least some key phrases to get by. It's no different in Cancer Land. It starts with your annual mammogram, which *screens* for irregularities in the breast. If anything irregular comes up you will undergo *diagnostic* tests to determine if cancer is present and to find out more information about the cancer. You will continue to be *monitored* with tests during and following your treatment to check for signs of recurrence.

I have listed some, but not all, of the key tests, reports, and results that you will need to know. I've also included terminology for breast cancer detection, diagnostics, and monitoring. For more terms, I suggest checking out the website of the American Cancer Society (www.cancer.org), Susan G. Komen Foundation (www.komen.org), or Breastcancer.org, which has a helpful downloadable document called "Your Guide to the Breast Cancer Pathology Report."

TESTS AND REPORTS: WHAT DO THEY MEAN?

Have your doctor write down the name of each test you are scheduled to receive and explain it to you carefully. Ask your doctor the following questions:

- What is the exact name of the test?
- What is its purpose and intended findings?
- How does it work and how long will it take?
- How do I prepare for it? (empty stomach, intake of fluids, injections required, and so on)
- Does it involve radiation?
- What kind of discomfort will I feel?
- What will the test tell us?
- When will we have the pathology report?
- Please explain the results carefully to me and provide a copy of the results in writing.

If you have any known allergies, make sure to alert the lab technician. For example, I discovered—after developing an itchy red rash from my core biopsy—that I was allergic to latex.

THE PATHOLOGY REPORT

A *pathologist* will analyze your test results and will prepare a *pathology report* for each test for your doctor to review with you. (This is not to be referred to as a pathological report, which is what I kept calling it in my cancer-confused brain.) The reports may not all be completed at the same time since tissue analysis may take longer with some reports. It is best to schedule your meeting with your doctor after all the reports are in. This should be a face-to-face meeting. This way, your doctor can carefully explain the results, show (or draw) diagrams and pictures, and provide whatever else you need to understand the information. Make sure that all of your doctors and nurse practitioners have copies of the pathology reports, including all second or third opinions (these should be kept in your binder).

KEY TERMS

To help decipher some key terms, I turned to Margaret Chen, MD, FACS, Attending Breast Surgeon, New York-Presbyterian, Columbia University Medical Center. She shares the following:

"Breast cancer is not a single type of cancer. It is a collection of diseases with different behavioral and biological characteristics," says Dr. Chen. "Thanks to the advancement of *epigenetics,* the study of cancer cell progression, we can now look further into the genetic expression of a cancer and how its DNA interacts with proteins. The goal is to help understand the pathogenesis (origins) of the cancer, how aggressive it is, and how to treat it."

1. Screening Tests

The inside of your breast is composed of *lobules* (milk-producing glands) and *ducts* (tubes that carry the milk to the nipple). These are surrounded by fatty, fibrous, and glandular tissues. *Dense* breasts have less fatty tissue and more glandular tissue. Studies have shown that dense breasts are six times more likely to develop cancer and can make it harder for mammograms to detect breast cancers.[1]

According to the website Breastcancer.org, "One way to measure breast density is the thickness of tissue on a mammogram. Another categorizes breast patterns into four types depending on which type of tissue makes up most of the breast. Still, no one method of measuring breast density has been agreed upon by doctors."[2]

Mammogram: the most common screening test for breast cancer. The American Cancer Society recommends that you have annual mammograms beginning at age forty, but if you have a family history of breast cancer, you may need to start screening earlier. Uncomfortable? Yes. Worth it? Yes. One hundred percent reliable? No. But it is currently the best form of screening available when used in combination with self-examinations and regular breast examinations by a health care professional. Studies have shown that annual mammograms have reduced the risk of dying from breast cancer by 35 percent in women over the age of fifty. If your mammogram reveals a suspicious abnormality, you may get a *diagnostic mammogram,* which will screen the area in more detail.

BI-RADS (breast imaging-reporting and data system): The American College of Radiology's (ACR) standardized breast imaging terminology and reporting system was created to assess and classify test results for mammograms, ultrasounds, and MRIs of the breast to determine the level of suspicion for possible breast cancer. BI-RADS is scaled from zero (additional evaluation is needed) to six (known malignancy).

Mass: a suspicious lump that could be a tumor, a fluid-filled cyst, or an abscess. A *tumor* is an abnormal mass or lump that may be either *benign* (noncancerous) or malignant. A tumor that tests *malignant* is a *carcinoma* (cancer).

Your doctors should have reviewed several detailed photos and illustrations of a woman's breast (healthy and not) with you so you get the complete picture.

2. Diagnostic Tests

If your mammograms reveal suspicious growths you will undergo *metastatic workups* (diagnostic tests) to evaluate the carcinoma and see if it has *metastasized* (spread) elsewhere in your body. I am listing these tests in alphabetical order, not necessarily in the order they will occur.

Biopsy: the removal of tissue cells to review under a microscope. There are many types of biopsies. A few key ones to know are listed below:

- *Fine needle biopsy* (a.k.a. fine needle aspiration): fluid, cells, or tissue are removed with a fine needle. This is the least invasive biopsy.

- *Core needle biopsy*: a slightly larger, hollow core needle is used to remove a larger sample of tissue (cores) from the tumor. This is an in-office procedure; however, even though my breast was numbed, the procedure felt like I was being repeatedly bitten or shot in the breast. I guess that's why they call the instrument a "biopsy gun."

- *Incisional biopsy*: removing tissue by incision. These are less common than the other biopsies.

- *Excisional biopsy*: a surgical procedure in which the entire tumor is removed.

- *Sentinel node biopsy*: blue radioactive dye or radioactive tracer is injected into the tumor during surgery. The first lymph node that picks up the dye is removed. If it contains any microscopic particles of cancer, more lymph nodes will need to be removed. One of the benefits of a sentinel node biopsy is that it could reduce the risk of *lymphedema* (abnormal swelling of the arm).

Blood test: During treatment you will have blood taken and tested regularly to check your white and red blood cell and blood platelet counts. Many chemotherapy drugs may lower your blood and blood platelet counts, which can increase your risk for anemia (low red blood cell count), infection (low white blood cell count), or bleeding (low blood platelet count), not to mention cause you extreme fatigue and other symptoms that can put you at further health risk. If your counts are too low, your medical oncologist may prescribe medications depending on the specific blood count to counter the risk.

Bone scan: an imaging test to determine if cancer has traveled to the bone. Your doctor may order a bone scan test at the time of diagnosis and during and after treatment. This is not to be confused with a *bone density test,* which evaluates bone strength and risk for osteoporosis (thinning of the bones).

CT (CAT) Scan (computer tomography scan): computerized X-ray imaging that enables doctors to look at your internal organs. You lie on a gurney that passes into a narrow X-ray machine for a few loud and nerve-racking moments. Depending on the type of scan, you may be injected with *contrast solution* (dye). CT machines are very sensitive to metal so you will remove all jewelry and should alert the technician if you have any metal parts in your body.

Chest X-ray: These will determine whether any cancer has spread to the lungs. If you develop a cough (as I did after my chemotherapy ended), chest X-rays will also check for pneumonia or other inflammation in the chest and lung area.

MRI (magnetic resonance imaging): imaging technology that uses magnets and waves to examine inside the body. These are used for gathering more information about the breast area prior to surgery and for monitoring for recurrence after treatment.

PET Scan (positron emission tomography): a computerized X-ray imaging that can obtain images of the body's cells. These are used to determine if the cancer has spread to the lymph nodes or other parts of the body and to assess how metastatic breast cancer is responding to treatment.

Ultrasound (sonography): an imaging test using high frequency sound waves to check whether an abnormality found on a mammogram is *solid* (fibroid or cancer) or *fluid filled* (benign cyst). This is usually one of the first diagnostic tests you will undergo.

3. Monitoring

After treatment, you will undergo monitoring tests. They include, but are not limited to, the following:

Blood marker: A blood marker test evaluates how the body is responding during and after treatment and can check blood proteins to detect if there is any cancer progression. This monitoring test is administered post-treatment. You will also have regular *blood tests* (see under #2, Diagnostic Tests).

Bone scans and *bone density tests* (see Diagnostic Tests, *Bone Scan*).

Chest examinations: Your doctor will manually examine your chest wall and surrounding area for any suspicious masses. Your doctor should also teach you how to conduct a *self-examination of your breast area post-mastectomy*.

Mammogram: You will continue to screen with mammograms unless you have a double mastectomy.

I detail post-treatment health tests in chapter 22, "Post-Treatment."

4. Reports

Your pathology report will analyze tissue removed from your body and explain the nature of your specific cancer. Listed below are a few basic terms to know:

Benign: Absence of cancer (what we all want!).

Stage: Following your surgery, your cancer will be *diagnostically staged* on a scale from 0 to IV based on the size of the cancer, whether it is invasive or noninvasive, whether it was also detected in the lymph nodes, and whether the cancer has spread elsewhere in the body.

Lymphatic system: your body's internal network of tissues and organs that produce, store, and carry white blood cells to fight infection. It also houses lymph fluid, which helps filter and clear bacteria, viruses, and cancer cells out of your body.

Lymph node (a.k.a. lymph gland): Lymph nodes (nodules of lymph tissue) are located throughout your lymphatic system and are the "vacuum cleaners" for your lymphatic system, keeping it clean of unwanted substances (see above).

Malignant: Invasive and progressive (not good!).

Margins: The pathologist reviews your surgical margins, which are the normal rims of tissue around the cancer that was removed during surgery. Having "clear margins" means that no cancer cells were found. It may mean that no additional surgery is needed. Having "close" or "positive" margins means that more surgery may be needed to remove cancer cells.

Metastasis: Cancer has spread to other internal organs, bones, or lymph nodes in other parts of the body.

Recurrence: Cancer can *recur* (return) in a localized area of the chest or in lymph nodes adjacent to the breast.

Type of Cancer

Your pathology report will contain a combination of acronyms identifying your type of cancer. *Noninvasive* cancers are contained in the milk duct or lobules in the breast (carcinoma in situ). *Invasive* cancers may spread to (invade) normal tissues. The most common classifications of breast cancer are as follows:

Ductal Carcinoma In Situ (DCIS): Cancer cells are contained in the milk duct of the breast and have not spread to surrounding tissue. This is the most common type of *noninvasive* breast cancer.

Invasive Ductal Carcinoma (IDC): Cancer cells start in the milk duct but can spread into the surrounding breast tissue. This is the most common type of breast cancer.

Invasive Lobular Carcinoma (ILC): Cancer cells start in the milk-producing glands of the breast but can spread into the surrounding breast tissue.

Lobular Carcinoma In Situ (LCIS): While not really cancer, LCIS is defined as such when abnormal cells occur in the milk-producing glands of the breast (lobules) and have not spread to surrounding breast tissue. LCIS tends to be asymptomatic. An LCIS diagnosis increases a person's risk of developing invasive breast cancer, so surveillance is recommended.

Estrogen receptors: A type of protein in some cancer cells that attracts estrogen. When estrogen attaches to the cells, the cancers can grow. There are also *progesterone receptor* proteins that can attract cancer cells.

- *Estrogen receptor-positive* (ER+): Breast cells that are estrogen receptor-positive depend on estrogen to grow. Antiestrogen endocrine therapy is used to block the receptors to shrink or eliminate cancer cells. Most breast cancers are estrogen receptor positive.

- *Estrogen receptor-negative (ER-):* These cancer cells do not rely on estrogen to grow; therefore, antiestrogen endocrine therapy is not required.

- *Progesterone receptor (PR):* If cancer is progesterone receptor-positive (PR+), the presence of progesterone in your system can accelerate cancer growth.

Human epidermal growth factor receptor 2 (HER2/neu): a protein in the cancer cell that helps determine aggressiveness. A HER2/neu-positive receptor indicates that breast cancer cells could grow faster or spread, as opposed to a HER2/neu-negative receptor. Several lab tests delineate the HER2 receptor even further. These enable your oncologist to select the best targeted therapy to fight your specific condition.

Triple Negative: estrogen receptor (ER), progesterone receptor (PR), and human epidermal growth factor receptor 2 (HER2) all test negative. This type of cancer is generally not responsive to hormone receptor targeted treatments but it can be responsive to chemotherapy. Triple negative cancer can be more aggressive than other types of breast cancers and more likely to recur depending on the stage of diagnosis.

NOTES

1. Judith White, "Breast Density and Cancer Risk: What Is the Relationship?" Oxford Journals, *Journal of the National Cancer Institute*, 2000, vol. 92, issue 6, 443, doi: 10.1093/jnci/92.6.443.

2. Breastcancer.org, "Having Dense Breasts," http://www.breastcancer.org/risk/factors/dense_breasts. Last modified on May 1, 2013.

Nothing but the Breast

PREPARING FOR YOUR SURGERY

"I read Peggy Huddleston's Prepare for Surgery: Heal Faster *and listened to her relaxation CD."*

—*Lisa R.*, diagnosed 2012

PRETEND YOU ARE CLIMBING MOUNT EVEREST. WHAT DO YOU do first? Get organized. Do your research. Hire the best guide. And get in shape! Your cancer journey is no different!

When word of your diagnosis reaches family and friends, everyone will call with a recommendation for "the best breast surgeon," "the best breast man," and "the best hospital facility or research center." It can be helpful, especially when someone offers to make a call to get you an appointment with that must-see surgeon or oncologist, but it can also be overwhelming.

Who you choose has to make sense for you and not just for your friends and family. As I said to one caring friend, "But I live in New York, and my situation is not dire. I can't travel to Pennsylvania on a regular basis to see the person you say is the best in the world." Watch the hype factor. Just because a physician is rated highly by a local magazine or receives multiple awards, it does not mean that he or she is the right doctor for you. And Aunt Mildred's breast surgeon may not appeal to you either.

First, find a board-certified breast oncology surgeon and a

board-certified breast reconstruction specialist (if you are having a mastectomy and considering reconstruction). Start by making a list of doctors. Include their contact information and availability and the name of the person who recommended them, and then do some research. While I did not spend a lot of time online researching breast cancer, I did spend time researching the breast surgeons that people had recommended. And I asked hospitals for recommendations and bios for doctors. My health insurance agent, Howard Goldstein, directed me to Castle Connolly (www.casteleconnolly.com), which publishes a directory of leading doctors by specialty throughout the United States. Online rating systems such as Healthgrades.com can provide information on the doctor and his or her track record. Online ratings are not always accurate, however, and could be misleading since you have no information about who is writing about and rating the doctor. I follow travel and restaurant rating sites and know how variable they can be based on the person writing the review. If you use a hospital referral service, make sure you are speaking with someone at the hospital and not an outsourced phone bank. Ask to speak with an office or department manager just to be certain.

DO NOT SWEAT: THE DOCTOR WILL BE IN . . . EVENTUALLY!

Getting appointments with doctors can be nerve-racking. This is especially true in August (when I was diagnosed), when it seems like every doctor you want to schedule is on vacation. After convincing myself that an army of ninja cancer cells would not be advancing through my body within the next three weeks, I made as many "next available" appointments as I could for early September for the doctors I really wanted to see and then did what everyone else seemed to be doing. I took an already-scheduled vacation to chill out and de-stress at a friend's home in the south of France rather than cancel the trip and wait to sweat it out in the city. My motto was always "Keep going! Don't stop doing what makes you happy just because you have an unwelcome visitor in your body."

SELECTING A SURGEON

Find a board-certified breast oncology surgeon and schedule a consultation. Arrange for your lab reports, mammogram reports, and test films or slides to be sent in before the visit so he or she (mine was a she) has time to review them. Make sure you get his or her medical identification number if you need a primary care physician referral.

Your final selection for a surgeon should be based on the following criteria:

KNOWLEDGE AND EXPERIENCE

This goes beyond a doctor's "outstanding reputation" in the field of medicine. Many survivors I spoke with reported that some of the more famous doctors they met were also some of the least sensitive and communicative. Research online and see if your potential doctors have written articles or books on breast cancer or participated in seminars. And you can ask to see photos of their work when you meet. Don't be shy about this. Would you buy a piece of artwork without looking at it?

COMMUNICATION, CHEMISTRY, AND CONFIDENCE

- Does he or she look you in the eye? Does he or she answer your questions clearly? Does he or she listen to you and not cut you off?

- Do you like the way he or she explains everything to you? One doctor I met with showed me a PowerPoint presentation of a breast on a computer, and I did not connect.

- Is she considerate of your time? If you are waiting for what seems like an eternity to meet with the doctor, chances are that it is a preview of things to come. Some doctors will have their assistants call you to let you know they are running behind.

- How accessible is the doctor? Does he or she offer you her cell phone number or email address to make it possible to answer questions or address emergencies outside of office hours? Is his or her assistant friendly and helpful?

- Does he or she participate in your health insurance coverage?

- Ask for references. Can you speak with other patients he or she has treated?

THE MEDICAL FACILITY

- What is the center's reputation in the field of cancer?

- Do you like the ambiance of the medical center? Do they welcome you warmly or do you feel as though you are being herded around?

- How long does everyone keep you waiting?

- What is the billing procedure and how flexible are they on pay-ment plans?

- What is the culture of the medical center? Does it have a reputa-tion for being aggressive when treating a disease? Is it "my way or the highway"? Request a treatment plan.

I advise seeking a second opinion, and most survivors will agree. You will want to know every single option available to you, and having at least two expert opinions will help you make your decision with confidence. I interviewed three breast surgeons at three separate and excellent medi-cal facilities. All recommended a double mastectomy with an option for reconstruction. Because I was planning immediate reconstruction after my mastectomy, I interviewed breast reconstruction surgeons at the same time since the two procedures would be done one right after the other. All the doctors were outstanding but the two who connected with me most were breast surgeon Dr. Alexandra Heerdt and breast reconstructive sur-geon Dr. Joseph Disa, both at Memorial Sloan-Kettering Cancer Center.

The job of breast surgeons is pretty straightforward. They will review and decipher the X-rays, charts, and lab reports, and will recommend addi-tional testing. They will "stage" the cancer and explain it to you and recom-mend the surgery and follow-up treatment that she believes will be best for your condition. Long after your lumps or breasts are gone, you will continue to see your breast surgeon for six-month checkups and eventually for annual visits for about ten years. The breast surgeon's job is to make sure that no recurrence is lurking under your chest wall, incisions, or chest muscle.

MY MIND IS IN A FOG. WHAT DO I ASK?

Do not meet with the doctors alone. Bring a family member or friend. Your mind is spinning. You will only hear half of what the doctor is saying. Take notes. Have the person who accompanies you take notes as well and then compare them after you leave.

Ask if you can tape the conversation. Have your doctor draw pictures of your breast and illustrate the differences between lobular, ductal, in situ, tumor location, and other terms.

You should have ready the following questions to ask your breast surgeon:

- What exactly do you know and not know about my condition based on current tests?

- Will you please explain—slowly—the terminology (ductal, lobular, invasive, infiltrating, poorly differentiated, multifocal, in situ, margins, and so on) I need to know?

- What are the characteristics of my type of cancer? Does it tend to be less or more aggressive?

- What is my staging?

- What is my preliminary prognosis?

- What kind of surgery do you recommend? Do I have options and what are the benefits and risks?

- Do you recommend that I have more tests before proceeding with surgery? If so, what kind?

- What exactly is the surgical procedure you recommend and how will it impact my body? What is the success rate?

- What will be my "downtime" after the surgery and treatment?

- What is the chance of recurrence with this kind of cancer, with and without follow up treatments?

- When will you know if I need chemotherapy or radiation?

- When will you know if I am estrogen receptor-positive or negative?

- How will being estrogen receptor-positive or negative affect the course of treatment you recommend?

- Do you recommend metastatic staging tests and, if so, when?

- If there is a recurrence, where is it most likely to take place?

- What types of tests will I need in order to be monitored for a recurrence?

- Will I need mammograms in the future? What tests will I need?

- Do you recommend genetic testing?

- What would be the advantage of genetic testing? Are there disadvantages to this?

- Is there any option to avoid surgery altogether and just start with treatment to spare my breasts?

ATTENTION! YOUR SURGERY IS NOW CONFIRMED

Based on your tests, your breast surgeon will recommend the best surgical option for you between a lumpectomy and mastectomy.

LUMPECTOMY

Your surgeon may recommend a lumpectomy (breast preservation surgery) over mastectomy depending on a number of factors: size and location of tumor, size of tumor in relation to the breast, type of cancer, and any prior health conditions you may have. The procedure involves removing the tumor and the healthy tissue around it. Usually radiation is the course of treatment following a lumpectomy.

If your surgeon recommends a lumpectomy, here are some questions to ask:

- How much of my breast will be removed?
- Will any lymph nodes be removed? How long will I need to stay in the hospital, and what kind of downtime do I have at home?
- How will the lumpectomy change the shape, size, feel, and sensitivity of my breast?
- Are there reconstructive options for my breast? If so, what are they?
- What course of treatment will be required after my lumpectomy, and how soon will it start after my surgery?
- How often will I need to continue undergoing tests such as mammograms or biopsies after my lumpectomy?
- What physical activities can I do after my lumpectomy?
- Can I nurse a baby?
- When can I drive a car again?
- Will I lose any sensitivity in my breast and, if so, will it be permanent?
- What happens if the cancer recurs in the same breast?

MASTECTOMY

A mastectomy is the surgical removal of the breast. In a *simple mastectomy*, the entire breast, but no other tissue, is removed. Occasionally, a sentinel lymph node also may be removed at the time of a simple mastectomy. In a *modified radical mastectomy*, the surgeon removes the entire breast and the lymph nodes in the armpit. A *bilateral mastectomy* is the removal of both breasts. Your surgeon will discuss with you the procedure he or she recommends based on the type of cancer you have. If you are planning to have immediate breast reconstruction, ask your surgeon about your options for a skin- or nipple-sparing mastectomy, which helps preserve the skin around your breast.

One Breast or Two?

I liked my breasts just fine, but I did not like the idea that what was now lurking inside them could potentially kill me. Once I was told I had tumors in both breasts, my acceptance of a double mastectomy was pretty solid. Looking back, if I was told I would only need to lose one breast, I would ask my surgeon whether or not I should have removed both. This is a tad controversial because removing a noncancerous breast is considered prophylactic (since you are removing a healthy appendage). But my state of mind was this: (1) I did not want any chance of cancer spreading to the second breast, (2) I did not want to ever face the option of needing a second mastectomy, and (3) I did not want to risk being lopsided or uneven after reconstruction.

Discuss your options with your breast surgeon and weigh the pros and cons on having a single or double mastectomy. Ask if there are any other options or treatment combinations. One survivor told me she was so fearful about having a mastectomy that she chose undergoing chemotherapy first followed by a lumpectomy to preserve her breast.

If a mastectomy is the route you are taking, the following are some questions to ask your surgeon:

- If my cancer is in one breast, do I have the option of having the other breast removed, and what would be the benefit?

- Is there an option for a nipple-sparing mastectomy?

- Aside from my breast(s), what else will be removed (lymph nodes, muscle, surrounding tissues, and so on)?

- How will removing lymph nodes affect my lymphatic system and my arm mobility?

- What other presurgical tests are required?

- What are my reconstruction options?

- Does the breast surgeon work directly with a reconstruction surgeon?

- What should I expect during recovery?

- What are the possible complications?

- How long will I be in the hospital?

- How long will it take after surgery to receive my pathology report? Will it be sent to me automatically or do I need to request it from a special department?

- Will you send my pathology report to another hospital for a second analysis?

- What will the pathology report tell me about my type of cancer?

- Do you have other patients that have had similar treatments that I may speak with about the procedure? You can ask to see pictures showing the results of the procedure.

- What foods should I eat and not eat presurgery?

- What about exercise before and after surgery?

- How long will I be out of commission after surgery?

- When can I resume normal activities (e.g., work, driving, exercise, lifting anything over six to ten pounds)?

- When will I regain sensation in my chest area?

- What is the chance of recurrence in the breast area after a mastectomy?

- What kind of testing will I require after my mastectomy to check for a recurrence?

- After my surgery, when can I use deodorant/antiperspirant and are there specific ingredients I should avoid?

- When can I shave the hair under my arms or have my armpits waxed?

- How often will I see you for follow-up visits?

- Will you provide me with an emergency number and contact information for your assistant?

OTHER OPTIONS FOR TREATING BREAST CANCER TUMORS

For early stage breast cancer with tumors smaller than two centimeters in diameter there are some new ways to treat the tumor while preserving the breast. Columbia University Medical Center breast surgeons Dr. Sheldon Feldman and Dr. Margaret Chen outlined some noninvasive procedures currently under study: *percutaneous ablation* using cryotherapy to freeze the tumor, lasers to heat the tumor, and other thermal ablative methods such as radio frequency and high-intensity focused ultrasounds. In studies for each procedure the tumors were destroyed. The procedures take place in-office with minimal downtime.

WE CAN REBUILD!

The good news is that you have a number of great options for reconstructive surgery that can make you feel whole again. Most reconstruction options can occur the same day as your breast surgery if your doctors agree. I devote Chapter 6 in this book to reconstruction.

PREPARING FOR SURGERY

A few weeks before your surgery, you will visit the hospital for presurgical testing. It's also smart to book any personal maintenance appointments such as a haircut and color, waxing, or manicures and pedicures for before the surgery. If you are not a fan of hairy armpits, get yours waxed. You may not be able to wax or shave under your arms for a very long time. (See my list of questions for the surgeon.)

Try to schedule surgery for the morning. You can't eat or drink after 11:00 p.m. the night before, so if you have surgery in the later afternoon (like I did) your blood sugar may drop and you may become irritable. No one wants to feel cranky before walking into the operating room!

Your doctor will give you a detailed document ahead of time what to do on the night before your surgery. You should also prepare your home in advance. These are a few recommendations to help you prepare for your surgery:

INQUIRE ABOUT INOCULATIONS

If flu season is about to start, ask your surgeon whether you should be getting a shot before surgery or treatment. Likewise, if you live in an area with Lyme disease, discuss inoculation. Remember, you are about to venture into a new stage in your life, so you want to plan and do as much as possible before the journey to protect yourself after it.

Stock These Ten Items in Your Bathroom:

- A working thermometer
- Gauze and bandages (Ask your hospital for samples.)
- Unscented lotion for sensitive skin (Eucerin, Lubriderm, Abolene)
- Aspirin, acetaminophen, and Ibuprofen (Discuss which pills you can take for pain with your doctor because some of these are not advised before or after surgery.)
- A doctor-approved stool softener for constipation
- Corticosteroid topical cream for rashes or itching
- Antibiotic cream (Your hospital will give you samples.)
- Baby wipes or other unscented disposable body wipes (They will be your best option for cleaning your body when you cannot shower.)
- Biotene mouth rinse for dry mouth
- Hypoallergenic, fragrance-free cleanser and moisturizer for both face and body

PREP YOUR HOME

The nicest gift a friend can give you prior to surgery or treatment is a professional home cleaning service so you don't have to think about it. Your towels and linens should be freshly laundered and ready for you. Have plenty of sturdy bed pillows to prop you up and a small bell on the bedside table to ring if you need anything. After surgery you will not want to move around much.

If you have a pet, consider having it washed and groomed before you get home. Larger dogs that love to jump up and give you loving licks should be caged or kept in another room until you are stronger.

TAKE PHOTOS

"The best gift I ever gave myself was a boudoir photography session one day before my lumpectomy. I wanted to document what I looked like before I underwent surgery."

—Nancy, diagnosed 2011

Some people take photos during a trip. For this journey, take photos of you and your loved ones before you go. I did this for a couple of reasons: First, I wanted to document what I looked like before cancer since I had no idea how I would look after. Second, I wanted to have a happy family photo to look at during treatment. Third, I wanted to capture a particular time in my life before moving on from it. I cherish the photos of me, David, and my Maltese dog, Chance (who is now no longer with us), and am thankful for Jennifer Mitchell, a professional photographer who did this for us as a gift out of friendship. Looking back, I wish I had taken photos of my bare chest to remember how it looked.

LAST MEAL: MAKE IT DELICIOUS! BUT EAT EARLY!

The night before surgery, eat a balanced meal and drink plenty of water but no alcohol. Rather than being a bundle of nerves, have a nice meal with foods you love because you need the sustenance and you won't feel like eating much after surgery.

WHAT TO PACK FOR THE HOSPITAL

Travel light; hopefully it will be a quick trip. Wear comfortable clothes that you can also wear on the way out plus a change of underwear. Here are my suggestions:

- Your health insurance card, photo ID, and medical information.
- A loose-fitting shirt or dress with a front enclosure that is easy to snap, button or zip. After surgery you will not be able to slip anything on or off easily, and you will have drains hanging off a specially designed bra.
- If you are wearing pants, make sure they are loose-fitting and easy to pull up (think drawstring or elastic band).
- Socks (your feet will get cold).
- A clean shawl or wrap—waiting rooms can be chilly!

- A light bathrobe for receiving guests—I did not bring one and just wore the hospital-provided surgical robe with a shawl.

- A toiletry kit with face wash, unscented hand and face cream, hand sanitizer, mouth rinse, a toothbrush toothpaste, lip balm, and breath mints or sugar-free candies for dry mouth. Take absolutely nothing with perfume, and there is no need for deodorant.

- Do not bring any valuables or jewelry, including your wedding ring or good luck bracelets. You have to remove everything for surgery.

- Your glasses—if you wear contact lenses, you will need to take them out.

- No need to wear a bra! I tossed mine out and started fresh after reconstruction.

- A lot of women bring a good luck item like a photo, bracelet, or stuffed animal. Just ask someone to hold on to it while you are in surgery.

- Water bottle with a straw (some hospitals will provide "sippy cups")

- Healthy snacks like KIND bars or granola bars for after the surgery

- You'll want distractions while you wait and wait: music, an iPad, books (not breast cancer books!), crossword puzzles, knitting, portable Scrabble, gossipy magazines, or a writing diary. Keep your mind and hands busy!

GOING IN

The walk to the surgery room can be nerve-racking, and it's not like you can run the other way. I heard drumbeats in my head. Have someone walk with you to keep you calm. It will be cold inside the operating room. Tell the technicians about any discomfort you have (aside from jittery nerves). Inside, you will be positioned on an operating table with your arms wide open, and will be secured and prepped for anesthesia. This is a great opportunity to visualize your next vacation to whatever destination you dream of visiting. My last vision before I drifted into la-la land was of palm trees swaying in a breeze.

COMING OUT

"No one prepared me for the pain after waking up from surgery."

—Christine B.

After coming out of surgery, you will remain in a recovery room until the surgeon decides you are ready to go to your hospital room. You will be groggy. You may be in pain. You may not be able to speak. Your surgeon may ask you some questions or tell you how things went. Make sure he or she repeats everything when you are less groggy and can respond better. I recall seeing my mother and husband in the recovery room staring at my chest, and I think my surgeon was admiring her handiwork with a big smile and a reassuring gaze. Or maybe it was a dream . . .

You will be provided with all sorts of pain medication. Take them. Your legs may be placed in special moving massage "booties." It feels pretty good! But if you have to get up to go to the bathroom, call a nurse. Do not attempt to get up or do anything by yourself! If you think you need to go to the bathroom, start calling for the nurse sooner rather than later. It's not like they appear at once like a magic genie out of bottle. One time I had to wait for quite a while and almost peed in my hospital bed. And ask for assistance inside the bathroom if you don't feel steady. I tried to flush the toilet with my foot while balancing my body against the wall when I walked myself to the bathroom. I would not advise this.

SITTING PRETTY

You will likely have visitors and receive gifts. This can be either very fun and social or very tiring depending on how you feel. Let people know ahead of time if you do not want visitors at the hospital. My nurses had me sitting up the day after surgery. On day two, I was walking slow laps up and down the halls, and I attended my first group session. We learned all sorts of arm exercises to regain mobility like "rotate your arms" and "crawl the wall." Even in the hospital I learned the importance of movement to rebuild my body.

GOING HOME

Pin your drains to belt loops
With a mastectomy bra, go up one size
Wear pull-up, not pull-down tops

—Lisa, diagnosed 2012

I almost didn't want to go home. The Evelyn Lauder Breast Cancer Center at Memorial Sloan-Kettering Cancer Center really did feel (sort of) like the Four Seasons . . . for hospitals. With the above-average hospital food, the afternoon tea service, arts and crafts, and a reading room filled with great books, I was more than comfortable! But, unlike a four-star hotel, it's the hospital's job to welcome you with open arms and then get you out quickly. When it's time to leave, have someone help collect your belongings and sign you out. Take the offer of a wheelchair and be rolled out like a queen, holding your flower arrangements.

At your (hopefully) cleaned and sanitized home, if your bedroom is on another level, have someone help you up or down the stairs, prop you into bed, and put everything you need within arm's reach. Do not attempt to do much of anything on your own. The bathroom should be cleared of slippery mats and have plenty of towels and access to medical supplies. It may be helpful to have a walking stick to steady you when you need to get up.

Nearly all survivors I spoke with said they wished they had known ahead of time about the level of pain and difficulty of movement they would experience after their mastectomies. Everyone's threshold for pain is different. One survivor said she felt like she was hit by a truck. For me, it was a lot of just massive soreness and aching, so I relied on the painkillers my doctor prescribed. What I did not expect was the loss of mobility and weakness in my upper chest and arms. I could not lift myself up or reach for anything. Even raising a glass of water to my mouth to take pain medication was hard. And the constipation from the painkillers was just as bad! I've had friends call me after their mastectomy in tears from the pain of being constipated from medications.

Firm pillows are important to prop you up. Getting in and out of bed is difficult due to pain and weakness in the arms and chest. Simple things like cutting up your food, getting dressed, and getting in and out of a car will not be easy at first. Have someone help you. Do not stress the chest area while it is healing.

POST SURGERY: MAMA'S GOT A SQUEEZE BALL SHE WEARS ON HER CHEST

With a mastectomy, no one really shares enough about the drains. Depending on your surgery, you will have anywhere from two to six small, round plastic drains hanging from thin tubes out of your chest area. They look like clear Christmas ornaments and may be hooked to a special mastectomy bra padded with large bandages and tape. The drains remove bodily fluids that collect after your surgery that need to be eliminated. The drains will be worn for nearly two weeks and will need to be emptied a few times a day. During this time you should wear loose-fitting clothes like smock tops or big shirts. The doctor or surgical nurse will review how to care for your drains with you and your caregiver. Follow the instructions carefully and make sure to always wear your surgical gloves when handling the drains to avoid risk of infection.

You will not be able to take a shower with drains hanging from your body. You can sponge bath around the drains or use baby wipes. You will be instructed to take notes about your drainage to make sure the drains are working properly. The color of the fluids will change from red to gold to hay colored and will decrease in level until one day you can have your surgeon remove them. Removal is a quick procedure with a slight pin-prick or burn. And when they are out, you feel like a free woman!

GOING OUT

When you feel sturdy enough, getting outside for a short walk and fresh air is a good idea. I went out to have my hair professionally washed and dried since I couldn't shower and my scalp was itchy. Some survivors told me they felt nervous stepping outside the first few times. I remember walking down the street shielding my chest with my arms, worried that someone would bump into me. You will not be able to drive a car until you regain enough strength and mobility in your arms to do so (and when you are off pain medications). Also, wearing a seat belt across your chest will be difficult. I found it hard to get in and out of a taxi since I could not lift myself with my arms. It was easier getting into a car with my butt first, and I usually asked the driver for help. It takes time, and it is OK to ask for help. Do not do anything to strain yourself. You should check with your surgeon before taking on any activity that could strain your chest area.

THE WAIT

It may take a few weeks for your surgeon to have the complete results back from your surgery. In my case, I needed to have more lymph nodes removed under my left armpit, requiring a second surgery. For others, your next stop is treatment options.

Survivor Wisdom

"The statue of Venus de Milo is considered one of the most beautiful images of a woman in the world and, yet, her arms are broken off."

—Charise Isis, The Grace Project

One of the hardest things is that first look in the mirror after surgery. Your heart will sink. One woman told me she had her husband cover the mirrors. Learning to adjust to your new body is going to take time. You will need to heal emotionally while your body is healing physically. If you choose to reconstruct, your body is going to change. Trust me, over time you will adjust. Once I was finished wearing my bulky mastectomy bra, I sent my husband to my favorite lingerie shop to buy beautiful soft slip-on camisoles to wear as a celebration of getting through the first step of the journey.

COOL PRODUCTS!

The mastectomy bras your hospital gives you will be functional but bulky. It's hard to wear clothes over them unless it's something loose or bulky (long scarves are great for hiding the bras!). For added comfort and style there are some newer options. The Masthead Bra was designed by a doctor who was also a mastectomy patient. This bra is soft and comfortable and features padded shoulders (great for helping clothes hang better), pockets for ice packs or prosthetics, and front closure for ease of entry. The Elizabeth Surgical Bra features patent-pending drain openings that accommodate different kinds of surgical drains and eliminate pinching or pain. More information on these products can be found at www.bfflco.com.

Treatment

THE **ONCOLOGY GODDESS** SPEAKS

"When my mom was going through treatment I gave her a bald Barbie doll dressed like an angel, which she called Grace."

—*Nancy*, diagnosed 2011

YOUR MEDICAL ONCOLOGIST: YOUR NEW BEST FRIEND FOR LIFE

Your relationship with your medical oncologist is intimate because she sees you half naked, and it is long term because you will remain under his or her care and observation for many years. Your medical oncologist is one of your chief warrior-strategists and will analyze your pathology reports and prescribe treatments that transform your system for several months to chase away the cancer. Like me, my medical oncologist, Maria Theodoulou, MD, was a woman with a strong personality. She was part mother hen and 100 percent all-knowing warrior-goddess of oncology—not the kind of person you want to argue with (though I often tried).

We went back and forth over my desire to go on a long-planned trip to Asia. She won; I cancelled the trip, and it was definitely the right decision. I peppered her with questions about her decisions for my treatment. She had all the right answers. I confided in her when my spirits were down. She listened and empathized. When I pressed her to let me take a therapeutic trip to Maui to celebrate my wedding anniversary, she made sure that I was in shape to go, and it was just the midway-through-chemo pick-me-up that David and I needed.

61

Your medical oncologist is your cancer confessional. Be open and honest with him or her about how you feel and report any unusual symptoms you are having and anything else you feel they should know. This is a person you need to be candid with at all times. If something feels wrong, let him or her know right away. You and your oncologist will meet before every treatment. He or she will continue to see you for years post-treatment to examine your chest, take blood tests, screen you for other cancers, check your bone density and lipid profile, and make sure your health maintenance is intact. He or she may request other tests to make sure there are no C-meanies lurking inside of you.

You will usually have your blood taken at these appointments. Remember to tell the nurse which arm to use if you have had lymph nodes removed.

SELECTING YOUR MEDICAL ONCOLOGIST

You should select your medical oncologist with the same thoroughness that you select your breast surgeon. You are not "assigned" a medical oncologist by your surgeon; you choose one. It helps when the breast surgeon and medical oncologist work at the same facility, but it is not a requirement.

Your medical oncologist will review and evaluate the pathology reports and decide if treatment is needed over a period of time to ensure that there are no additional cancer cells present. He or she will prescribe a mix of drugs to administer to you to attempt to eliminate any cancer that is present and to prevent it from spreading. You will want to know his or her track record on treating cancers similar to yours. I interviewed three oncologists hoping one of them would recommend something other than chemotherapy, but they all came back with the same answer. My chemotherapy was *adjuvant,* which means *protective.* Because microscopic particles of cancer were found in a tiny number of the twenty-three lymph nodes I had removed, a course of chemotherapy would potentially be my insurance policy to prevent the cancer from taking hold in another part of my body.

Questions to Ask Your Medical Oncologist:

- Based on the pathology reports, what do you believe is the most effective course of treatment and why?

- What does being estrogen receptor-positive or negative and HER2/neu-positive or negative mean for my type of cancer and its prognosis, and for the course of treatment you recommend? Does it make a difference?

- Is this pretty standard treatment for all breast cancer patients, or are there options for alternative treatment?

- Are there investigational treatments versus standard treatments?

- How effective is this treatment in preventing a local breast cancer recurrence?

- How effective is the treatment in protecting the cancer from spreading to other organs?

- How long will chemotherapy take?

- What are the drugs you will be prescribing, and what are the possible side effects for each one?

- What kind of immediate symptoms might I feel after each treatment?

- What are short-term side effects?

- What are the long-term side effects to my system?

- Will I lose my hair? If so, when will the hair loss start to happen?

- How will treatment restrict my daily activities?

- Should I avoid any activities (going to crowded shopping centers or theaters, riding public transportation, sports events, or getting a manicure, massage, or facial)?

- Will I be able to travel on an airplane?

- How can I best protect my immune system?

- What foods and medications interact with each of the drugs I'll be taking?

- What kind of medication will you provide to handle nausea and other symptoms?

- What if I have an allergic reaction to the treatment?

- What if the treatment does not work? How will you know?

- How long after treatment will I start feeling normal again?

- What long-term treatments will you recommend?

ONE MORE DECISION

Chemotherapy can take several months, and you may spend several hours in the chemo suite for each visit, depending on your drugs. Ask to tour the chemo facility where you will be treated. For me, a quiet, comfortable, private room, preferably with a window, was important.

HOW TO AVOID INFUSION CONFUSION

THE DRUGS

"Chemo kicked my butt but I managed to squeeze in (attending) five weddings between treatment."

—Sue, diagnosed 2010

"I wore eight pink crystal bracelets on my right wrist to start. At the end of each treatment I transferred one bracelet to my left wrist and then presented it to my daughter (age 12 at the time) when she came home from school. She knew when she had eight of them I'd be done. We eventually tied those bracelets together with a pink ribbon as a reminder of the journey we took together."

—Susan G., diagnosed 2010

Your oncologist will prescribe a custom cocktail of chemotherapy drugs or biologics (like Herceptin or endocrine therapy like antiestrogens) based on the kind of cancer you have (e.g., ER2-positive or negative or HER2/neu-positive or negative). The drugs may change midway through treatment based on the regimen and your body's tolerance. For example, I started with "dose dense AC-T," which is Adriamycin (it looked like cranberry juice) and Cytoxin (a clear liquid) for four sessions every two weeks, followed by Taxol. Because I had a massive allergic reaction to Taxol (this can happen, and your oncology nurse will monitor you during the infusion for an allergic reaction), we switched to Abraxane, an alternate form of Taxol that was administered every three weeks for four sessions.

During your chemotherapy regimen, your oncologist will prescribe other drugs, like antiemetics, to combat nausea. Your oncologist may prescribe an injection one day after your treatment that will boost your white blood cells and help you fight infection. The most common injections are Neulasta and Neupogen. Ask if you are a candidate for a white blood cell booster injection and which option is best for you. Your medical oncology team should also check to see if the shot is covered by your insurance plan because it is very expensive. The shot itself is a very fine needle.

Rather than haul myself up to the medical center, I asked my husband to administer it in just a few seconds. You may experience some slight pain, redness, or a mild fever. I noticed a mild shooting pain in my chest that quickly disappeared about an hour after receiving my shot.

Let your oncologist know about any side effects or unusual symptoms you may be having. I corresponded with a number of patients and many responded differently to the chemo. Their experiences ranged from "It wasn't as big a deal as I expected!" to "It nearly killed me!" For me, the cumulative effects of chemotherapy were harder by month four, when I experienced increasing bone pain and numbness in my hands and feet that only subsided with exercise. The fatigue was not as bad as I anticipated, and I was not nauseated thanks to my careful diet and the antinausea drugs my oncologist prescribed. Constipation was one of my biggest physical challenges after surgery and during treatment. I found that hydration and exercise helped move everything else through my body.

If you have side effects like constipation or loose bowels, sniffles, shivers, coughs, high fevers, dizziness, chronic pain, or rashes, let your oncologist know immediately. When you are undergoing chemotherapy, your immune system is completely compromised, and no symptom should go unreported.

MANAGING YOUR TIME AND ENERGY

"I dressed for chemo. I always wore red lipstick, a rockin' wig, and flowers in my hair. I made it an 'occasion'"

—Gina, diagnosed 2008

Schedule your chemotherapy time so it works for you. If you work full time, consider having chemo at the end of the day on a Thursday. If you want to spend quality weekend time with your family, schedule your chemo earlier in the week. Try to get in a workout the day you have chemo—it helps prepare your veins. Eat light; drink heavy (water, herbal teas, or juice) before you go. Take granola bars, almonds, or soda crackers to ward off nausea. Ice water can counter dry mouth and sores. Slices of fresh, juicy fruit can relieve a dry mouth, but be careful with acidic fruits, which can aggravate mouth sores.

It helps to have someone accompany you to each chemotherapy session. I used the time to catch up with friends. I dubbed my five o'clock late-afternoon treatment the "chemo cocktail hour" and invited friends to come visit with me. It was a helpful distraction. I wore makeup and a nice but comfortable outfit. Dressing the part you want to play makes a world of difference in how you feel about yourself.

Your wait before being called into the chemo suite can seem like an eternity. Nothing seems to run on time! Take a tote bag filled with supplies: a water bottle, a shawl or sweater, energy bars or fresh fruit, a book, your iPad or iPod loaded with music, a book of crossword puzzles, and fun magazines (nothing serious!). For chemo sessions that last several hours, you may find yourself alone. Pass the time by listening to music or books on tape or by playing games like Scrabble.

You may have a port, which is a small device inserted under the skin on your upper chest. The catheter is connected to your vein. A port is an alternative way to administer the drugs over time as opposed to the nurses repeatedly sticking needles in the veins in your arm. I did not want a port because I was concerned about infection or blockage (which can happen), but many patients prefer them if needles make them uneasy. Ask your oncologist and oncology nurse to check your veins to see if they can withstand multiple needle pricks.

Undergoing chemotherapy was more frightening to me than having the mastectomy, and it took more mental preparation and stamina. The idea of having toxic substances injected into my bloodstream turned my stomach even more than the prospect of losing my hair.

Visualization and meditation help when you prepare for chemo. I always stuck out my tongue and made the nurse smile when she was starting the infusion. But it still feels weird. At some point your eyes might sting or your sinuses might congest or your skin may tingle. By the time I got home my skin would pale and turn gray to alabaster.

Document your moods and your body's reaction to treatment. You may feel worse on day two or three than on day one. It's called the "steroid slump." The medication you take to fight nausea may wear off, and you may not be a very nice person to be around. Never mind that your entire hormonal balance may be turned upside down. The steroid slump was *totally unexpected*, and I was pretty nasty. At one point, my husband emailed me to ask me to stop shouting at everyone in the office. I made a New York taxi driver cry (and that is not easy to do!). I was a bundle of agitated nerves ready to strike at anyone. Once I realized this, I made sure my "slump" happened on a Saturday so no one had to deal with my altered personality. Fortunately the steroid slump is short lived, and not everyone experiences it.

Invite friends to join you at chemo and use the time to catch up and distract you from the drip. If you prefer to be alone, use the time to listen to music, read, meditate, or nap. However, if you are switching drugs on a particular treatment day you may want to be alone or with your caregiver. I had an allergic reaction to a new drug being administered midway through treatment and passed out. I'm glad that only my husband was with me during that particular session because it was pretty scary!

AFTER TREATMENT

You will continue to see your oncologist every three to six months, during which time she will examine your chest wall and muscles and review how you are feeling. If you have moved on to antiestrogen therapies, your oncologist will check your blood, update your health maintenance, and may request additional tests such as a mammogram (if you still have breasts), a bone density check, or a colonoscopy. Keep notes and tell her about any changes in your body or symptoms.

SELF-MONITORING

Just as you examined your breasts regularly before you were diagnosed with cancer, you will want to continue with self-examinations after treatment. Ask your doctor how to examine your chest area and what to look for. This list may include lumps or irregularities beneath the chest wall, around an incision scar, or under an armpit. It also includes changes in your breast shape or consistency. You should report any persistent symptoms like a cough, intense or chronic pain, rashes, shortness of breath, or dizziness. You should have a professional look at *anything* out of the ordinary.

RADIATION THERAPY

I did not undergo radiation therapy, so I conducted interviews with women who did. I also turned to radiation oncologist Elizabeth Chabner Thompson, MD, MPH, who contributed her expertise to this section.

Dr. Thompson's experience working with patients led her to create BFFL Co (Best Friends For Life), a line of garments and accessories for breast cancer patients. The following are her answers.

WHAT IS RADIATION THERAPY?

"Radiation therapy is an 'adjuvant,' or accompanying form of treatment, for women with breast cancer. It is rarely recommended alone and usually follows a lumpectomy or mastectomy. Radiation therapy involves the treatment of cancer patients with high energy X-rays (much higher energy than the X-rays involved with diagnostic X-rays or CT). These X-rays are photos, electrons, or possibly protons and they are delivered by a linear accelerator in a designated treatment center. The high-energy X-rays or 'radiation' intend to kill any cancer cells that may have evaded removal by the surgeon or that exist in the adjacent lymph node chains. Even if your pathology is 'clean margins,' data from large studies have taught us that radiation after a lumpectomy reduces local recurrence and affords patients the same long-term survival as a mastectomy. Radiation is also used in other circumstances (chest wall involvement or recurrence or palliative therapy for metastasis), so keep an open mind when you see your radiation oncologist."

SELECTING A RADIATION ONCOLOGIST

"Your medical team will include a radiation oncologist (the physician) and a radiation therapist, who positions you on the machine and turns the beam on and off.

"You will want to research your radiation oncologist with the same due diligence as you did your breast surgeon. Think of your surgeon, radiation oncologist, and medical oncologist as a team. Ideally, they will speak with each other when formulating your treatment plan.

"Your radiation oncologist will map out a plan for your treatment based on your pathology, operative note, scans, and your medical records. Your treatment plan may involve a lumpectomy, then radiation, and then chemotherapy, or it may involve neoadjuvant chemotherapy before surgery and then radiation, or some other sequencing of the three modalities. Keep an open mind and ask questions."

"*Experience*: In most situations, your referring surgeon or medical oncologist will recommend a colleague to administer your radiation therapy. Even so, online reviews, academic records, reputation, and personality are all important factors in finding the right physician. You don't have to be in love with your physician, but you should feel that you can candidly discuss your medical condition and that you trust this person. Ask other women who live locally for references, and don't be afraid to seek a second opinion. No physician should be offended by your seeking a second opinion. It's your prerogative as a patient."

"*Location and timing:* Radiation is a daily treatment for three to seven weeks. You *must* show up for every treatment because radiation works on a fractionated basis, which means it is delivered in small doses over a period of time. You can expect to be in the department for about thirty minutes each day. This time includes getting changed for treatment, waiting for your turn on the machine, seeing a nurse or physician if necessary, and changing back into your clothes. Delays can occur because of machine maintenance or emergency patients, so it's a good idea to warn those waiting for you that you may not be 'on time' getting out of treatment. If you work and need to keep the treatments to outside work hours, make sure to let your physician and therapist know about your time constraints so you can be the first or last patient of the day. The actual treatment time 'on the table' is usually five to ten minutes. You may decide to choose a treatment center closer to your home or office instead of going to your primary hospital."

"*Insurance:* Make sure that the treatment facility accepts your insurance and that you understand what you may need to pay out of pocket."

"*Physician–Patient Chemistry:* The radiation oncologist determines the total dosage, treatment course, and radiation fields and formulates a plan with a radiation physicist. Careful consideration is always given to adjacent organs such as the heart and lungs. You want a smart person writing your prescription. Your radiation oncologist or a physician from his or her team will see you once a week for a status check. If you have concerns, side effects, or medical issues in between the status checks, make sure to notify the nurse or the machine therapist, so that they can alert your physician. A physician does not see all patients every single day."

Different Types of Radiation and Machines

"Some facilities have newer treatment machines with different energies and different types of radiation. It is important to discuss this with the radiation oncologist. There are new modalities available now, such as *intraoperative radiation therapy*, which is done at the time of the lumpectomy, or *accelerated partial breast irradiation* (APBI) using a SAVI or Mammosite system which can shorten your length of treatment to between five and seven days. With either of these types of treatment, radiation is delivered internally, versus externally, through a catheter attached to a specific device inserted into your breast)

"Make sure to ask questions and make sure that you understand what the physicians are recommending."

PREPARING FOR RADIATION TREATMENTS

You will need to make sure that you have clean, dry skin with no lotions, crèmes, or deodorants on your skin before your daily treatment. This includes the approved medications that your physician might recommend. You can put on your medicated creams after your daily treatment. Do not wear sunscreen before treatment! Wear comfortable cotton clothing and a supportive bra such as the Masthead Estelle or Davi Bra, so that your breasts will be supported when they are tender or swollen. And with any treatment, maintaining a sensible diet, staying well hydrated, and getting regular exercise and enough sleep will make a difference in how you feel.

"Safe" Creams and Sunscreens

Everyone will have recommendations for you, but it's your physician who should decide what you put on your skin. Many preparations that you find in drugstores, naturopathic shops, or on the Internet will claim that they are safe, but ultimately few of these will be doctor-approved. Sunscreens can contain metals such as zinc and other chemicals that will irritate your skin. Keep your skin covered with a cotton shirt and make sure that the fabric is thick enough to block the sun's rays.

Tattoos

In order to align the procedure properly and create a permanent record of your treatment, you will most likely have one or two (maybe more) permanent India ink tattoos placed on your chest or side under your arm. These marks are intended to facilitate daily setup and to help future radiation oncologists, who may not have your records, make important treatment decisions.

Nutrition

Proper nutrition is imperative for your body to repair its normal tissues. This is not the time to begin a new diet or dramatically change your eating habits. Some radiation oncologists will ask you to discontinue all additive vitamins because some may interfere with radiation's ability to kill cancer cells. It's best to discuss this with your physician and not rely on the Internet or a friend for advice.

RISKS AND SIDE EFFECTS

Your radiation oncologist will discuss the risks and side effects of treatment with you. Most of your immediate or short-term side effects will involve your skin in and around the area that has been treated. Always discuss your side effects with your physician.

Redness or Rash

You won't see anything for the first two weeks, and then your skin will become red (erythematous). You may develop a red, bumpy rash in the treatment field. Many radiation oncologists will recommend over-the-counter hydrocortisone cream for this rash, so it's not a bad idea to have this in your medicine cabinet. The red, peeling skin does not happen to everyone, but it is common. Your skin will heal. Aquaphor and Eucerin are excellent, safe skin preparations and moisturizers. Lindi Skin makes a great product called the Skin Cooler Roller, which feels great after treatment to cool down hot, tender skin.

Fatigue

Many patients describe fatigue associated with treatment. This is completely normal. Based on when the fatigue settles in, decide if there is a better time of day for you to undergo treatment. And keep moving by walking or doing light exercise.

Long-Term Side Effects

These include possible damage to the heart and lungs, which lie immediately below the chest wall. Radiation oncologists keep this in mind during planning and attempt to minimize these long-term side effects. In addition, skin firmness or contracture around a reconstruction implant are long-term risks that you should address with your physician. Lastly, if you have any suspicion of lymphedema (swelling of the arm) after surgery, you should make an appointment with a lymphedema specialist to evaluate and take measurements. If there is any indication of swelling in your affected arm, you should begin a lymphedema reduction program.

Radiation To The Breast Will Not Cause Infertility

Your physician will ask you to take a pregnancy test and to avoid trying to get pregnant while having radiation. Milk production in a radiated breast may be compromised. If you do become pregnant after completing radiation, you should discuss this with your OB-GYN.

FOLLOW-UP CARE

You will have a follow-up appointment with your radiation oncologist for three weeks or, in some cases, up to three months after completing treatment. You will then have regular follow-ups with your physician to monitor your skin and potential long-term side effects. If you were to develop a recurrence or cancer in another area of your body, it would be beneficial to have kept records of your prior treatment and maintained a relationship with your radiation oncologist.

ENDOCRINE THERAPY

Just when you think you are over the treatment hump with radiation and chemotherapy, your oncologist will inform you that it is time for more drugs, and for a longer period of time. Endocrine therapy (often referred to as hormone therapy) is an important part of your treatment if your cancer is estrogen receptor-positive and/or progesterone receptor-positive (most are). Since hormone receptor-positive breast cancer needs estrogen to grow, these drugs work by blocking or inhibiting the production of estrogen in your body. The therapy helps you by (a) reducing the risk of recurrence, either locally or elsewhere in the body, (b) reducing the risk of breast cancer death, and (c) reducing the risk of a new breast cancer developing in your remaining or other breast, depending on the surgery you had.

The kind of endocrine therapy your oncologist prescribes and for what length of time will depend on a few things, such as whether you are pre- or postmenopausal and the stage of your cancer. You will take these drugs for at least five years and in some cases as long as ten years.

EXAMPLES OF ENDOCRINE THERAPY

Tamoxifen is used for women who are either premenopausal or postmenopausal. Tamoxifen is an estrogen blocker, which means it prevents estrogen from attaching to the cancer cell.

Aromatese Inhibitors lower the level of estrogen in your body. Aromatese inhibitors only work in postmenopausal women

Ovarian suppression drugs basically put your ovaries to sleep. These are used for premenopausal women. Sometimes they are prescribed in combination with tamoxifen.

Your medical oncologist will decide which drugs you should take. Again, drugs and dosages may change depending on your type of cancer and your body's reaction.

For premenopausal women:
Tamoxifen (alone)
Tamoxifen plus ovarian suppression drug
Arimedex plus ovarian suppression drug

Ovarian suppression drugs:
Goserelin (generic) or Zoladex (brand name) (both injections)
Leuprolide (generic) or Lupron (brand name)

For post-menopausal women (all pills):
Anastrozole (generic) or Arimidex (brand name)
Letrozole (generic) or Femara (brand name)
Exemestane (generic) or Aromasin (brand name)

SIDE EFFECTS

Each drug can produce different side effects, ranging from hot flashes or numbness to joint pain and thinning hair and bones. Many women report weight gain, which is primarily caused by having a slower metabolism rather than by the drugs themselves. You should discuss potential side effects with your oncologist and registered dietitian or nutritionist to see what vitamins and supplements you can safely take to counter negative side effects and reduce other health risks like osteoporosis. Also, you may need to avoid some foods or beverages that hinder the effects of the medication. If any medication is causing you extreme complications, discuss this and other options you have with your oncologist.

Questions to Ask Your Oncologist

- What course of endocrine therapy treatment do you recommend and why?
- How do they work for my type of cancer?
- How long will I be on this medication?
- What kind of side effects should I expect and how can I alleviate them?
- Are there any foods, vitamins, or supplements that may interact with the medication that I should avoid?
- Should I take a bone density test?
- Do I need to take pills or vitamins to strengthen my bone density?
- What risk(s) does this medication have of causing me to contract other forms of cancer?

If you are taking Herceptin for HER2/neu-positive cancer, also ask:

- How long do I have to take Herceptin? (The standard is one year.)
- How do I monitor my cardiac function?

AN INTEGRATIVE APPROACH: NATUROPATHIC ONCOLOGY

Naturopathic oncology offers an integrative approach to managing your cancer in conjunction with conventional treatment to help make treatment more effective and mitigate any side effects. Like conventional treatment, the goal of naturopathic oncology is to effectively reduce the cancer's risk of spreading or recurrence. Naturopathic oncology is also an option for women who are unable to take conventional treatment or who are unwilling to undergo it. Health care coverage for naturopathic medical treatment may vary by state and by policy, so check with your provider.

DEFINITION

A naturopathic oncologist is a physician who is board certified in naturopathic oncology. The certification requires completing a medical residency program or having at least five years' experience in a cancer-based naturopathic practice. A Fellow of the American Board of Naturopathic

Oncology (FABNO) designation means that the naturopathic physician has passed stringent examinations established by the Board of Medical Examiners (BOMEX) under the American Board of Naturopathic Oncology (ABNO).

A naturopathic oncologist will work with your primary oncologist to learn about your condition and what chemotherapy agents are being used. Your naturopathic oncologist will work collaboratively with your doctors during treatment and will continue to work with you after treatment, prescribing a regimen of lifestyle changes to help you rejuvenate your body.

For the section on naturopathic oncology, I turned to Lise Alschuler, ND, FABNO, a highly regarded naturopathic oncologist based in Arizona, and coauthor along with Karolyn Gazella of *The Definitive Guide to Cancer: an Integrative Approach to Prevention, Treatment and Healing* and *Five to Thrive: Your Cutting Edge Cancer Prevention Plan*. Dr. Alschuler was diagnosed with breast cancer in 2008 and underwent chemotherapy and radiation and continues with hormone therapy. She has applied her own experiences to her integrative approach to prevention and fighting recurrence (see www.drlise.net and www.fivetothrive.com).

The Five to Thrive program is based on five integrated steps to managing your well-being:

Spirit: Maintaining a positive attitude and reducing stress. This includes keeping active and avoiding potentially toxic situations.

Movement: Studies have shown that exercising three and a half hours a week can help significantly reduce your risk of recurrence.[1, 2] Dr. Alschuler advises patients to make movement a way of life. "The key is to make sure you are doing something you enjoy and can tolerate. Find something you like to do and get into a routine," she says. Yoga, which is both strength building and meditative, is a good choice. Some studios offer "gentle yoga" classes for cancer patients. Other easy forms of exercise are Pilates, qigong, tai chi, and walking.

Rejuvenation: "The body needs time to rejuvenate after being subjected to harsh treatments. If we burn the candle too fast, we set ourselves up for disease," says Dr. Alschuler. Sleep is a rejuvenator, as are meditation, deep breathing, and other relaxation techniques. Another suggestion is to move away from the computer and stop checking your emails so often. Turn off the news on TV if it upsets you.

Diet: Dr. Alschuler stresses the importance of diet in helping feed and build healthy cellular tissue. In the next chapter, I will delve into diet and nutrition further with two oncology nutritionists.

Supplements: Your oncologist will most likely instruct you to stop taking all vitamins and supplements since some can interfere with your treatment. However, Dr. Alschuler points out that certain supplements will complement and not counteract your treatment. "You need to seek the advice of an integrative practitioner who has done the research and who understands how supplements interact with treatment to help support it and also counter negative side effects. Antioxidants must be matched to both the patient and to the treatment."

"I consulted with an acupuncturist who told me to be gentle to my system and gave me a great natural prune paste for constipation."

—Susan, diagnosed 2005

"My naturopathic doctor recommended drinking pure aloe juice for the intense sore throat I developed using radiation, and soothing rice protein shakes for energy."

—Melanie, diagnosed 2008

NOTES

1. National Center for Health Statistics, *Health, United States, 2009, with Special Feature on Medical Technology* (Hyattsville, Maryland, 2010), http://www.cdc.gov/nchs/data/hus/hus09.pdf.

2. U.S. Department of Health and Human Services, "2008 Physical Activity Guidelines for Americans," http://www.fitness.gov/be-active/physical-activity-guidelines-for-americansx.

The Road to Reconstruction

6

"OF COURSE **THESE** BREASTS **ARE FAKE**—MY REAL ONES **TRIED TO KILL ME**."

I DIDN'T HAVE MUCH TIME TO MOURN THE LOSS OF MY BREASTS because I opted for a mastectomy with immediate reconstruction. Knowing we could rebuild my chest gave me hope that my body would be whole again. I started interviewing reconstruction surgeons at the same time I was selecting my breast surgeon.

Breast reconstruction is an integral part of breast cancer care, and you should discuss it with your physicians. Reconstruction is your choice. Some women choose not to reconstruct because they don't want foreign objects in their body or to have any more surgeries. And some women may not be good candidates for reconstruction for medical reasons. The good news is that you have a choice and you have several options, since advancements in reconstruction have come so far.

The Women's Health and Cancer Rights Act (WHCRA) was passed in 1998, requiring group health plans, health insurance companies, and HMOs to provide coverage for reconstructive surgery following mastectomies. The coverage includes (and I quote from the "Your Rights After A Mastectomy" website hosted by the United States Department of Labor) "all stages of reconstruction of the breast on which the mastectomy was performed, surgery and reconstruction of the other breast to produce a symmetrical appearance, [and] prostheses and treatment of physical complications of the mastectomy, including lymphedema."[1]

The website does point out that coverage by a "church plan" or "governmental plan" may not be subject to this law, and the extent of your coverage may be limited by your specific policy. As with anything related to your health insurance, ask to speak with an administrator or an assigned caseworker and request a written, detailed description for all mastectomy-, reconstruction-, and treatment-related provisions, conditions, and exclusions, including whether you need a second medical opinion for reconstruction.

What amazes me is that the WHCRA was not passed *until 1998*, and, before then, women had to agonize between the choice of paying significantly out of pocket to reconstruct or living with their scars and flat chest whether they wanted to or not.

According to a report in the January 2013 issue of the *Journal of Plastic and Reconstructive Surgery* published by the American Society of Plastic Surgeons (ASPS), "The trend toward immediate reconstruction and implant use signals a 'paradigm shift' in breast reconstruction in the United States." The report was based on a ten-year study (1998–2008, so after WHCRA was passed) by ASPS member-surgeon Evan Matros, MD, and colleagues at Memorial Sloan-Kettering Cancer Center. Results showed that "out of approximately 178,600 mastectomies, 51,400 were followed by immediate breast reconstruction. From the late 1990s to the late 2000s, the rate of immediate reconstruction after mastectomy increased from 21 to 38 percent—an average increase of five percent per year."[2]

This says two things: First, that the WHCRA has made a big difference in the lives of women undergoing mastectomies, with more choosing immediate reconstruction at a small but steady increase each year. Second, that still more than half of women undergoing mastectomies do not reconstruct. I will address options for reconstruction at the end of this chapter.

CHOOSING A RECONSTRUCTIVE SURGEON

First, discuss with your breast surgeon if reconstruction is an option for you based on your medical history and cancer diagnosis. Have your breast surgeon recommend a plastic surgeon who specializes in breast reconstruction after mastectomy. It's important that the two surgeons know how to work together since reconstructive surgery usually takes place right after your mastectomy while you are under anesthesia. It's not like you can be wheeled to another medical center. You can choose to have reconstructive surgery later, but that means a separate surgery. Knowing I could have new breasts after losing my old ones gave me hope and something to look forward to.

YOUR RECONSTRUCTION SURGEON: THE FIXER

When you interview reconstructive surgeons you should base your decision on the following:

Chemistry: Is he empathetic or brusque? I actually know of one patient who was told, "You should be grateful to be alive" by a reconstruction surgeon she interviewed.

Communication: Does he or she explain all of your options and how long the actual reconstruction process takes for each procedure? Does she take time to answer all of your questions?

Handiwork: Ask to see before and after photos of different procedures and preferably photos close to your body type and age. Now that I've gone through reconstruction myself, I would take this one step further and ask to see and feel the reconstructed breasts of an actual patient. Photos do not tell the full story but the touch test does.

Questions to Ask Your Breast Reconstruction Surgeon

- What are my breast reconstruction options? Here, the surgeon should explain the following things for type of reconstruction:
    - Procedure and length of time it takes
    - Risks
    - Pros and cons for each option (both medically and aesthetically)
    - What postsurgical procedures are needed and for how many months
    - Downtime and side effects from surgery
    - Long-term effects, especially after radiation
- What are the most natural-looking and natural-feeling reconstruction options?
- Are any particular procedures your specialty?
- What is the best reconstruction option for my body type and condition?

- When will reconstruction take place? Some procedures, like tissue flap reconstruction, occur immediately after the surgeon removes your breasts. Your course of treatment may also affect when you can reconstruct.

- When should I have reconstruction if I am having radiation? This is tough because often when you go in for your mastectomy, you don't know yet what your follow-up treatment will be. Radiation could affect the shape and texture of your reconstructed breast and the skin around it.

- What are my options for areola and nipple reconstruction?

- Will my breasts regain sensitivity?

- What physical limitations will I have after surgery?

- Will I have any limitations over the long term (e.g., lifting heavy items)?

- What happens to my breasts if I lose or gain weight?

- Will my new breasts have any additional risk for breast cancer recurrence?

- Will I need to continue getting mammograms?

- What is the risk of my breasts rupturing or leaking (with implants)?

- What if I have an allergic reaction or other complication (with implants)?

- If I already have a breast implant (in my remaining breast, for single mastectomies), should we remove it and put in a new implant to match my new breast?

- Will additional surgical procedures be covered by my health insurance if I need to replace my implants or undergo further surgery to address any physical or cosmetic complications from treatment?

- What if I had a tummy tuck? Is the tissue flap procedure an option?

- What do I need to do to prepare for my reconstruction? How long will I need downtime after surgery?

- How will chest X-rays and other radiation affect my breasts?

- What if I am unhappy with the results? Can I switch out my implants? Can I remove my implants and undergo a tissue and fat transplant to rebuild new breasts?

- What happens to my breast skin and chest wall if I choose to have my implants removed?

YOUR OPTIONS

Once you select your surgeon you will confirm the procedure you want. A nurse will take photos of your breasts from every possible angle. Your breast surgeon and your reconstruction surgeon will need to coordinate schedules to find a day and time they can perform surgery on you together. So make sure they are connected from the start.

I found choosing my new breasts both exciting and nerve-racking. Facing decisions about my mastectomy was comparatively easy: I had cancer in two breasts and three tumors in total; everything needed to go. Done! But reconstruction offered more options and the chance to decide how my body would look and how I would feel about it afterward.

Every woman has a different opinion of her breasts. I happened to love my 36B "originals" and hated losing them to cancer. But a friend said to me, "You can replace your breasts, but you cannot replace you." Today, I have beautiful, symmetrical, and permanent chest scars and two perfectly shaped breasts that are more Barbie than bouncy, a bit larger (my choice!), firmer, and more sporty than sexy. But above all, they are healthy!

BREAST IMPLANTS

According to the same 2013 ASPS study mentioned above, implants are the most common form of breast reconstruction, growing by 11 percent each year during the ten years that the study was conducted.

The great thing about implants is that you can actually choose your breast shape and size. That's a concept I liked: breast shopping! I took my husband with me to meet with my breast reconstruction surgeon: the handsome, skilled, and sharply dressed Dr. Joseph Disa at Memorial Sloan-Kettering. Once I consulted with him, I was happy to put my new breasts in his hands.

The nurse discussed my options (silicone versus saline) and asked if I wanted to see sample photos and feel the implants. Sure! Do I go bigger, fuller, or stay the same size? After touching and squeezing the implants, I chose a natural-looking "shaped cohesive silicone gel implant" named the 410. This implant is also referred to as the "Gummy Bear," and the reason is obvious once you feel them.

Here is what you learn along the way: The road to reconstruction with implants can be long and rather painful. You need to be patient. It is a multipart process involving a number of procedures.

After your mastectomy, the reconstructive surgeon implants tissue expanders under the skin and chest muscle. Think of them as balloons waiting to be blown up over the course of several months. Every few weeks you visit your surgeon to have a saltwater solution injected into the breast area to fill the expander. You choose the frequency of your visits and the size you want to become. After each session you can feel your skin stretching like it has been put on a rack. Your clothes, which hang flat and shapeless after a mastectomy, start to fill out . . . and beyond, depending on how large you expand. You need to be overinflated to reach your intended size. The expanded breast *mound* is really hard! At one point my breasts felt and looked like petrified hamburger buns. By the last injection I looked like I had cantaloupes sprouting from my chest. Another survivor described it as having "half of a coconut embedded in my forehead." I started seeing a physical therapist to deal with the back pain and inward rolling shoulders caused by the stretching.

During this time it helps to wear loose tops, draping jackets, and long scarves or a shawl to detract from your chest as it expands. This is particularly true if you have had a single mastectomy and are temporarily lopsided. You can also purchase shoulder pads or breast prostheses to wear until your chest evens out.

Transfer surgery, when my actual implant was inserted into the now very-expanded breast pocket took place about eight weeks after my last chemotherapy treatment, once my oncologist gave the green light for the surgery. The surgery was less painful than my mastectomy and required less downtime. You are sent home wearing a surgical bra for a few weeks and need to be very careful about lifting anything or wearing tight clothes. You cannot wear an underwire bra for a few weeks.

You should keep exercising throughout the reconstruction process, but some workouts are better than others. For example, weight lifting, swimming, high-impact aerobics, or anything that will build up your chest muscles are not recommended. Neither are push-ups, certain yoga positions, or overstretching the chest and arm area. Most likely you will be given a list of approved chest exercises.

BUT WAIT! THERE'S MORE!

You can choose to have your areola created from your own skin (most commonly the lower abdomen area), which requires another surgery, or you can have your areola tattooed on, which is an in-office procedure. With a tattoo you can choose the size and color of your new areola. It's like mixing a cosmetic foundation or liquid blush and having the doctor apply it.

Finally, you are "topped off" with nipples. Mine were created from the scar tissue on my breasts in another surgery. The key with rebuilding nipples is not to go for "perky and pointy" unless you plan to always wear a bra. Remember, your new nipples just need to look good and work with all of your clothing options.

SALINE AND SILICONE IMPLANTS: PROS AND CONS

Implants are about look, feel, durability, and psychology. You need to be comfortable with having a foreign object inside of you. Because reconstructive implants are inserted between the chest muscle and the skin, many patients say they feel like something alien is sitting inside their chest. In my case, I often feel a light tugging or stretching around my breasts and under my armpits like rubber bands wound around my chest and under my armpit. It's like wearing a too-tight bra. Sometimes my breasts tingle, and I have to be careful not to scratch my breast skin, which still has no feeling. When I go swimming, the implants stay cold after the rest of my body warms up, which can cause some shivers. Here are some pros and cons of each type of implant. Discuss each with your reconstruction surgeon.

Silicone versus Saline

Breast implants are made from two materials. Saline implants contain a saltwater solution encased in a solid shell of silicone. Silicone implants are composed of silicone gel encased in silicone. There are two versions of silicone implants. The first is round and soft; the second, a *cohesive gel implant*, is firmer and more breast shaped.

Some doctors and women say that silicone implants look more natural than saline. The newer (FDA-approved in 2012) cohesive gel 410

"Gummy Bear" implants have a lovely teardrop breast shape rather than a round orb shape. They look natural, but they do not move and are much firmer. The cleavage is more "lift and separate" versus "va-va voom!" Some women may like the idea of not having swinging breasts, especially if they do not like wearing a bra and are athletic. Others may want that "Victoria's Secret look" with deep cleavage. Some women told me that they switched out their implants due to discomfort. "They sat too high on my chest," said two women. Some had their breasts redone because they didn't like seeing the striations from the implant when they leaned over, or because their breasts changed shape after radiation.

Pros of Implants

- Both saline and silicone implants feel and move like a natural breast.

- They are durable.

- Implants come in different shapes and sizes for you to select. (Ask to feel them and see photos of women who have the implants. I would also speak with women who have the implants you are considering.)

- Some implants are firmer than others. You can choose a style that suits your lifestyle and aesthetic goal.

- Implants do not change shape or size. If you lose or gain weight, your breasts will stay the same.

- Recovery time from surgery is shorter than it is with other reconstruction options.

- No scientific proof links breast implants and autoimmune disorders or diseases. The Institute of Medicine (IOM) of the National Academy of Sciences was commissioned by the federal government in 1997 to conduct an extensive study on breast implants. Its findings, published in 1999, confirmed there was no link.[3-5]

Cons of Implants

- There is a risk of infection, rejection, or allergic reaction.

- There is a slight risk of rupturing or leaking.

- If you are thin-skinned in the chest area, you may see the implants moving or see thin striations of liquid, which some women do not like.

- Saline implants have a slightly higher risk of *capsular contraction*, which is a hardening around the implant.

- Implants can change shape or harden during radiation. Discuss this with your surgeon and radiation oncologist.

- Some breast implants may need to be replaced at some point; the average life span is reportedly at least ten years. If you need to repair or replace your implants, the procedure should be covered by your health insurance under the WHCRA Act.

Things I Did Not Know until I Had My Implants

- You may always feel the implant tugging inside your chest.

- Lying on the stomach is not comfortable. (If I get a massage, I request towels to pad my chest area.)

- The skin covering your implanted breasts will have little feeling. You can feel pressure, poking, and pinching but not much else. Be careful about potential burns, scrapes, or cuts that you may not feel.

- Implants are sensitive to temperature since they are placed right under the chest skin with no fat to insulate them. Your breasts may feel colder in the winter or after taking a swim. It feels pretty weird and a bit clammy. I asked my breast surgeon about putting hand warmers in my bras during the winter. She advised me against this saying that you could burn your breast since it has no feeling. It's better to cup your hand over your breast or keep a warm scarf close at hand.

- You may find your breasts tingling and itching. These are your severed nerve endings acting up. It's annoying, but do not go crazy scratching your breasts. Since you can't feel your breast skin, you could harm yourself.

- Implants are heavy. You may feel the weight in your shoulders or upper back. I find myself correcting my posture and relying on upper back and shoulder exercises to strengthen and stretch my tight chest area.

- Tissue expanders contain a small amount of metal and could be detected during routine airport safety screenings. It's best to travel with a note from your reconstructive surgeon. I have never set off an airport security system, but it's best to be prepared rather than try to explain it yourself!

- Implants look great in clothes, but you may need to have some older clothes tailored to fit your new breast shape.

NATURAL-TISSUE BREASTS

Another option is *autologous* (taken from your own tissue, cells, or DNA) reconstruction, where your breast is rebuilt from fat, tissue, and sometimes muscle from another part of your body, such as your abdomen, back, buttocks, or inner thighs. This is a longer, more-invasive surgery option that usually takes place immediately following your mastectomy unless for some reason you are delaying reconstruction.

This is a nice, natural option if you are a candidate with enough body fat to form new breasts. An added bonus is the effect of a tummy tuck once fat is removed from your abdomen. Many women told me they loved having a flatter stomach.

A few types of tissue transfer surgery are available to you depending on your body (as in the availability of fat).

TRAM flap reconstruction: Transverse rectus abdominus myocutaneous or TRAM flap surgery uses skin, fat, and muscle tissue from the lower abdomen to create a new breast. This is a good procedure if you carry a good amount of belly fat. You will have a stomach scar, and you do run the risk of weaker abdominal muscles. The bonus is the flatter stomach along with the natural and sensitive new breasts.

DIEP flap reconstruction: Deep inferior epigastric perforators or DIEP flap surgery uses abdominal skin and fat to reconstruct but leaves the muscle in place. This is an even more complex surgery with more risk. But you can preserve the stomach muscle, which can help offset any long-term discomfort.

SIEA flap reconstruction: Superficial inferior epigastric artery or SIEA flap surgery uses skin, fat tissue, and blood vessels from the abdomen.

This surgery is riskier with a potential for blood clots.

SGAP and IGAP reconstruction: Superficial and inferior gluteal artery perforator, or SGAP and IGAP surgeries, take skin, fat, and tissue from the buttocks. Again, it is a complicated surgery. There are a few bonuses: The surgery can be repeated (using the other buttock) and because no muscle is used it is a nice alternative to abdominal surgery if you are athletic.

Lattisimus dorsi reconstruction: This surgery transfers skin, fat, and muscle from the back to the chest area.

TUG flap reconstruction: Transverse upper gracilis flap surgery uses fat, skin, and muscle from your inner thigh.

Pros of Natural-Tissue Breasts

- You are using your own skin and tissue versus implanting a foreign object.
- Your body can't reject its natural tissue.
- Breast looks and feels natural.
- Breast will regain normal sensation once your nerves regenerate.
- You have the "bonus" of a tummy tuck or butt tuck, depending on the procedure.
- If you gain or lose weight, your breast size will adapt to the change. (This is also a "con" if you want to keep the same size breast despite your weight.)

Cons of Natural-Tissue Breasts

- It is a more complicated surgery with added risks (infection, blood clots, and necrosis of the transferred tissue).
- Your recovery time will be longer, and you will have more drains to deal with.
- There is additional scarring on your body.
- With TRAM flap surgery, you run the risk of having weaker stomach muscles, which can also cause strain on your back.
- Breast shape and size may be affected by radiation therapy.
- Most of these surgeries cannot be redone.

RECONSTRUCTION THROUGH AUTOLOGOUS FAT TRANSFER

Another option for reconstruction is autologous fat grafting, a procedure using needles similar to those used in liposuction to transfer fat to the breast from another area of the body. According to Jeffrey Hartog, DMD, MD, director of The Bouganvillea Clinique in Orlando, Florida, the procedure can be initiated at the time of the mastectomy: "Fat can be placed into the muscle, under the muscle, and peripherally under the skin to begin the creation of the breast mound. I have demonstrated that this approach leads to much better healing and less scar contraction of the mastectomy site, making subsequent reconstruction easier." For total breast reconstruction, the process requires a series of fat grafts over a period of several months for up to a year to reach completion and may be initiated at the time of the mastectomy.

Dr. Hartog noted that autologous fat transfer can be beneficial for lumpectomies, total mastectomy reconstruction, rebuilding deformed breasts, and particularly reconstruction in radiated tissue: "Fat is also beneficial to resolve pain from radiation and can change scarred radiated tissue to normal soft pliable tissue. Fat grafting is frequently used to salvage reconstructions that have had complications using other procedures."

While autologous fat grafting is a less-common form of reconstruction, Dr. Hartog believes the procedure will emerge as a preferred option for many patients. "In 2013 the Food and Drug Administration, as part of an ongoing study, approved a key component of the procedure, the BRAVA external expansion device, as a B1 reimbursable device when used in combination with fat grafting.[6] This is important as insurance acceptance is a key component in the patient choice." The BRAVA device, developed by Dr. Roger Khouri at the Miami Breast Center, is a space-age-looking gel-like bra that serves as an external breast tissue expander (like a suction cup). Patients wear the BRAVA device in the weeks prior to and following the fat transfer procedure.

One of Dr. Hartog's patients who is satisfied with the procedure is his wife Michelle, a registered nurse and breast cancer survivor, who helps guide patients through the reconstruction process at his clinic.

Pros of Autologous Fat Transfer

- Less surgery and potential complications from surgery
- Less scarring since procedure is done through needle insertion

- Recuperation is similar to any liposuction procedure, with some soreness and bruising
- Natural look
- Breast will have sensation
- Like a natural breast, size will change with normal weight gain and loss
- Does not interfere with follow up mammograms

Cons of Autologous Fat Transfer

- Risk of fat necrosis needs to be studied more fully for possible oncologic risk: "There is broad clinical applicability of autologous fat grafting for breast reconstruction. Complications were few and there was no evidence of interference with follow-up treatment for breast cancer. Oncology safety remains unclear."[7]

In reference to the last point, I also refer to the ASPS "2012 Post-Mastectomy Fat Graft/Fat Transfer Guiding Principles" and other studies,"[8-12] which states, "Evidence suggests that in post-mastectomy breast reconstruction patients, fat grafting does not increase the risk of breast cancer recurrence." So, discuss this option and its pros and cons with your surgeon.

Survivor Wisdom

During the months after my reconstructive surgery and even sometimes now, I had a love/hate relationship with my 410 "Gummy Bears." They looked great, but the pulling was bothering me, and they did not move. They felt like stuffed animals hanging off my chest. It was like wearing a tight sports bra all the time. I longed for pillowy breasts, not pokers. I tried massaging them, but nothing loosened them up.

I debated back and forth whether to have them exchanged for softer silicone gels. In fact, I became a little obsessed. My husband caught me fondling bags of gummy candies in the supermarket aisle for a touch test. I stared at other women's breasts.

"The problem is that I forgot what real breasts feel like, and I can't just go ask a woman if I can feel her breasts," I complained to Dr. Disa, who I decided was also part therapist when it came to breast reconstruction issues. He said he had a patient who was unhappy with her silicone gels because of rippling and was considering a switch to "Gummy Bear" implants. He told me that if we were both open to the idea, he would introduce us so that we could talk about the pros and cons of our respective breast implants.

The woman, who had her implant surgery just a few months after mine, called me. We compared breast characteristics and commiserated. And then we said to each other, "To heck with it! Let's just meet and check out each other's breasts. To switch implants is a big decision and another surgery to consider."

And that is how I ended up topless in a bathroom at Memorial Sloan-Kettering feeling another woman's breasts in the middle of the afternoon. Strange? Yes! Worth it? Yes!

It was worth it because seeing a silicone gel implant in a photo or hanging from the fingertips of a doctor's aide just does not tell the full story of how it will look and feel in your body. I think every woman considering breast reconstruction should ask to feel the breasts of at least one woman who underwent the procedure that she is considering. It is not kinky or weird. It helps you make a smart, clear decision about what is going on in your chest. "Feel research" is a good thing.

In the end, I canceled my surgery to exchange my implants. After speaking with several women and doing more research, I was not convinced that switching would make enough of a difference, and I was worried that I might have to live with seeing striations under my thin, fair chest skin. Also, I was a little surgery shy. I have no idea what the other woman decided.

TIPS

- Talk to fellow survivors about their experience with reconstruction to get their opinions and insights.

- Take the touch test: Feel your breasts and then feel the implant options to make sure you select the option that feels best for you.

- Try to feel other reconstructed breasts. Pictures only tell half the story.

- Ask your breast reconstruction surgeon to show you photos of his or her work.

- Throw out or donate all of your old bras and buy yourself the most beautiful lingerie you can afford. Have a friend throw you a lingerie party when you finish reconstruction!

AFTER RECONSTRUCTION: REGAINING MOBILITY AND STRENGTH

When you can resume normal activities after reconstruction will depend on you and the kind of procedure you have. For most it is a matter of weeks, but make sure your surgeon examines you first. Some women reported that they could hit the tennis courts or golf course with ease. Others have a more difficult time. I couldn't lift heavy pots or pans (*no cooking!*) or pull myself into a cab, much less swing a tennis racket. I wasn't able to hold myself up in the water when I tried to take a swim. My arms and chest area were that weak. After consulting my doctor, I signed up for physical therapy to strengthen my upper body and improve my mobility. This helped. But what helped even more was working with a Pilates instructor. I credit this technique for strengthening my upper body, arms, and core. Safe body manipulation also helps to break down residual scar tissue. If you get a massage, make sure to tell the masseuse that you have had reconstructive surgery and also which arm is at risk for lymphedema. Better yet, go to someone whose expertise is in working with mastectomy patients.

AN EXPERT WEIGHS IN

- "Mastectomy with reconstruction is like having a giant rotator cuff injury," says Dr. Brian Nathanson, a self-described "fascia-ist." Soft tissue therapy on the fascia is his specialty. At his office, New England Physical Care, in Norwalk, Connecticut, he treats a variety of patients for muscular or joint-related discomfort, scar tissue, and related chronic pain using a trademarked, instrument-assisted Graston Technique. Twenty percent of his patients have been treated for breast cancer and usually come to him suffering from scar tissue on the fascia (the tough, fibrous tissue located between the muscle and outer skin) after a mastectomy and/or reconstruction.

- "After breast cancer surgery, a patient's fascia is scarred and knotted. There is limited mobility, something I refer to as 'broken wing syndrome.' I will maneuver the fascia using a combination of deep tissue massage and myofascial release and some pretty fierce-looking instruments to break up the scars and help patients regain mobility in the rotator cuff and arms. The therapy usually takes between six and twelve treatments and possibly more for patients who undergo radiation."

Dr. Nathanson works closely with breast reconstruction surgeons. "I have two types of breast cancer clients. The first come in before or after reconstruction. I work around the tissue expanders. I also see women years after their reconstruction who come in with a condition called 'radiculopathy,' where a nerve may be trapped in the scar tissue or a bulging disc."

The goal is to help a woman regain all of her mobility and help eliminate any residual pain or discomfort. Dr. Nathanson will also provide instructions for simple stretching exercises a patient can do at home. He notes that it is important to ease back into being active and doing activities you love. "Pick up your child. Have a workout. Ride your bike. Don't live in fear."

MY EXPERIENCE

When I met with Dr. Nathanson, he spent a good amount of time working my chronically tight rotator cuff and latissimus dorsi muscles, as well as the top of my pectorals and shoulders. The Graston Technique tool he used on me looked like a giant stainless steel butter knife, and when he applied oil to my body and started scraping the knife on my skin, all I could think of was buttering toast. I could hear and feel the scraping movement, which also made me feel like my fascia tissue was undergoing microdermabrasion. Afterward my body was anything but "toast." It was mildly sore in a good way, like my fascia had been given a good workout in order to soften and limber up. My range of motion was better.

NOTES

1. U.S. Department of Labor, "Your Rights After a Mastectomy: Women's Health and Cancer Rights Act of 1998," http://www.dol.gov/ebsa/publications/whcra.html.

2. Claudia R. Albornoz, Peter B. Bach, Babak J. Mehrara, Joseph J. Disa, Andrea L. Pusic, Colleen M. McCarthy, Peter G. Cordeiro, and Evan Matros, "A Paradigm Shift in U.S. Breast Reconstruction Increasing Implant Rates," *Plastic & Reconstructive Surgery*, January 2013, vol. 131, issue 1, 15–23, doi: 10.1097/PRS.0b013e3182729cde.

3. Institute of Medicine of the National Academies, "Safety of Silicone Breast Implants," 1999, http://www.iom.edu/Reports/1999/Safety-of-Silicone-Breast-Implants.aspx.

4. United States Institute of Medicine, "Information for Women about the Safety of Silicone Breast Implants," edited by M. Grigg, S. Bondurant, V. L. Ernster, et al. (Washington DC: United States National Academies Press, 2000), http://www.ncbi.nlm.nih.gov/books/NBK44775/. A report of a study by the Institute of Medicine, National Center for Biotechnology Information, and the United States National Library of Medicine, Bethesda, Maryland.

5. Breast Implant Safety.org, "Risks Related to Breast Implants," http://www.breastimplantsafety.org/SafetyRisksandBenefits/risks.php.

6. BioPortfolio, "Breast Reconstruction and Augmentation with Brava Enhanced Autologous Fat Micro Grafting," http://www.bioportfolio.com/resources/trial/100050/Breast-Reconstruction-And-Augmentation-With-Brava-Enhanced-Autologous-Fat-Micro-Grafting.html.

7. American Society of Plastic Surgeons (ASPS), "Post-Mastectomy Fat/Fat Transfer ASPS Guiding Principles," 2012, http://www.plasticsurgery.org/x1673.xml?google=Post-mastectomy+fat&x=0&y=0. Accessed June 27, 2013.

8. E. Delay, R. Sinna, T. Delaporte, et al., "Patient information before aesthetic lipomodeling (lipoaugmentation): a French plastic surgeon's perspective," *Aesthetic Surgery Journal*, 2009, 29, 386–95. See also http://www.ncbi.nlm.nih.gov/pubmed/19825467 or doi: 10.1016/j.asj.2009.08.007.

9. I. Sarfati, T. Ihrai, G. Kaufman, et al., "Adipose-tissue grafting to the post-mastectomy irradiated chest wall: preparing the ground for implant reconstruction," *Journal of Plastic, Reconstructive & Aesthetic Surgery*, September 2011, 64 (9), 1161–66. See also http://www.ncbi.nlm.nih.gov/pubmed/21514910 or doi: 10.1016/j.bjps.2011.03.031.

10. A. K. Seth, E. M. Hirsch, J. Y. Kim, and N. A. Fine, "Long-term outcomes following fat grafting in prosthetic breast reconstruction: a comparative analysis." *Journal of Plastic, Reconstructive & Aesthetic Surgery*, November 2012, 130 (5), 984–90.

11. J. Y. Petit, E. Botteri, V. Lohsiriwat, et al., "Locoregional recurrence risk after lipofilling in breast cancer patients," Oxford Journals, *Annals of Oncology*, 2011, http://www.ncbi.nlm.nih.gov/pubmed/21610155.

12. G. Rigotti, A. Marchi, P. Stringhini, et al., "Determining the oncological risk of autologous lipoaspirate grafting for post-mastectomy breast reconstruction," *Journal of Plastic, Reconstructive & Aesthetic Surgery*, August 2010, 34 (4), 475–80. See also http://www.ncbi.nlm.nih.gov/pubmed/20333521 or doi: 10.1007/s00266-010-9481-2.

Your Option to Reconstruction

7

"*I wish more women were told about their options. There are some very good alternatives to reconstruction if you know where to look and what to ask.*"

—*Kate Rubien,* CMF, cancer survivor

Underneath It All

THE TEN-YEAR ASPS SURVEY REPORTED THAT 21 TO 38 percent of women who undergo mastectomies choose reconstructive surgery. That means more than half still do not reconstruct. Their best option is a breast prosthesis.

Under the WHCRA, your health insurance is required to cover at least one silicone breast prosthesis and two mastectomy bras (some cover more bras), provided that you have a written prescription for a medical breast prosthesis from your doctor. You should check with your insurer to confirm exactly what is and is not covered and for what amounts and the wording that is required on the prescription.

Shopping for a breast prosthesis is an emotional experience that needs to be treated with sensitivity by an experienced, certified mastectomy fitter (CMF) who has a prerequisite 500 hours of bra-fitting experience and who has passed an examination on the subject. Since 2009, Medicare has required that all shops selling medical breast prostheses must be accredited. This is important to know if you plan to file for insurance coverage since policies may require that you purchase your prosthesis from an accredited provider.

Looking online at outlets that sell breast prostheses, I skipped over anything with the utilitarian words *surgical products* or *orthotics*. These kinds of stores usually sell a limited number of utilitarian prostheses and are not exactly warm and fuzzy. Instead, go for quality and style and find a specialist who works in a store that caters to women who have had mastectomies.

I turned to SHARE for a list of providers and found Underneath It All, an elegant salon on Fifth Avenue in Manhattan that specializes in mastectomy bras, breast prostheses, lingerie, bathing suits, and wigs. Developed in 1993 by Carol Art Keane, a breast cancer survivor, Underneath It All is the perfect shop for the woman who wants a knowledgeable and caring team to help her choose her breast wardrobe. I met with Carol's partners and CMFs, Kate Rubien and Christina Faraj. Kate is a breast cancer survivor and Christina's mother had breast cancer. Here is what I learned:

WHY DO YOU NEED A PROSTHESIS?

Whether you have a single or double mastectomy there are some important reasons for wearing a breast prosthesis, and they are not all about your appearance. Sure, your clothes will hang better, and you will feel more balanced. But there's more to it, which is why they are called "medical" prostheses:

- A prosthesis will support your posture and help prevent poor skeletal alignment, slumping shoulders, and potential back pain and breastbone problems.

- It prevents your bra from shifting and tugging if you had a single mastectomy, which can cause discomfort in the shoulder and chest area.

- It protects the scar area on your chest.

You will need to be completely healed from your surgery before being fitted for a prosthesis. For your visit, plan to wear a form-fitting top rather than a loose shirt so you can better see how the prosthesis will fit in your clothes.

THE BRA COMES FIRST

You most likely will only need one visit for a fitting. First, you need to be fitted for a bra, which serves as the foundation to hold the prosthesis in place. It's really no different than shopping for a regular bra, and there are many styles to choose from if you are going to the right store. Underneath It All sells beautiful and sexy lace bras with discreet pockets as well as sportier bras for your workouts. Your fitter will decide the best size for you. (You may think you know this but let the fitter measure you and give recommendations!)

OPTIONS

Today's prostheses are lightweight yet supportive and are made from high-quality medical-grade silicone. Unlike cup sizes, prostheses come in sizes from 0 to 14. Like bras, there are many varieties and styles. There are different shapes, sizes, and color tones to match to a woman's body and skin tone. Prostheses come in "left side," "right side," and different symmetries to provide the best match for your body's needs. The texture feels like a real breast. Most slip into pockets in mastectomy bras, bathing suits, and camisoles. Some more expensive versions are self-adhesive. There are also breast forms for after surgery and swimming, press-on areola and nipples in different sizes and skin tones, and just about every possible form, filler, or enhancer for partial reconstructions, lumpectomies, and balancing out uneven breasts after surgery. Kate even showed me "nipple covers" for when you want your "headlights off."

CARE

Most prostheses and fillers are hand washable in cold water and have a two-year warranty. Some pieces may have a shorter warranty. Check the warranty and check your insurance. Medicare issues the guidelines, and coverage for replacement is usually based on a two-year warranty. This includes one prosthesis (for a single mastectomy) or one set (for a double mastectomy). Kate suggests having your bra and prosthesis refitted annually, especially if you lose or gain weight, since this will affect the size you may need.

To find a certified mastectomy fitter where you live, Kate and Christina suggest looking at manufacturers' websites to see which outlets they recommend. Amoena is one of the world's largest manufacturers of quality prostheses and offers store locators on its website (www.amoena .us; Twitter: @amoena.us).

Nordstrom department stores around the United States sell breast prostheses, bras, and accessories and provide trained fitters (www.nordstrom.com, 1-888-282-6060).

Land's End offers a collection of mastectomy swimwear and has a special hotline and trained fit experts to assist in selecting a prosthetic swimsuit (www.landsend.com, 1-800-963-4816).

If you live in or plan to visit New York, Underneath It All is located at 320 Fifth Avenue at 33rd Street (www.underneathitallnyc.com, 212-717-1976).

A list of manufacturers and retail outlets can also be found on the American Cancer Society website: http://www.cancer.org/cancer/breast cancer/moreinformation/breast-prostheses-and-hair-loss-accessories-list.

Your Best Defense:

HYDRATE, GYRATE, AND MASTICATE!

MAKING HEALTHY CHANGES TO FIGHT CANCER IS A PRELUDE to making lifestyle changes to live a healthier and longer life. Cancer is just the kick in the butt to make the commitment faster if you have not done so already. The best defense is what I call the Holy Trinity of Healthy Living:

- Hydrate: Drink plenty of water and healthy liquids

- Gyrate: Move and exercise daily

- Masticate: Maintain a balanced and nutritionally sound eating plan

More sleep and less stress are the final two factors of healthy living, but I find I can manage on less sleep and deal with more stress when I adhere to my holy trinity.

Raise a Glass to Your Health

8

CHEMICALS, DRUGS, AND STRESS ALL DEHYDRATE YOU inside and out. Staying hydrated will help your body function better and enable you to eliminate waste. Staying hydrated can also help ward off nausea, dizziness, chemo brain, and dry skin. Hydration is important for properly flushing toxins out of your system; given what chemotherapy is putting into your system, you will definitely want to get rid of the by-products!

Pure still water or ice water is best, but if you need more taste, try flavored water or fresh fruit juices. Decaffeinated herbal teas can be useful, but some may have ingredients that interfere with your treatment. Check with your oncologist and nutritionist to see if there are any herbs that you should avoid. In general, try to go for fresh, sugar-free or low in sugar, caffeine-free, and low-sodium options. Here are a few more delicious ways to stay hydrated:

TWELVE WAYS TO HYDRATE

- Add slices of cucumber, oranges, or lemons to chilled still or sparkling water.
- Add fresh fruit juices to club soda or ginger ale or ginger beer.
- Blend fresh fruit and coconut water for a refreshing smoothie.

- Keep sliced fresh fruit in small, portion-controlled bags in the refrigerator.

- Pour fresh juices or cider into ice cube trays and pop out for a pick-me-up refresher.

- Freeze grapes (one of my favorites).

- Infuse slices of fresh ginger or lemon in hot water.

- Drink fresh fruit juices like watermelon, pineapple, and honeydew and add refreshing mint.

- Juice up some of your favorite vegetables.

- Buy sugar-free popsicles or make homemade fruit pops.

- Make homemade granitas or shaved ice with fresh fruit juices or agave syrups.

- Warm vegetable consommé for a soothing broth.

AVOID

- Caffeinated beverages (tea, coffee, soda)

- Sodas or any sugary beverages (including high-sugar juices)

- Enhanced energy drinks

If people ask you what they can bring you, tell them fresh-peeled fruit salads, fresh juices to chill and serve, and fresh soups that are easy to heat and easy to digest. Sugar-free or all-natural popsicles, pudding pops, and sorbets are also nice treats, but watch out for products made with artificial sweeteners. Some can worsen diarrhea. Review your medications with your oncologist and nutritionist to make sure you avoid anything that might interfere with their effectiveness. Grapefruit is one example. Some herbal teas or green tea may be off-limits.

Fight Fatigue

GET MOVING!

THE DAY AFTER MY MASTECTOMY, MY NURSES CAME IN and said, "Time to get up." There was no lying around. First I was sitting up, and by day three they had me walking . . . slowly, but walking nonetheless. A group of us tethered to our IV bags sat in a session where we were taught all sorts of exercises to regain motion in our upper bodies. The message was: Get moving; heal faster.

I decided not to take this fight lying down. Once I had my surgeon's approval, I ramped up my exercise program to thirty to forty minutes of light cardio and fifteen to twenty minutes of core work and stretching. I exercised about sixty minutes a day, four times a week. I could not afford a personal trainer, so I created my own program based on articles in magazines. Once the weather warmed up, I coaxed my husband to take walks with me. It gave us time to be together and unwind. As a result, I had more energy and was able to get through my surgeries, chemotherapy, and recovery with less interruption to my life.

BUT I CAN'T LIFT MY HEAD OFF THE PILLOW!

Everyone's cancer experience is different, and some may have a more difficult time with treatment than others. But I believe that for everyone, expending energy will help generate more energy. Even on my most fatigue-infused days, I forced myself to get up and move. Even twenty to thirty minutes made a difference. I also started early to get in better shape before my mastectomy. I tackled my cancer journey by training hard in advance, just like I trained hard to get in shape and build my endurance for the high altitudes and rough trails of the mountains I trekked in Asia and South America. Get in shape early to build your strength and stamina.

It is widely documented that regular exercise, a healthy diet, reduced stress, and plenty of sleep are the pillars of maintaining good health. If you haven't started yet, take a hard look at what's stopping you and ask yourself how important those obstacles are to your life and to your well-being. Your head and the rest of your body will feel a lot better if you get up and move. Do what you can, but don't overdo it. If you feel dizzy or nauseated, stop. And stay out of hot showers, saunas, and steam rooms at the gym until you are finished with treatment. The high temperatures could make you dizzy and faint, and the heat dries out your super-sensitive skin.

You don't need to join a gym or spend a lot of money to exercise. Take a walk or exercise at home. Here are five easy things to pick up at a sports retailer or a discount store like TJ Maxx for working out at home:

- Yoga mat or exercise mat for stretching and floor exercises. Make sure to clean it after each use. You can purchase a natural disinfectant spray from an organic foods store or supermarket, or create your own. I like to mix a half of cup of white vinegar in a spray bottle with water and a dew drops of lavender oil. If the smell of vinegar is unappealing, another option is two tablespoons Dr. Bronner's Magic Soap (I like the citrus orange scent) in a spray bottle with water.

- Resistance bands: These usually come in packs with different levels of resistance and a manual showing difference exercises. What I love about bands is that they don't take up space in your home, they are lightweight and pack easily in a suitcase, and they are versatile for working arms, legs and core muscles. You can always book an appointment with a trainer who can teach you exercises to do at home.

- Small exercise ball: I use the ball for arm lifts and rotations and thigh and stomach crunches.

- Plastic water bottles: Fill and use as light free weights. Or buy light two- or three-pound weights.

- Exercise videos that you can easily follow at home, or a Wii Fit program.

Many women I spoke with credit Pilates, yoga, dance, and swimming with helping them regain their range of motion in their arms and stay in shape. I had trouble swimming for months. My arms could not hold my weight in the water. So I focused on water exercises at my neighborhood YMCA and worked out regularly on a reclining stationary bicycle since it required nothing from my arms. After working with a physical therapist for three months, I started Pilates, which made a world of difference. Today, I take an integrative approach, combining cardio, core stability and strengthening, dance movement, light weights, and stretching. I find aerobic exercise helps alleviate the stiffness and mild arthritic-like pain I experience from taking Arimidex and helps maintain my energy throughout the day. My energy and focus on the days I exercise is much better than on the days I do not.

MOVEMENT PROGRAMS FOR BREAST CANCER PATIENTS

If you need motivation, there are many programs and classes across the country to help women and men get moving during and after treatment. Moving for Life is a nonprofit organization that provides aerobic exercise classes incorporating specific movements designed to help with the physical and emotional side effects of cancer treatment. The program was created by Martha Eddy, CMA, RSMT (a certified movement analyst and a registered somatic movement therapist). Skilled movement professionals must undergo a rigorous one-hundred-hour training program to become a Moving for Life certified instructor and holistic "Cancer Exercise Specialist." Moving for Life has certified instructors around the country and has put out a *Dance to Recovery* DVD. The program is open to anyone undergoing or finished with treatment.

"Aerobic exercise is critical for helping train your cells to get back into commission after cancer treatment. Efficient cellular metabolism counteracts fatigue. Livestrong research has shown that fatigue is the number one complaint by cancer patients in the United States. Aerobic exercise will help increase your energy," says Dr. Eddy.

Moving for Life's approach to aerobic exercise also addresses other body and mind side effects from treatment, including range of motion, lymphedema, neuropathy, joint pain, body mass index (weight gain or weight loss), anxiety and stress, and body image. "We take an integrative approach, customizing movements that lead to regaining a strong, capable sense of self. We include somatic education activities to help you listen to your body. This bodily awareness reduces the chance of injury. Private somatic movement therapy sessions using MFL include touch, movement repatterning, and relaxation."

Survivor Wisdom: EMPOWERED CANCER FIGHTERS MAKE NO EXCUSES!

If you say you are too busy taking care of your family, remember: taking care of yourself properly may give you more time to spend with your family in the long run. So do it for them if not for yourself.

If you say you are too busy with work just remind yourself that jobs and clients come and go. No one is indispensable. Work a full day if you feel up to it, but don't let work stress you out and do not run yourself ragged.

Moderate exercise will not only build up your energy reserves, it will make you feel better emotionally. Motion impacts emotion.

Chew on This

NUTRITION AND DIET ESSENTIALS

What foods did you crave during treatment?

"*Avocados*" —*Joyce*, diagnosed 2012

"*Pineapples*" —*Melanie*, diagnosed 2008

"*Coconut water and milk*" —*Debbie*, diagnosed 2009 and 2011

"*Oatmeal*" —*Karol*, diagnosed 2007

ALMOST EVERY CANCER SURVIVOR AND EXPERT I SPOKE with said that diet, exercise, and reduced stress are the key factors in staying healthy during and after treatment. Being both a cancer patient and a food industry professional, I made diet a top priority during treatment. It was kind of a "push-me-pull-you" reasoning: I wanted to stay healthy and I didn't want to get sick. I wanted the food going into my body to be as pure as possible to counteract the toxins being pushed into my system.

You wouldn't drive your car on empty or fill your tank with the wrong gas. So why would you treat your body any differently? Food is the fuel to keep your body engine running, and during cancer treatment you may need more and higher-quality fuel.

I still ended up losing some weight, but I also maintained a healthy weight, and that is important. I advise consulting with a registered dietitian who is a certified specialist in oncology nutrition (CSO) at the start of your diagnosis and throughout treatment to devise a sensible eating plan. For this section I consulted with Susan Bratton, founder of Meals to Heal (an oncology nutrition service that delivers nourishing, balanced, and delicious customized meals to the patient's home). For eating and nutrition tips, I spoke with Jessica Iannotta (Meals to Heal) and Holly Mills (FreshView Nutrition). Both are registered dietitians (RD), certified dietitian-nutritionists (CDN), and certified specialists in oncology (CSO), which means they have each completed at least two years of professional experience, have demonstrated a minimum of 2000 hours of nutrition practice in oncology, and have successfully passed a national certification examination every five years.

THE IMPORTANCE OF DIET AND NUTRITION MANAGEMENT TO CANCER TREATMENT

"Diet and nutrition will not cure cancer; however, proper nutrition can strengthen the body's immune system, prevent weight loss and malnutrition, and improve the patient's quality of life and clinical outcomes. In developing Meals to Heal, I conducted extensive research on the subject of oncology-related nutrition to assess the types and frequency of nutritional issues experienced by cancer patients as well as the impediments to their receiving proper nutrition. What I found was startling: Poor nutrition is pervasive in cancer patients, and it is indicated in 50 to 80 percent of all cancer cases. Malnutrition is the number-two secondary diagnosis in cancer patients, and 30 percent of all cancer deaths are due to severe malnutrition. I also found that if nutritional issues are addressed, a patient's clinical and quality of life outcomes improve. Not only does the patient respond better to treatment but she will *feel* better," said Susan.

"A hallmark study found that 'widespread agreement' exists that preventing, mitigating, and managing nutritional issues is essential in high-quality effective cancer care. Patients should undergo early and ongoing nutritional screening, assessment, counseling, and interventions to determine what specific micro- and macronutrients, food, supplements and vitamins they may need.[1-7]

"A separate study found that malnutrition in cancer patients has long been associated with adverse outcomes, reduced immune response, increased treatment toxicity, greater and more severe side effects, diminished quality of life, increased length of hospital stay, and reduced survival."[8-9]

Furthermore, "a study published by the American Society of Clinical Oncology reported that identification of nutrition problems and treatment of nutrition-related symptoms were shown to stabilize or reverse weight loss in 50–88 percent of cancer patients."[10]

Finally, a number of studies have shown that nutritional counseling also improves clinical and quality of life outcomes. Both the *Journal of Clinical Oncology* and the *Journal of the American Dietetic Association* have published articles showing that dietary counseling improves dietary intake, nutritional status, and quality of life and reduces or lessens the impact of treatment side effects and, in some studies, radiation-induced morbidity."[11–13]

"In short, just like going to chemotherapy or radiation, patients should consider proper nutrition—both eating right and getting nutritional counseling (an essential part of their cancer journey) both before and after treatment," Susan summarized.

KITCHEN WISDOM FOR CANCER PATIENTS

from Jessica Iannotta and Holly Mills (Meals to Heal)

"Work with your registered dietitian to create a nutrition framework that best suits your needs. Every woman begins her cancer journey at a different place. An oncology dietitian will begin by evaluating your current nutritional status and helping you set individualized goals to maintain optimal nutrition through cancer treatment and beyond," said Jessica.

She continues, "Evaluate your diet and goals. Make small changes at first and adjust as you go. Remember, when everything else seems like it is out of control, your nutrition is something that you can control! Optimizing your nutritional intake empowers you to take control of your health."

BUILDING IMMUNITY: JESSICA IANNOTTA'S TIPS

- *Consume adequate protein.* Protein is your body's building block to repair damaged cells and rebuild your immune system. Choose lean meats, poultry, turkey, eggs, fish, yogurt, cheese, tofu, beans, and nuts. Speak with your registered dietitian if you are concerned about your protein intake.

- *Consume more antioxidant-rich fruits and vegetables* full of vitamins C, E, and beta-carotene. *Vitamin C* can be found in foods such as citrus fruits (oranges, grapefruit), green and red peppers, kiwis, tomatoes, broccoli, and fortified foods. *Vitamin E* can be found in foods such as wheat germ, vegetable oils, nuts, and seeds. *Beta-carotene* can be found in foods such as carrots, sweet potatoes, cantaloupe, red peppers, mangoes, and broccoli.

- *Consume more colorful fruits and vegetables* full of phytochemicals such as lycopene, lutein, and ursolic acid, which are known to enhance immunity, repair damage, and fight disease. *Lycopene* can be found in tomatoes, watermelon, and red grapefruit. *Lutein* can be found in dark green leafy vegetables like spinach. *Ursolic acid* can be found in cranberries, prunes, and apples.

- *Cook with flavorful herbs and spices* such as ginger and turmeric. Ginger can be added to soups, stir-fry, and homemade tea. Turmeric is used to make curry, casseroles, soups, and stews.

- *Organic versus nonorganic*: Fruits and vegetables have numerous health benefits whether or not they are organic. To reduce exposure to pesticides, some choose to buy organic. Be aware that organic foods can be more expensive and spoil more easily. If you cannot afford organic, the benefits of any fruits and vegetables outweigh any risk of pesticide exposure, and organic foods are not a mandatory component of a cancer-fighting diet. Be sure to wash fruits and vegetables well. If you can afford to buy *some* organic, the Environmental Working Group's recommendations are a great place to start.

- *Avoid processed foods, convenience foods, and fast foods,* which do not contain the healthful properties of a cancer-fighting diet and contain excessive sodium, preservatives, and saturated fats.

- *Always ask*: What foods interfere with my medication? Grapefruit is a common food that can interact with certain medications and interfere with drug metabolism in the body. It is also important to avoid any questionable herbal ingredients in larger quantities that may interfere with chemotherapy treatments. This may include herbal and green teas. Most important, supplemental forms of antioxidants, herbals, and botanicals also have the potential to inhibit the effectiveness of chemotherapy by being potent antioxidants and protecting cellular damage. It is important to discuss individual herbs and supplements with your registered dietitian and health care team, who can help you make an informed decision.

THE ENVIRONMENTAL WORKING GROUP'S 2013 SHOPPER GUIDE TO PESTICIDES IN PRODUCE

Dirty Dozen (produce with the highest pesticide residue)	Clean Fifteen (produce with the lowest pesticide residue)
Apples	Asparagus
Celery	Avocados
Cherry tomatoes	Cabbage
Cucumbers	Cantaloupe
Grapes	Eggplant
Hot peppers	Grapefruit
Nectarines (imported)	Kiwi
Peaches	Mangos
Potatoes	Mushrooms
Spinach	Onions
Strawberries	Papayas
Sweet bell peppers	Pineapples
	Sweet corn
	Sweet peas (frozen)
	Sweet potatoes

The great thing about working with a registered dietitian who is a certified specialist in oncology is that you won't waste your time or money buying foods that you think you need but really don't. It's like when we buy expensive beauty creams that don't make that big of a difference. The stuff you read on the Internet can make it even more confusing. Your nutritionist will pare it down and make a plan for you. I asked Jessica to enlighten me, and here is what she shared:

I Was Told to Avoid Fatty Foods. What Are Some "Good Fats"?

"Because fat is a necessary component of cells, organs, nerves, and tissues, your body does need fat in order to function optimally. There are two types of fat: unsaturated fats and saturated fats. It is best to choose more unsaturated fats and fewer saturated fats.

- *Unsaturated fats* are usually liquid at room temperature. Certain polyunsaturated fats like *omega-3 fatty acids* can actually help promote heart health. They decrease inflammation in your body, helping protect against many chronic diseases, such as cardiovascular disease and cancer. Sources of unsaturated fat include olive oil, canola oil, and flaxseed, and fatty fish like wild salmon, fish oil supplements, walnuts, and almonds.

- By contrast, *saturated fats*, like butter, lard, and coconut oil, are solid at room temperature and can increase your serum cholesterol. Saturated fats are more likely to lead to the buildup of 'bad' cholesterol (LDL) in your blood stream, contributing to the blockage and inflammation of your arteries and blood vessels. *Trans fats* have similar negative cardiovascular effects as saturated fats. In fact, they not only increase 'bad' LDL cholesterol but also decrease good HDL cholesterol."

How Can You Add More Healthy Fat to Your Diet?

- Consume more omega-3 fatty acids from sources such as wild salmon, tuna, and mackerel, walnuts, flax, canola oil, and omega-fortified eggs. Fish oil supplements that contain both EPA and DHA can be taken under the guidance of your physician.

- Consume monounsaturated fat from sources such as avocados, olive oil, and almonds.

- Speak with your registered dietitian if you have specific questions about your dietary fat intake."

I Keep Reading That Sugar Is Evil, but I Love My Dark Chocolate!

"All foods are acceptable in moderation. Try to avoid highly processed and artificial sweeteners such as high-fructose corn syrup, aspartame, acesulfame potassium, and sucralose, and instead choose natural sweeteners such as raw sugar, honey, real maple syrup, fruit, and agave," says Jessica.

What About Miracle Foods like Açai and Flax?

Jessica continues, "There will always be the latest and greatest miracle food. However, if you focus too much on these foods, you may miss out on the benefits of all of the other healthy and delicious foods! You should also be sure that the foundation of your diet is healthy and well balanced, because any new antioxidant-rich food will not make any difference unless you are already eating a healthy cancer-fighting diet packed with fruits, vegetables, grains, legumes, and lean protein. Essentially there is no magic bullet or miracle food. For example, açai berries may be rich in antioxidants, but so are blueberries, especially the wild kind, which are a great addition to smoothies, yogurt, waffles, and muffins. Flaxseed is a good source of alpha-linolenic acid, a type of omega-3 fatty acid and dietary fiber, but so are walnuts and heart-healthy salmon. Flax should be used in one to two tablespoon portions per day, as too much may contribute to gas and bloating, especially if added quickly."

To Eat Soy or Not to Eat Soy?

Jessica responds: "This is probably one of the biggest questions that breast cancer patients ask. Soy foods contain isoflavones, which are phytoestrogens that are similar in structure to human estrogen. The majority of human studies demonstrate that, in moderation, soy is likely safe. However, there are many factors that come into play, such as age at the time of diagnosis, menopausal status, weight status, and family history. The consensus is that one to three servings of soy foods per day are considered safe. There is no need to add soy suddenly to your diet, as it should always be consumed in moderation within the context of a healthy, well-balanced diet. It is most important to avoid processed sources of soy such as soy powders, shakes, and supplements. These products contain isolated soy protein that may be in a form that is too potent and does not provide the same benefit as the whole food. They also do not have any data that demonstrate their safety. If you have questions about your specific soy intake, speak with your registered dietitian and health care team."

What If I Am a Vegan?

Holly Mills responds: "You can remain a vegan during treatment and recovery, but you need to work with an RD or nurse practitioner to make sure you consume adequate protein, especially after surgery or during chemotherapy when your protein needs are higher. Additionally, a vegan diet may be deficient in micronutrients like vitamin B12 and iron. An RD can work with you to make sure you are getting the nutrients you need."

MANAGING YOUR DIET TO COPE WITH SIDE EFFECTS

The challenge for me was deciding how to maintain a healthy diet when I was hypersensitive to smells, and many foods tasted off or metallic, which is a common problem with patients. I also wanted to avoid throwing it all up or having discomfort from bloating and constipation, which seemed to be a constant issue. Fortunately I grew up in the Deep South, where my mother cooked bland boiled vegetables and unseasoned broiled white-meat chicken, and that is what I craved during treatment. Boiled spinach, green beans, and squash were my comfort foods. I preferred fresh pineapples, papayas, and just about any juicy fruits. I also ate smaller, more frequent portions.

I asked Jessica how to handle diet and the common side effects of treatment. Here are her tips:

Loss of Appetite

"Although you may not feel like eating, keep in mind that getting adequate nutrition and maintaining a healthy weight are important parts of your recovery. Take advantage of the times when you do have an appetite and try to consume small frequent meals and snacks throughout the day. Eat in enjoyable surroundings, and make meals look less overwhelming by placing them on smaller plates rather than larger plates."

Changes in Your Palate

"During cancer treatment, foods you usually like may become unappealing. You may also find that foods taste bland, bitter, or metallic. Try rinsing your mouth with one to two ounces of baking soda rinse before and after meals (one quart water, three quarters of a teaspoon salt, and one teaspoon baking soda). If red meats taste strange, try substituting other proteins such as chicken, turkey, fish, eggs, dairy, beans, or tofu. Eat foods that smell and look good to you. Some patients report a metallic taste in their mouths, so it may be helpful to avoid using metal utensils. Instead, use plastic utensils. Avoid hot foods to reduce strong odors, and serve food at room temperature."

Managing Nausea

If you have ever had food poisoning or experienced sea sickness, you know that once you start tossing your cookies it never seems to end. Envision merging both conditions together and you have nausea from chemotherapy! When I asked my cancer mentor how she managed nausea, her advice was this, "Stay ahead of the nausea so it doesn't grab you from behind." While nothing can totally prevent nausea, and everyone's reaction is different, here are a few things to try:

- Take your oncologist-prescribed antinausea medicine as directed.
- Drink water—still or sparkling—and soothing herbal teas like ginger.
- Lie down and put a cool damp washcloth over your face.
- Try deep breathing techniques.
- If you have mild nausea, try an over-the-counter remedy like ginger candies, teas, and pills, with physician approval.
- If you have extreme nausea, contact your doctor and keep hydrated.

The last thing you want to do when nauseated is eat. Here is Jessica's advice for preventing or managing nausea: "Nausea is sometimes described as an unsettling or queasy feeling in the stomach and can be experienced with or without vomiting. Having an empty stomach may make nausea and vomiting worse, so be sure to eat regular meals and snacks. Eat small, frequent meals (five to six times a day) instead of three large meals, and avoid greasy or spicy foods and food with strong odors. Eat foods such as crackers, toast, or clear broth that may be easier on your stomach. Try ginger teas, ginger snaps/cookies, or gingerroot in soups."

Fatigue

Jessica says, "Fatigue is one of the most common side effects experienced by patients receiving treatment for cancer. It is usually described as feeling very weak, tired, or having a lack of energy. Choose foods high in protein and calories, which provide lots of energy. Try nutritional supplements or liquid meal replacements if recommended by your physician and health care team. Address underlying anemia if that is a contributing factor.

Constipation

Holly Mills weighs in: "Management of constipation includes adequate fluid and fiber intake and regular physical activity. I encourage patients to consume between eight and ten cups of fluid daily as long as they have not been advised to restrict fluids for another medical condition. Adequate fluid intake is essential for bowel regularity and the prevention of constipation. Eating dietary fiber found in foods like whole grains, beans, fruit, and vegetables is important. I recommend patients consume at least twenty-five grams of fiber daily. For those patients whose diets are unusually low in fiber, I encourage them to slowly introduce fiber into their diet and drink of plenty of water. Suddenly adding large amounts of fiber to your diet without adequate fluid intake may result in abdominal bloating or gas.

"Additional remedies for constipation management include warm prune juice, a cup of coffee, whole flaxseeds, and Senna tea. For those individuals interested in trying Senna tea, I advise speaking to your health care team first. This product is for short-term use only. It is not recommended to take Senna tea on a regular basis for bowel regularity.

"Heavy doses of pain medication and nausea medication may require the need for over-the-counter stool softeners or prescription medication. I communicate regularly with the medical team to discuss patient cases including treatment plans and side effects. My patients may not tell their oncologists everything they tell me so it is important to communicate with their doctors."

Diarrhea

Jessica says, "Diarrhea occurs when you are having frequent loose, soft, or watery bowel movements, and it can quickly lead to dehydration. Avoid foods high in fiber, greasy or fatty foods, raw vegetables, and caffeine. Be sure to stay hydrated. Drink a minimum of eight to ten eight-ounce glasses of fluid per day, such as water, clear beverages like broth or juices, Gatorade, or decaffeinated tea. Consume foods rich in potassium such as fruit juices and nectars, bananas, and potatoes (without skin) to help replenish the potassium that can be depleted with diarrhea. Consume foods high in pectin and soluble fiber such as applesauce, baked apples, bananas, and oatmeal, all of which can help bind the stool and make it more formed."

Extreme Weight Loss

Jessica says, "Cancer and its treatment can have a profound effect on a patient's nutritional status due to biochemical changes (such as an increase in metabolism and inflammation) or as a result of the cancer hindering the digestive system's ability to properly absorb nutrients. Treatment side effects can further impact nutritional status by impeding patients' ability to consume whole food. All of these factors can result in weight loss and malnutrition. It is important for cancer patients and caregivers to proactively focus on preventing weight loss and malnutrition, beginning at the time of diagnosis, because both result in poor outcomes and because both are hard to reverse."

Jessica recommends including more calorie- and protein-rich foods to your diet if your appetite is decreased. Here are some examples:

Sources of additional calories: Add extra butter, oil, mayonnaise, sauces, dressing, gravy, honey, jam, cheese, and nuts to your meals. Drink high-calorie liquids such as juice, milkshakes, smoothies, and protein drinks. Include nutrient-dense snacks such as yogurt, cheese and crackers, peanut butter and crackers, or trail mix. Try nutritional supplements or liquid meal replacements if approved by your physician and health care team.

Sources of additional protein: Add poultry, meat, fish, eggs, yogurt, cheese, beans, and nuts to your meals and snacks. High protein snacks such as peanut butter crackers, granola bars, nuts, yogurt, pudding, and cheese can be helpful. Mixing dried milk powder in gravies, soups, and sauces can also add extra protein. Try nutritional supplements or protein powders if recommended by your physician and health care team. Be sure to speak with your registered dietitian and health care team to determine which would be the most appropriate for you.

Weight Gain

"Steroids make you gain weight. Wish I had known."

—Tracey, diagnosed 2002

Some treatments, medications, and steroids make you gain weight. Stress eating and inactivity can also make the pounds creep up on you.

Holly says, "When I meet with patients in the middle of treatment, I usually tell them to focus on weight maintenance. However, I will review their diets and level of physical activity. A lot of people don't realize they may gain weight, so I work with them on appropriate techniques that they can start implementing during treatment, such as making healthier food choices and eating smaller portions. I encourage patients to see me for weight loss recommendations after their treatment is over and not during. I do not promote a lot of lifestyle changes during treatment. However, I advocate continuing a relationship with a registered dietitian post-treatment for weight management counseling, as being overweight is a risk factor for recurrence."

Diet Management

Both Jessica and Holly recommend keeping a food diary to track what you are eating to help you manage your weight and identify foods or eating patterns that may be aggravating your symptoms. Your registered dietitian can provide the most individualized recommendations for you by looking at several days' worth of your typical food intake.

No Time or Energy to Cook?

The last thing you probably want to do is stand over a stove. If your caregiver is a decent cook, you are a lucky! If not, this is a good time to rally all those friends who rushed you after surgery and ask them to help out with grocery shopping. Assign them days to prepare and deliver healthy dishes. Also, give them a checklist of what you can and cannot eat. Some supermarkets now have personal shoppers who will purchase what you want and arrange for home delivery. Meals to Heal will develop a customized plan developed by an oncology dietitian and will deliver meals to your home (service is available in the continental United States.

TIME SAVERS: JESSICA IANNOTTA'S
HEALTHY DIET SHOPPING LIST

Category	Food	Purchasing Pointers
FRUITS	Berries	Buy fresh or frozen blueberries, blackberries, cranberries, raspberries, and strawberries.
	Citrus fruits	Buy lemons, oranges, and tangerines.
VEGETABLES	Cruciferous vegetables	Buy broccoli, Brussels sprouts, cabbage, cauliflower, or kale.

	Tomatoes	Choose cooked tomato products more often than raw, as heat helps to release more lycopene.
PROTEIN	Fish	Sardines, mackerel, wild salmon, and tuna are high in omega-3s.
	Legumes	Buy lentils, dried beans, and peas. Canned legumes are an acceptable alternative.
	Nuts (Brazil nuts, walnuts, almonds)	Make sure to buy nuts that are not roasted or salted.
GRAINS	Whole grains	Buy grain products that are ideally 100% whole grain or that list a whole grain ingredient first.
DAIRY	Yogurt	Select a low-fat yogurt with a variety of active cultures.
OTHER	Tea	Buy green, black, white, or oolong tea to brew. Bottle, decaffeinated, or instant powdered provide minimal flavonoids.

TIME SAVERS: JESSICA IANNOTTA'S EASY AND HEALTHY SNACKS AND MEALS

Designed with Anne Pesek, RD, CD

Jessica says, "The following snack and meal ideas require minimal preparation and are loaded with fruits and vegetables, whole grains, and lean proteins—all of which are an important part of a healthy diet during and after cancer treatment."

- Cottage cheese and fruit plate
- Pudding popsicle: prepare low-fat pudding and freeze in popsicle molds (or freeze low-fat pudding singles)
- Yogurt parfait: mix together plain yogurt with honey and top with cereal or nuts
- Fruit parfait: mix yogurt with dried fruits and nuts (one ounce each)
- Homemade healthy granola bars: recipe provided at the end of this list
- Cheese on whole grain crackers or toast
- Toaster waffle with yogurt and berries
- Whole grain pasta salad: mix together whole grain pasta noodles, olive or canola oil, and steamed vegetables
- Hummus and raw vegetables or pita bread
- Homemade trail mix: mix together your choice of nuts, dried fruit, crackers, and pretzels
- Baked sweet potato
- Rice cake or crackers topped with peanut butter and banana
- Hard-boiled egg on one slice of whole grain bread or an English muffin
- Power smoothie: place 1 cup low-fat yogurt, 1 banana, 1 tablespoon peanut butter, and ice in a blender, and mix until smooth

Healthy Granola Bars

Recipe provided by Jessica Iannotta

Ingredients

2 cups rolled oats
¾ cup packed brown sugar
¾ teaspoon ground cinnamon
1 cup all-purpose flour (or whole wheat flour)
¾ cup dried fruit (or ½ cup dried fruit + ¼ cup chopped nuts)

¾ teaspoon salt
½ cup honey
1 egg, beaten (or two egg whites)
½ cup canola oil
2 teaspoons vanilla extract

Directions

1. Preheat the oven to 350°F. Generously grease a 9x13 baking pan.

2. In a large bowl, mix together the oats, brown sugar, cinnamon, flour, dried fruit, and salt. Make a well in the center, and pour in the honey, egg, oil, and vanilla. Mix well using your hands. Pat the mixture evenly into the prepared pan.

3. Bake for 30–35 minutes in the preheated oven, until the bars begin to turn golden at the edges. Cool for 5 minutes, then cut into bars while still warm. Do not allow the bars to cool completely before cutting, or they will be too hard to cut.

Note: All fruit suggestions are interchangeable depending on your preferences or specific needs. Certain foods on this list may not be appropriate to meet your individual requirements. If you have any questions, speak with your registered dietitian or physician about your individual nutrition needs.

Easy, Healthy Meals

Jessica provided these easy and healthy meal suggestions. Most take fifteen minutes to prepare. Personally I found steamed or lightly sautéed leafy greens to be soothing on my stomach and intestinal tract and tried to have a serving with every meal. Try spinach, kale, collards, bok choy, Swiss chard, or whatever is in season and make sure to wash thoroughly before cooking.

- Grilled chicken breast with brown rice
- Whole grain flatbread sandwich: fill with cheese and choice of fruits or vegetables
- Grilled tuna with steamed vegetables
- Whole grain rice with plain nuts, choice of steamed vegetables, olive or canola oil, and dried fruit
- Whole grain pita with egg salad, tuna salad, or chicken salad, and fresh vegetables
- Salad with fresh vegetables, cottage cheese, and beans

- Turkey burger on a whole grain bun

- Egg white omelet: fill with low-fat cheese and a mix of vegetables

- Whole grain pasta with olive or canola oil and steamed vegetables or beans

- Chicken and vegetable stir-fry over instant brown rice

- Cheese and vegetable quesadilla (for extra protein, add grilled chicken)

- Roasted vegetable wrap: make with choice of roasted vegetables and cheese (for extra protein, add grilled chicken)

- Stuffed peppers: fill with instant rice and mixed vegetables

- Whole grain bagel or flatbread: serve open-faced and top with roasted vegetables and low-fat cheese

- Minestrone, lentil, or any hearty soup (with beans, vegetables, noodles, rice, and lean meat if desired)

CAN I GET YOU A DRINK?

I work in the wine, spirits, and food business. During my treatment I organized wine tastings. I attended a cocktail conference in New Orleans. I was the token teetotaler in the room among hundreds of happy cocktailians. You should avoid consuming alcohol during treatment. First, it is extremely dehydrating. Second, alcohol can wreak havoc in your already compromised system and can irritate mouth sores. Third, wine or champagne probably won't taste good to you anyway.

After treatment, discuss with your medical oncologist if and when you can resume drinking wine, beer, or cocktails. While many medical and nutrition experts advise breast cancer survivors to avoid alcohol consumption, my fellow wine lovers, don't despair. While much has been reported about the link between alcohol consumption increasing the risk of breast cancer, according to a study released in April 2013 by the Fred Hutchinson Cancer Research Center in Seattle, "the relationship between alcohol consumption and breast cancer survival is less clear." Furthermore, the study concluded "Overall alcohol consumption before diagnosis was not associated with disease-specific survival, but we found a suggestion favoring moderate consumption."[14] The study indicates that moderate consumption of alcohol may be beneficial in reducing the risk of dying from cardiovascular disease, a major cause of mortality among breast cancer survivors. Alcohol consumption and your health is something to address with both your doctor and nutritionist after treatment has concluded, and moderation is always a smart approach.

There are some delicious options to alcohol-free cocktails. Natalie Bovis, "The Liquid Muse," wrote a book for expectant mothers called *Pregatinis: Mixology for the Mom-to-Be* that is filled with refreshing alcohol-free drinks. I asked her to recommend a few thirst-quenching options for fearless and fabulous cancer chicks. The recipes she shared are easy, refreshing, and have ingredients that can help with queasy chemo tummies.

Soothing Ginger Tea

Ginger is a great stomach soother. This recipe makes two servings:

1 heaping teaspoon of freshly grated ginger (or one organic ginger tea bag)
Small bunch of fresh mint
1 teaspoon lavender or wildflower honey

1. Pour two cups of boiling water over mint and ginger (or tea bag) in a teapot. Let steep five minutes. Add honey. Serve in teacups or mugs.

Kingston Krush

There's a famous song that says, "Put the lime in the coconut and you'll feel better." This one adds açai juice, which is rich in antioxidants.

3 ounces coconut water
1 ½ ounces açai juice
¼ ounce lime juice
½ teaspoon coconut flakes

1. Pour all ingredients in a mixing glass. Shake with ice, and then strain into a cocktail glass. Sprinkle with coconut flakes.

Pineapple Paradise

Pineapples* help quench those dry mouth days. Ginger beer, which contrary to its name is an alcohol-free beverage, is a stomach soother, as are the bitters.

1½ ounces pineapple juice

Dash Angostura bitters (optional)
Ginger beer
Pineapple wedges

1. Pour the juice, bitters, and ginger beer into a tumbler glass filled with ice. Garnish with a pineapple wedge.

*Note: Pineapples, though thirst-quenching, are acidic. If you have mouth sores, you may want to avoid them. Rinse your mouth with water after drinking or eating acidic foods.

Apricot Gingerini

Both ginger and clove can ease the stomach. White grape juice is a refresher.

2 ½ ounces white grape juice
3 ounces apricot nectar
1 ounce ginger-infused simple syrup
¼ teaspoon ground clove

1. Pour juices, ginger-infused simple syrup, and most of the ground clove into a mixing glass filled with ice. Shake vigorously and strain into a martini glass. Garnish with remaining clove.

Credit: Recipes excerpted with permission from Preggatinis: Mixology for the Mom-to-Be by Natalie Bovis *(Guilford, CT: Globe Pequot Press/© 2009).*

NUTRITION AND FOOD SAFETY NOTES FOR THE CAREGIVER

Susan Bratton watched some close friends suffer through cancer and endure numerous difficulties with food intake and diet management. As a result of these experiences, she was inspired to start Meals to Heal, seeking to help people like her friends with cancer and their caregivers get access to proper nutrition and nutritional resources. Susan notes that frequently the responsibility and concern for feeding the patient falls on the caregiver. "Caregivers are the unsung heroes of the cancer care world, often worrying on behalf of the patient about a wide range of things impacting her during treatment. Sometimes the diagnosis and the treatment become almost too much to handle, and the burden of confronting and addressing other important things like childcare, finances, nutrition, and other details falls on the caregiver. It is important for caregivers to focus on taking care of themselves also. This includes getting proper rest, eating right, and exercising."

SUSAN'S TIPS FOR CAREGIVERS

- Accompany the patient to meet with the RD-CSO and ask questions. Be actively involved in helping manage her diet and nutritional intake.

- Plan meals a week in advance to make shopping for groceries more efficient and reduce the number of trips to the store.

- Be flexible and patient. Her dislikes and side effects change daily. What she prefers one day she may not want on another day. Many caregivers become frustrated and anxious when the patient does not eat or does not like what the caregiver prepares. It's important to take a deep breath and realize it is not a rejection of your effort but, rather, a side effect of cancer that is as frustrating for the patient as it is for the caregiver.

- Pushing a patient to eat can create conflict. If the patient does not feel like eating or can't eat, try to encourage her to eat smaller bites more frequently, which makes the eating process more manageable.

- Keep the kitchen clean and utensils sanitized. Food safety is essential for a compromised immune system. Thoroughly wash fruits and vegetables as well as the chopping board. We recommend disinfecting with diluted bleach solution (generally one tablespoon per one gallon warm water) and then rinsing thoroughly. Make sure not to cross contaminate, and use separate cutting boards for meat and vegetables.

- Take extra caution when storing leftovers. Make sure to place in a container, seal tightly, and do not leave them in the refrigerator for longer than two days. Our rule of thumb is: "When in doubt, throw it out!"

- Take caution with—or avoid altogether—salad bars and open buffet tables when dining out, as they can harbor germs.

NOTES

1. K. S. Mann, "Education and Health Promotion for New Patients with Cancer," *Clinical Journal of Oncology Nursing*, February 2011, 15 (1) 55–61, PMID: 21278041. See also http://ons.metapress.com/content/ j27748r57t128647/ or doi: 10.1188/11.CJON.55-51.

2. National Cancer Institute, "Nutrition in Cancer Care," 2011, http://www. cancer.gov/cancertopics/pdq/supportivecare/nutrition/Patient.

3. F. D. Ottery, "Rethinking nutritional support of the cancer patient: the new field of nutritional oncology," *Seminars in Oncology*, 1994, 21 (6), 770–78, PMID: 7992092. PDF available for a nominal fee at http://pubget.com/ paper/7992092/Rethinking_nutritional_support_of_the_cancer_patient__ the_new_field_of_nutritional_oncology.

4. K. McMahon, G. Decker, and F. D. Ottery, "Integrating proactive nutritional assessment in clinical practices to prevent complications and cost," *Seminars in Oncology*, 1998, 25 (2 Suppl 6), 20–27, PMID: 9625379.

5. J. Bauer, S. Capra, and M. Ferguson, "Use of the scored Patient-Generated Subjective Global Assessment (PG-SGA) as a nutrition assessment tool in patients with cancer," *European Journal of Clinical Nutrition*, 2002, 56 (8), 779–85, PMID: 12122555. See also http://www.ncbi.nlm.nih.gov/ pubmed/12122555.

6. H. C. Lukaski, "Requirements for clinical use of bioelectrical impedance analysis (BIA)," *Annals of the New York Academy of Sciences*, 1999, 73:72–76, PMID: 10372152.

7. D. T. Dempsey and J. L. Mullen, "Prognostic value of nutritional indices," *Journal of Parenteral and Enteral Nutrition*, 1987, 11 (5 Suppl), 109S–114, PMID: 3312690.

8. D. T. Dempsey, J. L. Mullen, and G. P. Buzby, "The link between nutritional status and clinical outcome: can nutritional intervention modify it?" *Academy of Clinical Nutrition*, 1988, 47 (2 Suppl), 352–56, PMID: 3124596.

9. McMahon, et al, "Integrating proactive nutritional assessment."

10. D. Holder, "Nursing management of nutrition in cancer and palliative care," *British Journal of Nursing*, 2003, 12:667–68, 670, 672–74.

11. F. D. Ottery, S. Kasenic, S. DeBolt, et al. "Volunteer network accrues: 1900 patients in 6 months to validate standardized nutritional triage," *Proceedings of the American Society of Clinical Oncology*, 17:A-282, 73a.

12. P. Ravasco, I. Monteiro-Grillo, P. M. Vidal, et al. "Dietary counseling improves patient outcomes: a prospective, randomized, controlled trial in colorectal cancer patients undergoing radiotherapy," *Journal of Clinical Oncology*, 2005, 23 (7), 1431–38, PMID: 15684319.

13. E. A. Isenring, J. D. Bauer, and S. Capra, "Nutrition support using the American Dietetic Association medical nutrition therapy protocol for radiation oncology patients improves dietary intake compared with standard practice," *Journal of the American Dietetic Association*, 2007, 107 (3), 404–12, PMID: 17324657.

14. Polly A. Newcomb, Ellen Kampman, Amy Trentham-Dietz, Kathleen M. Egan, Linda J. Tutus, John A. Baron, John M. Hampton, Michael N. Passarelli, and Walter C. Willett (Fred Hutchinson Cancer Research Center), "Alcohol Consumption before and after Breast Cancer Diagnosis: Associations with Survival From Breast Cancer, Cardiovascular Disease, and Other Causes," *Journal of Clinical Oncology*, 2013, 31 (16), 1939–46, doi:10.1200/ JCO.2012.46.5765.

Staying Fearless & Fabulous during Treatment

"When the Japanese mend broken objects, they aggrandize the damage by filling the cracks with gold. They believe that when something's suffered damage and has a history it becomes more beautiful."

—*Barbara Bloom*, artist

Launch a Positive Counteroffensive

"Don't let cancer define you. You are more than your diagnosis."
—*Susan*, diagnosed 2005

ATTITUDE IS EVERYTHING

Looking back at my experience, I tell people that I wore an invisible tiara and not a halo on my head. I was a Cancer Princess, not a Cancer Patient. A friend of mine actually sent me a cartoon drawing of a princess to put in my diary.

MAKE YOUR DAYS MATTER

I found it helpful to create a routine. I would focus on my cancer calls, appointments, follow-ups, and connecting with friends and loved ones in the morning. Then I would let it go and focus on the rest of my day-to-day business. I set aside specific allotments of time to send and answer emails, open mail and pay bills, run errands, and have couple time with my husband. Every hour had a purpose. Every day had a goal. At night, I did not answer the phone unless I was prepared to address questions about my health from concerned relatives or friends. If I did not want to talk about cancer, I told people I was choosing to have some "cancer-free" time and changed the subject. Most understood. By sticking to the routine I developed, I felt I still had some level of control in a situation that could have easily spun out of control. Sure, there were slips, but more than anything else there was stability.

GRIN AND BARE IT

First, try to get over any body inhibitions you have. You'll be stripping down for a number of doctors who will be touching you. It's just part of the protocol. This may be harder for some women, especially if your upbringing, cultural background, or religious beliefs make it taboo to have your naked body, much less your private parts, viewed or touched by anyone other than a spouse. But it is part of the breast cancer drill. Your breasts will be touched. If you are uncomfortable, have someone you trust accompany you to examinations.

Second, get in touch with your own body. You need to read any and all signs of changes as you go along and be comfortable discussing them. One of the most difficult things is learning to look at your new body in the mirror. I posted encouraging quotes and funny cards around my mirror. One of them read, "You are going to need a bigger tiara after this one." Another said, "Hello, Gorgeous."

BLUE IS NOT YOUR BEST COLOR

"Give yourself permission to cry but don't sit on your pity pot too long."

—Carol, diagnosed 2002

It's not easy keeping a positive attitude when the news is negative. But it makes a difference. It is normal to feel angry, sad, confused, depressed, and heartbroken. It is not so good to remain that way. Cancer is not contagious but moods are. How you convey your emotions will impact how others feel around you. I promised myself that for every negative emotion I would work on a positive one. Cry and then a call a friend who will make you laugh. Play with your child or your pet. Hug your husband or significant other, who is undergoing just as much emotional stress as you are and may need reassurance. Negative energy is exhausting. Blue is not your best color right now.

You have a choice. You can wallow in misery and be sad or you can say to yourself, "This is a major inconvenience, a detour I did not plan; but I will focus and get through it the best I can." Use meditation and creative visualization to free your mind to feel better.

IT'S OKAY TO BE A LITTLE SELFISH

Let people treat you. Allow yourself to be indulged for once. My friends delivered home-cooked meals, provided easy-to-wear post-mastectomy tops, gave me massages, brought me books and watercolors, went shopping for me, and did their best to make me laugh. And the gift of friendship was the best gift of all.

Be very clear with everyone if you need some quiet time, because having a steady stream of visitor and callers can be emotionally taxing and tiring. I, for one, enjoy selective solitude to reflect and write. I also kept working, which I found distracting and therapeutic since my work was something I could still control in my life. Politely let people know if you need time for yourself.

A Caring Attitude Is a Two-Way Street

IT'S OKAY TO BE PROTECTIVE OF YOUR SPACE AND EMOTIONS; you may want to withdraw. But you also need to put yourself in the shoes of those who are sharing your Cancer Land journey. It's rough for them as well and they may not always be able to "read" you.

Don't take it personally if well-wishers fall by the wayside as you undergo treatment. For some, watching a friend go through treatment is just plain difficult. Others just get caught up in their day-to-day lives. You will also reconnect with friends who you may not have seen or heard from in awhile and deepen relationships elsewhere. Some of my nicest letters and gifts came from acquaintances who heard the news and quietly just wanted to reach out to show their support.

BE GRACIOUS

"Take naps. Take walks. Accept all acts of human kindness and food. Pamper yourself and write thank-you notes."

—Peaches, diagnosed 2005

I was showered with gifts and cards and funny poems to cheer me up. I suggest you keep a diary of all the people who reached out, sent letters, and gave gifts or time to you. They are your special community of friends and it is important to stay in touch with them to share news of your progress and recovery and to thank them for being there for you.

Being a gracious giver and receiver is important because you will be amazed at some of the things people do for you!

Once your treatment is over, host a victory party with your share-givers to thank them for being there for you. Take pictures. Write notes. Celebrate! And mentally promise yourself you will be there for the people who were there for you.

YOU'VE BEEN PINKED!

You will be sitting pretty in pink. It's the official color for breast cancer, and people will give you a lot of pink gifts. So I hope you like pink. I made a list of the pink gifts I received: socks, scarves, turbans, shawls, robes, sweaters, blankets, makeup bags, purse holders, pepper spray, key chains, baseball caps, bedroom slippers, underwear, camisoles, and a beautiful pink "survivor ring" from my mother that I will cherish forever. But it's okay and not disloyal to the breast cancer cause to say after treatment is over that you no longer want to be attired in or gifted pink if it makes you sad or is just not your favorite color.

GIFT IDEAS FOR HER, POST SURGERY AND DURING TREATMENT

What was your favorite gift someone gave you?

"A juicer so I could make my own fresh juices."

—Gina, diagnosed 2008

"$500 cash tucked inside a pillow and a hand-knitted soft hat a stranger made for me."

—Peaches, diagnosed 2005

"A fresh breakfast basket and an iPad."

—Debbie, diagnosed 2009 and 2011

"After my mastectomy, two friends took the Acela to New York to spend the day with me. They shopped for groceries and took me to lunch. It was a beautiful day!"

—Melanie, diagnosed 2009

It's the hospital's job to get you in and out of the facility quickly. So it is better for well-wishers to deliver flowers and gifts directly to the patient's home so no one has to carry them out. The same goes for hospital visits. Hospitals are stressful and where you recuperate. It's a good time for the patient to rest and be quiet. Better to save your visits for her home. Here are some gift ideas before and after surgery or during treatment:

- Warm socks, soft scarves, shawls or a robe that wraps, loose cotton button-front pajamas or big shirts (avoid anything that she has to slip over her head)

- Stock up her refrigerator and freezer with fresh soups and prepared meals.

- A basket of healthy snacks such as almonds, dried fruits, trail mix, and energy bars.

- Soft knit hats or pretty cotton scarves for when she starts losing her hair.

- Gift certificates for hand and foot massages—ask if she is comfortable receiving a full-body massage before gifting a certificate for this service

- After surgery, when showering is an issue, the gift of a professional hair wash and blow-dry is the best!

- Funny cards or notes before or after each chemo session to lift her spirits.

- Chip in with friends to hire a regular maid service to do the cleaning and laundry.

- Buy her pretty underwear or a soft camisole top that she can easily slip on and off, or a sarong that easily wraps.

- Offer to run errands, drive carpool, walk the dog, or pick up dry cleaning.

- Books on tape are great for longer chemo sessions or when her eyes are tired.

- Remember, cancer treatment lasts awhile. Keep in touch with your friend throughout her treatment and not just during her surgery.

If your friend is facing a mountain of hospital bills or is unable to work, set up a special gift bank account for her and ask friends to contribute to it. Or join up with friends to buy her one very special gift. When a close friend was diagnosed with advanced breast cancer and was unable to work, a large group of her friends pooled our funds to replace her old worn-out bed, bought new pillows and linens, and picked up a nice used sofa bed for her sister to sleep on when she came to stay with her.

A Doctor's Inspired Gift

Give her a "surgery survival bag." The Double Mastectomy BFFLBag contains an Axilla-Pilla comfort pillow designed to support tender underarms, wound and drain care supplies, a skin care gift pack, toiletries, collapsible water bottle, amusements pack, KIND healthy snack bars, and a folder to organize your important papers, all packaged in a high quality duffel bag. BFFL also offers bags tailored for lumpectomies and chemotherapy, as well as other kinds of cancer surgeries (see www.bfflco.com).

CARING ADVICE FOR THE CAREGIVER

While you are absorbed in keeping your life in order detailing a plan of action, your caregiver—usually a spouse, partner or close loved one—is watching and waiting for signs for what to do next. Here are eight caregiver tips:

- Make sure you read up on her condition to understand what she is going through and take notes at every doctor's appointment.

- Take care of all of her food needs: Stock the cupboards and refrigerators with healthy foods. Realize she may not want to eat and don't assume what you want to cook will be something she will want to eat. Discuss what foods do and do not agree with her. Make sure anything she needs is by her bed or on her desk and within easy reach. Make sure she is not trying to lift bags, heavy books, or anything that could strain her chest area. One or both arms will be weak depending on her type of surgery.

- Monitor her medications and make sure she takes her pills as scheduled and stays well hydrated.

- Take her out for "date nights" if she is up for it and do not discuss cancer or medicine. It is important to make sure that she has a life outside of cancer.

- Don't assume anything and be prepared for everything. She will be emotional. Don't take it personally. She may want to go out; don't expect her to stay bedridden. She may seem "normal" but be sensitive to what may be going on inside her head.

- Be her sounding board and "PR person" to share the news, on her terms, with everyone else.

- Tell her she is beautiful every single day and don't be afraid to touch and embrace her. She will not break!

Before my mastectomy, my husband, David, went out and purchased pillows, a pink Snuggie, a bed tray, a night-light, and a Kindle (uploaded with *The Velveteen Rabbit*) so I could stay cozied up in bed during my convalescence. The thing is, I didn't want to lie around propped up in bed in a Snuggie and kept asking for my computer and Blackberry so I could write emails and work. That was me, and that is what I needed to stay connected with the non-cancer world.

Stress?

NOT NOW; I HAVE A **HEADACHE**!

"Just when the caterpillar thought the world was over, it became a butterfly."

—Proverb

WITH A CANCER DIAGNOSIS, YOUR STRESS LEVEL CAN CLIMB to Code Red. If you are living a fast-paced life, you may feel like you have been brought to a halt, like a door was slammed in your face. If your life is slow and easy, you may feel like your life is starting to spin out of control. Fear, anger, denial, and disillusionment are normal. But you gather your wits, accept the challenge, and start the fight.

Clinical psychologist Carla Marie Greco works with cancer patients. In a nutshell, here is what she shared with me: "A cancer diagnosis triggers a grieving process. It is generally understood that the five stages of grief involve denial, anger, bargaining, depression, and acceptance. These stages do not necessarily occur in a linear fashion, and a cancer patient may cycle in and out of the stages."

TIPS FOR MANAGING YOUR EMOTIONS, SANITY, AND STRESS

- *Face your anger*: Dr. Greco says, "It is a myth that anger is not okay. Once the numbness of the diagnosis wears off a bit, anger often rises as the wide impact of the diagnosis filters through the

141

mind and body. Some women believe that their natural anger is inappropriate and, therefore, feel that it should be 'hushed' or hidden. Stifling anger can create additional stress on the body and mind."

- *It's okay to feel disillusioned.* Dr. Greco says that "while everything may not have been 'perfect' prior to the diagnosis, the devastating news brings a new dimension to life. No longer are days and moments taken for granted. Instead, the moments become both more precious and more painful as life begins to feel very precarious and shaky."

- *Find creative outlets to clear your head.* Seek ways to steady your mind, be it a creative outlet like writing in a journal or drawing; a spiritual outlet like prayer or meditation; a physical outlet like deep breathing, yoga, or other form of movement; or a healthy distraction like a hobby.

- *Ask for and be willing to accept help.* "Family and friends are vital resources during breast cancer treatment. Many women are accustomed to 'doing it all,' and the idea of relying on others speaks of weakness and dependency. Get over it. Now is not the time to be Superwoman. Reach out to others for assistance. You might be surprised at how many people truly want to help. Get used to the idea that, while you are in treatment, you are definitely someone who is 'in need.' Don't apologize for it, don't be embarrassed about it, and don't judge yourself for it. Muster up all the gracious and gentle dignity you have, and accept offers of help," says Dr. Greco.

- *Accept your limitations*: "Be it your work, parenting, or shouldering household responsibilities during treatment, learn to acknowledge and accept your limitations. By being up front about your needs and limitations, the stress of 'not performing' at full speed will be one of the least of your concerns," says Dr. Greco.

- *Being selfish is okay*: "By far, the most important tip is that this time of your life is ALL about YOU. Put that idea front and center in your mind. This is NOT a selfish way of thinking. Remember, if you are out of balance and stressed, you will be less able to heal and thrive," says Dr. Greco.

- *Be relentless about relaxing*: "Relaxation is an important part of the treatment and recovery process," says Dr. Greco. Some of the ways I relaxed were listening to music, meditation, yoga stretches, playing Scrabble, curling up with my dog and my husband, watching funny movies, and reading fashion or travel magazines.

- *Make small changes in your day-to-day life to make a big impact on your stress levels:* Dr. Greco echoes my sentiment about making lists to organize and prioritize. She suggests making two lists: the first with all of your critical tasks or responsibilities such as going to your doctor's office, getting treatment, paying bills, tending to basic self care, cooking, cleaning, helping kids with homework, etc. The second list is all the things that you can afford to cut out. Evaluate the lists through your eyes and those of others, like your doctor, partner, or dearest friend and pare down the first list. Stick the list on your refrigerator or desk as a reminder that your day-to-day life will be much easier to manage when you "let go" of the nonessentials.

- *Take ten*: Dr. Greco says that some of her clients told her they count to ten when emotions and stress start to well up. "As many stressful situations arise during the treatment process, it is easy for tempers to flare. Rather than taking anger out on the medical staff or loved ones, remembering to 'count to ten' before responding to any irritating or provoking situation can be a relationship saver!"

Whatever it takes to de-stress, make time for it, even if it's only ten minutes. I am going to build on this and give you ten ways to "take ten" for yourself:

MELANIE'S "TAKE TEN" LIST

- Ten minutes to stretch every hour or so to relax tension and tight shoulders.

- Ten minutes to close your eyes and just breathe deeply and visualize a beautiful place you want to visit.

- Ten minutes to call a good friend and just gossip and laugh.

- Ten minutes to chat with and really listen to your children, spouse, or partner talk about what they are up to (no cancer talk!).

- Ten minutes to massage your dry, sensitive skin with luxurious unscented body cream or essential oils (better yet, have your partner do it!).

- Ten minutes to have your scalp massaged by a friend or loved one.

- Ten minutes to take a short walk, even if it is only around the yard or down the street and back.

- Ten minutes to write a letter or thank-you note to someone who has been helping you out.

- Ten minutes to clean out a drawer (or two) that has been piling up with junk (I did this a lot!).

- Ten minutes to write down ten things you want to do when have your normal life back.

This Is Your Brain on Chemo

FOR AN ADMITTED CONTROL FREAK LIKE ME, A SIDE EFFECT I was unprepared to deal with at first was a condition referred to as "chemo brain." No one gave me enough warning about this side effect of chemotherapy. My head felt like it had been sliced in two and put back together off-kilter. It was hard to concentrate. I would forget words or someone's name. My eyes would be blurry. By the end of the day my brain ached with fatigue. My emotions were all over the place. I call it "Chemotion." Some days you feel like you are losing your mind, and other days you are just fine.

The definition of "chemo brain" on the American Cancer Society website (www.cancer.org) is "a mental fog" or "mild cognitive impairment." It usually starts during treatment and lasts for some time after. Some women report experiencing it from a few months to a few years. But women undergoing hormone therapy may go from cancer treatment right into menopause, which can proffer other mental fogginess.

COPING WITH YOUR CHEMOTIONS

I hated having chemo brain. I countered the symptoms with exercise, water, sleep, and cognitive exercises like making lists to organize my thoughts, and I turned to writing for therapy and kept a diary to document my emotions and my progress. I made sure anything requiring major cognitive focus took place early in the day when I was fresh from waking up and my workout. I cleaned out drawers and closets, which somehow helped clear my mind.

TIPS FOR DEALING WITH CHEMO BRAIN

- Become familiar with your body's energy cycle while undergoing treatment and work with it rather than against it. If you need to rest, make the time. Do not overtax yourself.

- Take on bigger tasks during the times when your energy level and mind are at their best.

- Don't schedule anything too important (like reviewing budgets or paying bills) at the end of the day or when you are more fatigued.

- Watching a movie or TV may be easier than concentrating on reading a novel.

- Write down your thoughts or pick up some paints and express yourself.

- Pop on headphones and listen to music.

- Play board games or cards to get your mind to focus.

- Keep oxygenated through deep breathing and light exercise and stay hydrated.

- Some women seek out acupuncture to alleviate chemo brain.

- Remember: this too shall pass.

BLAME IT ON CHEMO BRAIN!

Here are some chemo brain experiences from me and a few others who were willing to share:

- Forget to pay your credit card bill? Whoops! Chemo brain! I paid the credit card bill twice or overpaid.

- Called people by the wrong names when looking straight at them.

- Want to get pushy sales people off the phone sooner? Excuse me, I have chemo brain.

- Forget where you left your keys, parked your car, or put that envelope of money?

- Not in the mood for sex? "Oh, honey, I am afraid I have major chemo brain!" Of course, sex may also be the best antidote for chemo brain!

- Can't serve jury duty! I can't go to that boring party or reunion.

- How dare you try and serve me with legal papers when I have chemo brain!

- Getting pulled over for driving too slow (this happened to me!). "Sorry, officer, I have chemo brain." He let me go.

A study led by UCLA's Jonsson Comprehensive Cancer Center published in April 2013 reports that "Approximately one out of five breast cancer patients treated for breast cancer [has] elevated memory and/or executive function complaints that were statistically significantly associated with domain domain-specific neuropsychological (NP) test performances and depressive symptoms."[1]

Survivor Wisdom

The effects of chemo can last quite a long time after the last treatment, so take it easy.

My chemo brain turned in to a menopause mental fog, which, fortunately, I have learned to manage through getting enough exercise and sleep.

NOTES

1. "Relating Neuropsychological Test Performance to Cognitive Complaints After Breast Cancer," Oxford Journals, *JNCI Journal of the National Cancer Institute*, April 2013, doi: 10.1093/jnci/djt112.

Don't Wig Out about the Hair

"Bald is best! Wigs get hot. It's a nice opportunity to get creative and learn news ways to tie old cotton T-shirts into twisty artful head wraps."

—*Peaches*, diagnosed 2005

AM I GOING TO LOSE MY HAIR?" IS ONE OF THE FIRST questions that crosses your mind when you are diagnosed with cancer. Discuss this with your medical oncologist. Not all chemotherapy drugs result in hair loss or thinning hair. However, Adriamycin (a.k.a. "the red devil"). Cytoxin, and Taxol—drugs used to treat breast cancers—do trigger hair loss. These drugs were my chemo cocktail. My oncologist warned me that my hair would "release" (the euphemism for "shed") after my second or third treatment. She was right. It started slowly and then kept going until I wanted to pull my hair out rather than see clumps in my hairbrush, on my clothes, and on the bed pillows.

I never had bad hair days until my hair started falling out. My stomach churned when I read cancer books with patients recalling how their hair came out in fistfuls and sloughed off in the shower. I don't even like seeing my husband's whiskers in the sink or dandruff on a dark sweater. How was I going to deal with my hair shedding and having a bald, scrawny head? Like everything else in Cancer Land, you deal with it.

WHY IS MY HAIR FALLING OUT?

The main purpose of chemotherapy is to kill cancer cells in your body. However, as the drugs are absorbed and if they are particularly aggressive, they will impact other healthy cells, including your skin and hair follicles, which basically go to sleep. Just remember: your hair follicles are not permanently dead; they are in deep hibernation like bears in the winter. A few weeks after treatment ends, the follicles will wake up, and your hair will grow back.

IS THERE ANY WAY TO PRESERVE MY HAIR?

Dr. Mario Lacouture is a board-certified dermatologist at Memorial Sloan-Kettering Cancer Center, where he specializes in dermatological issues for patients undergoing cancer treatment. Dr. Lacouture is author of *Dr. Lacouture's Skin Care Guide for People Living with Cancer* (Harborside Press, 2012). I refer to him as the doctor who puts the "couture" into designing a smart skin/hair/nail/dental plan for your cancer treatment.

I found his book so informative that I will continue to use it as a reference when dealing with dermatological issues. Dr. Lacouture addresses two "hair preservation" methods.[1]

COLD CAPS

There is some debate about the "cold cap" method of wearing an ice cap on your head during and after each chemotherapy treatment. The science behind this is the ice pack prevents the chemotherapy toxins from reaching the hair follicles on your head; therefore, your hair won't fall out. For more information on the cold cap, visit the Rapunzel Project website (www.rapunzelproject.org).

In his book, Dr. Lacouture notes that studies with patients using cold caps showed that "scalp hypothermia helps to reduce complete hair loss in fifty percent of people, but the technique does not work for everyone."

Medical science also says that if the chemotherapy drugs do not reach the hair follicles, there is a potential risk that any little lurking cancer cells in your head may not be destroyed. Also, the patient is at risk for hypothermia of the head as your veins constrict, not to mention a brain freeze-style headache, potential dizziness, and discomfort. And it is not 100 percent effective. Dr. Lacouture notes that "For these reasons, the cold cap method is not endorsed or used by leading oncology organizations or cancer centers."

MINOXIDIL FOR HAIR LOSS

In the same book, Dr. Lacouture discusses using prescription Minoxidil (Rogaine) on the scalp prior to and during chemotherapy to help with hair regrowth. There is a small chance for facial hair growth. Dr. Lacouture said this happens in about one out of every two hundred women and is a reversible condition. *Post-treatment,* and with your oncologist's approval, Dr. Lacouture suggests taking daily doses of vitamin B7 (Biotin/2.5 mg or 2,500 mcg) with 10 mg of orthosilicic acid to help with hair regrowth.

HAIR TODAY, GONE TOMORROW

Other cancer survivors and my husband all suggested that I shave my head once my hair started wilting. Instead, I cut my hair to chin length and conditioned it hoping that would help. But after round one of chemo, my hair became dull and listless, and five days after my second treatment I saw blonde hairs floating around me as I moved or touched my head. I stopped brushing my hair and wore lighter colors for about two weeks. And then one night I couldn't take it any longer and I told my husband, "Get the clippers."

Some women report a tingling sensation in the scalp, and they can feel the hair releasing. I didn't feel anything until my husband started shaving my head. My heart pounded and my scalp tickled as the clippers buzzed around my ears. It took longer than I expected, and when it was over I felt a combination of relief and sadness. I held my breath when I finally looked in the mirror and saw my tiny bald self for the first time. And then I reached for my new blonde crown of hair and placed it on my head. I stared at my reflection and said, "Cancer, you may be pretty damn ugly, but I'm going to be pretty darn amazing throughout this ordeal!" I said to David, "I want a tiara."

Some women suffer in silence while losing their hair, and others turn it into a hair happening.

One woman I spoke with threw a head-shaving party with her family and friends. Some rally their buddies to make it a girls' night in. Spouses or friends may shave in solidarity. My husband, who has an enviable head of hair, offered to shave his head. I said, "Absolutely not!" I saw no reason he should lose his head by shaving his hair to show support for me. I know it's a touching gesture, but there are better ways to show solidarity for your loved one. Give her a day of beauty or have a fun outing together, and don't talk about cancer or anything serious!

Don't go razor crazy and shave your head before chemo even starts. Wait until *after* you start losing your hair! If for some reason you have an allergic reaction to chemotherapy and cannot continue the treatment, you do not want to be stuck with a bald head. This happened to someone I know. We both agreed we would have a chuckle about it some day, but, in the meantime, she ended up having to undergo radiation instead and had to wait months for her hair grow back.

TAKING THE PLUNGE

First, decide if you even want to wear a wig. Some women prefer going *au naturel* or wearing other head gear like turbans and scarves. It's another one of the choices you can control. Then, check with your insurance company. Many will cover the cost of one "cranial prosthesis" for chemotherapy-induced hair loss during a twelve-month calendar period. Ask your oncologist or breast surgeon for a written prescription for your "cranial prosthesis" (it's all about the wording) and check with your health insurance carrier again to see how much of that prosthesis is actually covered so you have no surprises. If your insurance carrier does not offer this coverage (how dare they!), or if you do not have medical insurance, some wonderful organizations like Westchester County's The Wig Exchange will provide wigs to women facing chemotherapy-related hair loss.

My friend Valerie arranged one of the sweetest gifts. She contacted my friends and asked them to contribute to a wig fund for me. She said she wanted me to be as beautiful on the outside as I was on the inside. I can't even begin to tell you what a great idea this is for a friend who may not have the insurance to cover the "cranial prosthesis." My friend Laura hosted a dinner party for me and invited everyone who contributed to the wig fund so I could have an unveiling.

INVESTING IN A WIG

Your wig is a short-term investment with a long-term yield in the self-image department, and I am bullish on blue chip quality with minimal risk. The best people to ask about wigs are people who wear them or your hair stylist. You will want your hair stylist on board from the beginning so he or she can help shape the wig to complement your face. I researched online took friends' recommendations, and visited three wig salons. At each I tried on a lot of wigs but waited to make the final purchase. Do not purchase your wig impulsively; some salons have a no-return policy.

You may want to shop for a wig after your first treatment. Since some wigs are expensive you want to be 100 percent sure you will actually need one. Or you might prefer starting sooner in case you don't have the energy once you start chemo. Give yourself enough time to select the wig that makes you happy. Meet with a wig specialist while you still have hair so he can see your current hair color and style and recommend wigs that best match them (unless you want to try a totally new look). The stylist can recommend wigs for your skin tone and face shape and teach you how to adjust and affix the wig so it does not move around. It also gives you time to have the wig professionally styled and ready to wear. Once you have lost all of your hair you may want to have your wig refitted for your head. I ended up purchasing my primary wig before I started chemo so I could practice putting it on. Knowing I had a great head of hair ready for me eased my hair loss anxiety.

Questions You Should Have Answered
When Looking into Wig Suppliers

- Do they have specialists who work with cancer patients?

- Do they charge a consultation or "try on" fee?

- What is their return or exchange policy?

- Will they work with you on the necessary paperwork for insurance reimbursement?

- What kind of wig servicing do they offer (e.g., wash, style, pickup/delivery)?

- Will they restyle and resize the wig for you for free?

- What other services do they offer to help you? Some higher-end salons will style your old hair and new hair to match so your transition is seamless. Some will shave your head, prep your scalp, prep your new hair, and touch up your makeup, all on the same day. And they'll throw in a free glamour girl sleep turban to boot. This is very accommodating if you are a busy executive and trying to downplay your diagnosis.

I visited three wig salons in New York City to find hair that I liked. My favorite place was Barry Hendrickson's Bitz-N-Pieces, a brightly lit showroom whose walls were lined with photos of famous women who I had no idea even wore wigs. I was seduced by a glamorous natural human hair wig that was simply Clairol golden blonde perfect! It became my main mane for work and social nights out. My husband and I called it the "Rolls Royce." At Helena's in Chelsea, I purchased a synthetic hair wig for my outdoor walks and workouts and for when the "Rolls Royce" was in the shop. We called it "the SUV." There are also mail-order catalogs like Paula Young that offer a wide selection of wigs, deliver nationally, and have a nice return policy.

MAKE IT A BEAUTY OUTING, BUT DON'T LOSE YOUR HEAD BUYING THE WRONG WIG

Shopping for a wig can provide some nice retail therapy, but make sure to take someone with you to give you an outside opinion. Schedule an appointment with a wig consultant that specializes in working with women dealing with cancer. Many offer valuable beauty advice beyond hair. Here are some factors to consider when making your purchase:

Comfort

The wig cap needs to be well made. Otherwise the wig will feel scratchy and uncomfortable. You can splurge and invest in a custom wig built for your head, but there are less-expensive options. A well-made, finely sewn lace cap that conforms to your head will be the most comfortable and practical and will have adjustable straps to tighten or loosen as needed. You will need to have your wig adjusted anyway after your hair falls out. "Comfort" also applies to the comfort level you feel when you place the wig on your head. If you feel in anyway uncomfortable or unattractive, the wig is not for you.

Look and Feel

In addition to a quality cap, you want quality hair. There are basically three types of wig hair: human hair, a blend of human and synthetic hair, and 100 percent synthetic hair.

Natural human hair wigs look and feel most like your real hair, but that doesn't mean the wig is higher in quality because the cap could still be poorly made. Human hair wigs also have a higher price tag. Human hair wigs need a lot of care in the styling department; they can be luscious and lovely but can also have too much hair for your face. I cringed when my stylist started cutting and shaping my very expensive new wig because

I saw dollar signs floating to the ground, but the styling was needed for the wig to look more natural on me.

Human hair wigs also require more maintenance. Like your own hair, human hair wigs do not hold up well under inclement weather. Every time they are washed they need to be styled. You can try and wash and style them yourself, but they will look a lot better when you send them out for a professional cleaning and grooming every few weeks. If you choose a human hair wig, I suggest that you purchase a spare wig to wear for bad weather or when your primary wig is out for a grooming.

Synthetic hair wigs can look very good, and their upkeep is easier. Synthetic wigs retain their style even in high humidity or inclement weather. You can easily wash a synthetic wig in the sink by rinsing it in cool water with a mild shampoo and popping it on a special wig stand to dry. The main downside to synthetic wigs is that the color and texture may not look or feel as natural as real human hair. You cannot style them like an all-natural wig but they usually don't require it. The materials in synthetic wigs can also be susceptible to high heat, so no blow-drying, curling, or straightening irons or leaning over your stove or an open flame.

Half human hair, half synthetic hair wigs offer the fuller natural look of human hair with the ability to be styled combined with the ease of maintenance of a synthetic wig. Use special wig shampoos to wash and air dry on a wig stand for best results.

Length, Color, and Style

Wig shopping can be a fun occasion to experiment with a new look if you have been sporting the same hairdo for years. You have to weigh the pros and cons of the look you want. If you are keeping your cancer diagnosis low key, go for a hair color, length, and style that match what you already have. If you want a new look, play a bit with cut, color, and style, but be sensible. You may not want to wear a pink bob or sport auburn hair for several months. You may want to purchase a more serious "true you" wig for work and a colorful play wig for leisure time.

Price

If your health insurance covers one medical hair prosthesis, buy whatever wig makes you feel and look your best and submit the receipt with your written prescription. But if you do not have insurance or don't want to make the initial monetary outlay required to buy the wig before the insurance check arrives, then go for a wig that is within your financial comfort level, fits well, and makes you feel good about how you look.

The price of a wig depends on its quality, workmanship, and type of hair, and can range from fifty dollars for a synthetic wig to a few thousand dollars for a super-quality human hair wig.

Accessories

Have your wig specialist show you how to fit your wig on your head and care for it at home. You will want to purchase a few wig care items (you can get them at any hair or wig salon) such as a Styrofoam wig stand, a portable collapsible wig stand for traveling, a wig brush, wig cap, and double-sided wig tape to keep everything in place. I kept getting the tape stuck in my new hair and finally gave up and plopped my wig on without any support.

Think seasonally when you shop for hair replacement accessories. I went through chemotherapy in the winter and wore cute, soft hats since my head was always cold, regardless of whether I was wearing my wig or not. But by summer, just as my hair started to grow out, I could not stand the scratchy heat from my wig. One sultry night while having dinner with my husband outside at a restaurant, I felt my head was going to fry in the city heat! I asked the waiter for a doggie bag, went to the ladies' room took off my wig and returned to the table to finish dinner with my freed scalp. The waiter did not even notice!

For summer, you can find some great "wig-hats"—baseball caps with hair hanging down. Wide brim hats are great for shielding both your scalp and your now-delicate skin. During my mid-chemo trip to Hawaii, I channeled "movie star" with my giant sun hat, big dark glasses, and body-shielding sarongs.

Someone told me to treat myself to an expensive silk scarf to wrap around my head. I didn't take her advice because (1) I did not want to spend the money, and (2) silk scarves slip off of bald heads. Cotton scarves and head wraps are easier to tie and will stay on your head. (I am sure some fashionable stylist who reads this will disagree, but several survivors shared this tip.)

CARING FOR YOUR SCALP

"I went for a facial, including my bald head, every three weeks!"

—Tracy, diagnosed 2002

You will learn to love the sensation of water trickling over your bare scalp. Just remember to take care of your scalp; it still needs to be cleansed with mild shampoo. Moisturize and massage your scalp with nourishing oils to keep it conditioned. Wear a wig cap if your scalp itches. And if you go outside with a bare head, wear a strong sunscreen! If you experience any other scalp conditions, consult your dermatologist.

GIVE YOUR HEAD A REST!

I thought I would be able to sleep in my wig. A fellow survivor told me, "You really will not want to wear your wig to bed!" She was right. The few times I tried wearing my SUV wig to bed, it slid around, covering part of my face. I just can't even imagine how it looked! I decided to give my head a rest and slept bare or with a soft cap to keep my head warm.

THE BALD AND THE BEAUTIFUL: AN EXPERT'S SURVIVOR WISDOM

Kate Conn is a breast cancer survivor who runs The Wig Exchange, a not-for-profit initiative based in Westchester County, New York, that recycles gently used, high-quality wigs for cancer patients. Their motto is "The gift of hair from women who've been there." Kate works with women to select wigs and shares her own survivor smarts. I asked her advice on wigs:

Kate says, "I suggest women don't feel obligated to spend a lot of money on their wig. I made that mistake. As I was about to start chemo, I felt like I had to have a custom human hair wig, and I spent about $2500 to do so. Now, for some women, especially working women, this might be the best way to go. But for me, a stay-at-home mom, it didn't make sense to spend that much because I didn't wear the wig all that often. And it still didn't look like my natural hair! It was a good wig, but it was still a wig. I wish that I would have just borrowed or purchased a less-expensive wig. That is one of the reasons we started The Wig Exchange—to help women find affordable options. Wigs are a practical item that will allow you to avoid unwanted questions and go about your business while under treatment without feeling as if your diagnosis is public information—they don't have to break the bank."

"I would advise women, whether they choose to use our service or not, that they look for a wig that will help them look how they did before they lost their hair. Make sure that it is comfortable and that it has warm colors in it. Warm colors will help your skin look healthier while you are in treatment. Synthetic wigs are a bit lighter in weight, so that might be more comfortable if you are in treatment over the summer."

To donate to or to inquire about getting a wig through The Wig Exchange, call 914-412-4884 or visit www.thewigexchange.org. The Wig Exchange is also working on a manual to help similar grassroots initiatives get started around the United States.

THE HAIR LOSS NO ONE DISCUSSES: BODY AND FACIAL HAIR

To get rid of body hair while in treatment, an electric shaver is safer than a handheld razor, which carries the risk of nicks that can lead to infection. Of course, with some chemotherapy treatments, hair loss is a full body experience. This means no more eyebrows, eyelashes, or body hair—north or south. I loved not having to tweeze, shave, snip, or wax.

But, as they say, "Eyes are the windows of the soul," and for many women, losing their eyebrows and eyelashes is like losing a part of their face and expression. It can be pretty devastating! Here are three options:

1. Consider buying a wig with bangs to detract from not having eyebrows. It's the same thought process as wearing bangs to hide forehead wrinkles.

2. Make an appointment at a makeup counter or salon to have a specialist show you how to deftly pencil in brows and line your eyes to properly frame them. Lashes of Love is a nationwide volunteer initiative to help teach women with cancer-related hair loss how to apply false eyelashes and line their eyes. I did this and came home with two sets of lashes (www.lashes-of-love.org).

3. If your brows grow in thinner (as was the case for me), have them professionally shaped and purchase a brow kit to use to fill them in. I use a brow brush, but some women prefer a brow pencil.

TEN POSITIVE THINGS ABOUT LOSING YOUR HAIR

- You will never have a bad hair day.

- You can change your looks with new wigs.

- You will save money on hair salon appointments.

- Wigs are fairly easy to maintain.

- You can smile when people tell you how great your hair looks.

- Being bald in the summer helps cool you down.

- Being bald in the winter means you will not have flat hat hair.

- No shaving, waxing, or tweezing required.

- Your hair will grow back faster than you think after treatment.

- Looking back, you will realize how short six to eight months of bald is compared to a lifetime of good health.

My favorite times were when people commented on my great haircut. "How do you keep your hair looking so nice in all this humidity?" the pretty blonde woman at the Chattanooga Zoo asked. "I have really good hair," I replied, smiling. And I did. I had the best hair of my life when I was in chemotherapy! You can focus on just being bald. Or you can focus on being bald, bold, and beautiful. I chose the latter.

THE FOLLICLE FOLLIES

You will celebrate when you see your first shadow of new hair. It happens pretty quickly and a bit strangely. It may grow back in a color or texture you may not like at first. My new hair was about four different colors, like seasoning salt with a lot of salt and pepper.

Just enjoy the experience of seeing your hair return and embrace it like a long-lost friend coming home to roost on your scalp. You cried enough when it was falling out! Why complain when it finally returns?

Your hair may grow back in curly or kinky. This is called "chemo curl." It can last about a year. Or it grows back straight, and you look like Julius Caesar. When it gets to be about one or two inches and starts sticking out of your wig on the sides, visit your hair stylist. I asked Kattia Solano, owner of Butterfly Studio Salon in New York City (www.butterflystudiosalon.com), which hosts a number of breast cancer initiatives, to weigh in on some of my hairier questions:

When Should You Consult with Your Hair Stylist?

Kattia: "Make an appointment as soon as you know you are going into treatment. It gives you and your stylist time to prepare for wig shopping

159

and set up a plan for hair cutting and maintenance. Your stylist can make sure that the shape and proportion of the wig is flattering and appears natural. It is important to make sure your wig's color has the right texture and weight to support your preferred style."

"If you decide to have fun with it and opt for something new, discuss with your stylist which styles will be more flattering to your face shape. Your stylist can adjust and tweak to customize the look of the wig on you or give it an update when you're ready for a change. The most important thing is perfecting the style of the wig with those finishing touches so that it frames the face as well as possible. I make sure to advise my clients that wigs can be uncomfortable so I wouldn't go crazy buying too many."

What Do You Tell Clients about Preparing for Hair Loss?

"Be gentle with the hair you have and give your scalp extra focus by nourishing and massaging it. I like to recommend the less chemical, more natural approach for shampoo and conditioner. I love the Rahua line, which has natural and organic ingredients to make your hair and scalp healthier all around. Work with what you have to get the appearance of fuller or more hair. I love using a styling product like Mousse Substantif by Kerastase, which gives hair a boost of collagen for instant volume no matter how you style it.

"I also like to educate my clients on other options, like synthetic fashion wigs to achieve a specific look, or using head scarves and fun hats as an alternative. My favorite is to tie a long, draping head scarf to one side because it looks and feels like you have hair. Wearing earrings is a great option too."

"Many people focus so much on the hair that they forget about all of the other things they can do to complete a beauty look and bring out what they have. Seeking the expertise of a makeup artist or aesthetician is very important because you can learn new techniques or tricks to bring out your beauty. If you can't frequent the salon for services, schedule a makeup lesson to learn about things like how to draw in or fill out eyebrows or how to apply lashes at home."

When Your Hair Starts Growing Back, How Should You Take Care of It?

"New-growth hair after chemotherapy is very tricky. I call it 'stick hair' because it's usually coarse and very dry. I advise my clients to keep this hair trimmed even as the regrowth process starts. Clients usually don't like to hear that because their main concern is growing their hair but it helps to trim the coarse ends. Post-chemo hair usually starts to grow pretty fast and grows out wavier and curlier than your natural texture. I would choose a single style and keep it up for a few months. During this phase it's about taming your layers and trying to make hair look less full or bulky and keeping it healthy. In-salon deep conditioning treatments, hair masks, and leave-in conditioners are highly recommended. Have your hair trimmed every six to eight weeks and work with your stylist on different ways to style your hair."

When Can You Start Coloring or Relaxing Your Hair Again?

Kattia: "If hair appears strong enough, you can color it once you have a few inches of growth. For more fragile strands, I would recommend cutting it a few times and waiting about three to five months after treatment for the more intensive services."

"I recommend INOA, which is an ammonia-free permanent hair color. It uses an oil-based delivery system and is optimized for scalp comfort. It covers grays while providing intense nourishment. Your hair looks and feels silkier and softer while giving hair much more shine than it had before the process. It's definitely a safer, gentler approach to hair color."

Some Survivors Tell Me Their Hair Is Thinner and More Fragile.

"I recommend FusioDose by Kerastase and its take-home set 'Homelab' to follow up with treatment benefits at home. It's a tailor-made system that can target specific hair needs to transform the hair from the inside out using made-to-measure, active ingredients. Results are instantaneous.

"To promote hair vitality and resistance, the Résistance Force Architecte hair cleansing system by Kerastase is a great option. Its advanced reconstructing formulas prevent breakage and split ends while strengthening and protecting.

"When hair is stronger and healthier, I like Age Premium Substantif too, for its collagen-infused formulas that leaves hair feeling thicker with more volume and body."

What About Hairpieces or Recommended Haircuts for Thinning Hair?

"Hotheads Extensions are really incredible for their gentle approach. These extensions bond to the hair using a weft adhesive and require no heat or tools. The tape does not pull, so there is no tension or damage. You don't feel them because the tracks are super thin and lay flat on the scalp. You can get as many or as few as you want to create fullness and, in some cases, a little bit of length."

"Shorter haircuts are always better for finer, thinner textures. Cuts that have clean lines like bobs are a fantastic option to create the appearance of more hair. Angles around the front of the face imitate layers. Short hair should be cut (more like cropped) shorter, close to, and around the shape of the head. With styling, stay away from rollers and defined styles. A more natural texture looks best."

What Vitamins or Supplements Do You Recommend for Healthier Hair (after Treatment and If Your Oncologist Approves)?

"My number one supplement recommendation right now is Viviscal. At the salon, we carry the 'professional' grade of these women's hair growth supplements and they really work! You get stronger, fuller, longer hair faster. It nourishes thinning hair and promotes hair to grow from within. Some clients report that you get more hair growing everywhere, which could be a benefit for some post-treatment. I love Viviscal because it's drug free, contains powerful antioxidants, and uses a unique Marine complex called AminoMar, which is not found anywhere else.

"Kerastase carries a line of nutrient-rich tablets called 'Densi-Recharge' with essential fatty acids and amino-vegetals to increase hair's density. Using this with 'Specific,' their leave-in intensive scalp treatment kit for thinning hair (technically created for those prone to hair loss), promises fuller, thicker locks in thirty days. The technology here is Arginine and Vitamin PP+B8."

Survivor Wisdom

About two months after my hair started to return, I tried self-coloring at home with a natural potion from a local hair supply store. I gave up. In month three of my new hair, I went to a professional salon and had a colorist turn it platinum blonde and gel it up. I decided to channel my inner hipster and go for a new look. I figured I had a new body, new hair, and a new life. So why not just go for a new look at the same time?

The responses were pretty funny! Friends who had not seen me in a long time would walk by me at events without recognizing me. A business associate actually came up and introduced herself to me!

Sometimes I would catch my reflection in the mirror and not recognize the woman looking back at me. Did the white-blonde burst of hair sprouting out of my scalp make me look old or young? What did I think? I decided to run with it and bought big, dark sunglasses, bright scarves, eye-catching earrings, and skinny jeans. I would dress younger to match my new hair and outlook. It worked! People would come up to me and say things like "Omigosh! You cut your hair! You look amazing!" or "Oh, I just love your new look! It makes you look so much younger!"; or "You look hot! If I weren't gay, I would hit on you!" (Seriously, a man said that to me at a wine tasting!)

I remember one friend started crying and hugging me when she first saw the new me. She was overwhelmed to see me looking so fit and healthy. I cried tears of happiness with her. My year of living chemically and surgically was almost over.

I actually went through wig withdrawal. I did not want to stop wearing my beautiful Rolls Royce of a wig with its perfect blonde hair. It was my safety net, my special survivor crown. When I wore the wig, I felt beautiful. It covered my bald scalp, detracted from the eyes with no lashes and brows, brightened the pale, sallow chemo skin, and masked the harsh reality of having cancer when I went out in public. When I finally packed up my wig, I realized it was an important step in moving past the worst part of my cancer journey.

HAIR REGROWTH

I'M SPROUTING HAIR LIKE A WEREWOLF!

Hair regrowth will vary by individual and by treatment. Some women report thinning hair from hormone therapy drugs. Tamoxifen may cause excess facial hair, which is what happened in my case. After being hairless for several months, suddenly I had blonde hairs sprouting from my face in excess!

Of the different hair removal methods, Dr. Lacouture recommends threading for facial hair. But, be careful if you have sensitive skin. I had my chin and cheeks threaded a few months after treatment and while taking tamoxifen to remove excess facial hair. It left my skin red and irritated for a few days. An electric shaver is another option. Dr. Lacouture advises against waxing or using chemical depilatories.

NOTE

1. Mario E. Lacouture, MD, "Preventing and Coping with Hair Loss," *Dr. Lacouture's Skin Care Guide for People Living with Cancer* (Cold Spring Harbor, New York: Harborside Press, 2012), 111–17.

The Best Defense for Looking Fabulous

16

SKIN, NAILS & ORAL CARE

"Pay close attention to what makes you feel beautiful, whatever that may be. Through the process you will find that cancer can never take away your true beauty."

—*Marlena*, diagnosed 2009

TAKING CARE OF YOUR SKIN, NAILS, TEETH, AND GUMS IS NOT just a skin-deep matter. There are real dangers lurking if you are not diligent. Treatment-related skin rashes, brittle nails, dry mouth, and mouth and gum sores can lead to infections—not to mention extreme discomfort. Again, I turned to Memorial Sloan-Kettering's Dr. Mario Lacouture for insights.

First, we will start with your body's largest organ, your skin.

I experienced four different skin rashes during my cancer journey. The first was an allergic reaction to latex after my core biopsy produced an itchy red rash in the area of the biopsy. It was treated topically with a *corticosteroid cream*. The second was an allergic reaction to an antibiotic which resulted in extreme redness and itching on both arms. The doctor switched antibiotics and prescribed an *antihistamine tablet*. The third was an allergic reaction to Taxol in which my injection arm turned red, the room spun, and I fainted. We switched chemo drugs. The last was cellulitis on my arm, which led to a visit to the emergency room and a round of antibiotics. What I learned is this: if your skin's color and/or texture are changing, if your skin is crawling and itching, or if your skin is heating up or turning cold, contact your doctor. Do not try and self-medicate and do not "wait it out."

On page 41 of his book, Dr. Lacouture notes that "Approximately eight percent of people living with cancer visit a dermatologist for a rash caused by chemotherapy or targeted therapies."

IS IT A RASH . . . OR IS IT MORE?

Briefly, here are the differences as explained by Dr. Lacouture in his book's second chapter,[1] "All Rashes Are Not Created Equal":

- *Allergic reaction*: This can be a red, itchy, and/or painful rash with or without bumps. It happens pretty quickly, and, once treated with the proper prescribed antihistamines and corticosteroids, it will disappear. It is important to document in your medical organizer the names (brand and generic) of any medication that gives you an allergic reaction so your physician can prescribe something else.

- *Rash from chemotherapy*: A rash can be red, yellow-white, or purple. It can be flat or raised, dry or oozy, smooth or scaly, itchy or painful, and have a number of other characteristics. Your physician will need to analyze the rash to determine the cause and treatment. A rash that is a side effect from treatment may take some time before it starts to appear. Rashes that can be treated with topical creams or soothing ointments usually fit into these categories: (a) inflammation, (b) itching, and (c) infection.[2]

- *Dry skin*: All cancer treatments will make your skin extremely dry and sensitive. You need to be diligent about moisturizing your face and body skin daily. If you want something heavier than a lotion, try a cream or, for even more lubrication, an emollient. Look for a hypoallergenic moisturizer that is free of fragrance, paraben, lanolin, preservatives, and alcohol, since these ingredients can irritate your skin. You do not need to slather on moisturizer—a quarter-sized dollop for each part of your body will work, and try to apply it within fifteen minutes after you shower. If your skin is itchy, do not scratch it; you might break the skin, which can lead to an infection.

- *Hive*: A hive is a red, raised, itchy welt. A hive can appear anywhere on the body and may be a sign of an allergic reaction. Hives can be treated with antihistamines or corticosteroids. However, a hive accompanied by shortness of breath or a drop in blood pressure could be a serious allergic reaction.

- *Blisters and sores*: These are common side effects from some treatments, especially in the hands and feet. Blisters in other areas may indicate an infection. Depending on their severity, they may be treated with topical ointments or oral medication.

- *Rosacea*: Pimple-like red bumps and a light rash most common on the face, rosacea can be a lifelong condition treatable through topical and oral medications, lasers (post-treatment), diet (avoid spicy food, red wine, and hot caffeinated beverages) and the avoidance of extreme heat or cold (e.g., saunas and steam rooms). Some cancer medications may make rosacea worse.

- *Discoloration*: Changes in skin color and texture are common side effects of radiation but are not limited to it. Some will disappear after treatment ends. Others are more permanent and will need to be treated by a dermatologist.

- *Scars:* All surgeries will leave scars. Some scars are more visible and "angry" than others. Some, like keloid scars, are hard and raised. If you know prior to your surgery and treatment that your skin has a tendency toward scarring and especially keloid scarring, tell your doctors. Scars should be treated early on with gels, silicone sheets, or ointments developed to reduce and soften the effects of scarring. There are several ways to lessen scarring post-treatment, including chemical peels, laser treatments, fillers, bleaching creams, and scar revision surgery.

Survivor Wisdom

If you see something, say something. With cancer, there is no such thing as a "mild skin condition" to try and treat yourself. Always advise your doctor of any changes in the skin texture, color, temperature, or sensation. And record every skin condition and how it was treated in your medical journal.

SKIN CARE

With ultrasensitive cancer skin, handle with care. Your tolerance to certain skin care products you are already using may change under treatment. This is also not a great time to switch skin care products unless necessary. You should perform a patch test for any new product by applying a small amount behind your ear or forearm and keeping it covered for two days and then monitoring your skin's reaction. Dr. Lacouture's book lists a number of allergens in different kinds of products, and stresses that just because a product is labeled "all-natural" or "chemical-free" doesn't mean that it has necessarily been allergy tested or dermatologist tested, which is what you want.[3] Always read the labels.

SOME TIPS

- Look for gentle cleansing and moisturizing skin care products that are labeled "hypoallergenic," "allergy tested," and "fragrance free." During the day, you may want to use a light cream or lotion that is water based. At night, you may choose to wear a heavier cream or emollient that has a higher percentage of oil versus water on your face and body for added lubrication, especially if your bedroom is low humidity.

- Avoid products with acids (harsh), paraben (possible allergen), or scrubbing particles that can scratch and tear sensitive skin.

- Face lotions and creams are designed for the more sensitive skin on the face. Stick with body lotions on the body.

- Wear a broad-spectrum (UVA and UVB protection) water-resistant sunscreen with a minimum sun protection (SPF) of 30. You should apply a quarter-sized amount to each body area thirty minutes before you go outside, and you should reapply every two hours, or every hour if swimming or sweating. Sunscreen should also be worn inside, since fluorescent lights can also damage the skin, and clear windows do not provide adequate sun protection. Your sunscreen should contain zinc and Helioplex or Mexoryl. Dr. Lacouture notes that para-aminobenzoic acid (PABA) is an allergen, so avoid this ingredient. This is the rule for applying sunscreen to all exposed body parts: If you cannot reach an area, ask someone to apply it for you.

- What do you apply first to your face? Dr. Lacouture recommends moisturizer, followed by sunscreen and finally concealers and makeup.

- Take short showers or baths in tepid or lukewarm water using fragrance-free soap for sensitive skin. No loofahs or brushes— they can spread bacteria.

- Use unscented soaps for sensitive skin versus antibacterial soaps, which can be drying.

- Avoid extreme heat in showers, baths, hot tubs, saunas, or steam rooms.

- Pat your skin dry. Do not rub. It's best to apply lotion or cream to your skin within fifteen minutes after a shower or bath while skin is still moist.

- Avoid scented body creams and perfumes; the smell may not appeal to you right now, and the alcohol in them is drying.

- Alcohol-free aloe gels and creams are soothing.

- Use aluminum-free deodorant. If you have hair under your arms, use an electric shaver and not a razor.

- If a product stings or gives you a rash, stop using it immediately and consult with your dermatologist.

POST-TREATMENT

Discuss with your oncologist and dermatologist when you can resume using certain products like alpha hydroxy acids, vitamin C serums, and other exfoliants. You should wait until your system is stronger before having any fillers or laser treatments. You may find yourself with some lingering side effects long after treatment. Here are a few:

Skin Discoloration

This is usually a result of radiation, so it is localized to the area that underwent radiation. Some patients, however, may have other skin discolorations from conventional treatment.

There are topical treatments such as hydroquinine and specific lasers that may be used to treat discoloration.

Rosacea

I developed rosacea, a persistent and lingering redness, on my cheeks from one of my cancer drugs. My dermatologist gave me a prescription ointment to apply daily and recommended that I avoid spicy food, red wine, caffeine, and saunas. Targeted lasers provide effective, but more expensive, treatment. Certain lasers also work on broken capillaries. However, none of this is permanent and your lifestyle choices may continue to aggravate the conditions (e.g., smoking, weight gain, diet). You may need to have multiple procedures in order to manage the condition and see optimal results.

Rough Textures and Spots

Rougher skin and spots can be the result of treatment or the onset of menopause and aging skin. You should discuss treatment options, from topical to laser, with your dermatologist, and see what works for you and what you can afford, since most treatments are not covered by health insurance.

Fibrosis is a thickening and tightening of an area of the skin that has been radiated. According to Dr. Lacouture, fibrosis occurs in thirty percent of patients treated with radiation for breast, head, and neck cancers. Dr. Lacouture said studies have shown that taking 1000 international units (IU) of vitamin E and 800 mg of the prescription drug pentoxifylline (brand name: Trental) can help alleviate symptoms.[4]

Surgical Scars

There are surgeries that can help reduce the appearance of surgical scars. In his book, Dr. Lacouture notes that massaging scars will not make them softer or look better, nor will rubbing with vitamin E oil or "scar minimizing" products containing onion extract. What can help are certain scar correction gels and silicone sheets and an emollient like cocoa butter or petroleum jelly, but they need to be used on fresh scars.[5]

Tattoos

Radiation tattoos can be removed through laser surgery.

HANDS AND NAILS

Dr. Lacouture notes that weak, brittle nails are the second most unanticipated side effect of cancer treatment. It's really no surprise since nails beds rely on healthy cells. My nails became brittle and ridged during chemotherapy, and they are still brittle because I am still taking Arimidex.

TIPS

- Do not bite your nails or cuticles.

- Keep your nails short. Trim or file them yourself or have a professional do it. My doctor advised against having mani-pedis to reduce any risk of contracting an infection. If you do go to a professional nail salon to have your nails trimmed, bring your own sanitized nail tools and do not have your cuticles cut. This can lead to infection.

- A licensed, board-certified podiatrist can trim your toenails and address foot care.

- Use plenty of unscented hand cream, olive oil, shea butter, or vitamin E oil to combat brittle nails. Use sunscreen on the backs of your hands for protection.

- Wear gloves to protect your nails while washing dishes or gardening, and wear warm gloves during cold weather.

- Use hand sanitizers like Purell to protect against germs. Most are drying, so carry hand cream or lotion to apply after sanitizing.

- Massage fingernails and toenails with cuticle cream to help prevent splitting and dryness.

- Your dermatologist can prescribe a nail strengthener or recommend one that is over the counter.

- If you choose to use nail color, look for a water-based polish that is formaldehyde-free. Dr. Lacouture suggests OPI or Sally Hansen.[6]

- Use gentle, acetone-free polish remover. There are some nice polish removers for sensitive skin.

- Avoid acrylics or gels as they can sometimes trap bacteria.

- Some salon nail drying machines contain ultraviolet (UV) lights and should be avoided.

- If your nail darkens and splits from the bed, do not remove it yourself. Go to your doctor or a licensed podiatrist and have them handle it.

- If you have scaly feet or calluses, lubricate them with a thick moisturizer containing salicylic acid, urea, or ammonium lactate and then wear socks to bed to soften overnight.

- If you have blisters or lesions, do not pick or pop them. Leave treatment to your physician.

- Discoloration or oozing liquid or pus around the nail may be a sign of a nail fungus or infection. Contact your physician.

- If you see anything suspicious, notify your doctor. Do not self-treat.

Building Stronger Nails After Treatment

After your treatment ends and with your oncologist's approval, taking daily doses of 2.5 mg (2500 mcg) vitamin B7 (biotin) along 10 mg of orthosilicic acid can help strengthen nails, according to Dr. Lacouture.

PUT YOUR MONEY WHERE YOUR MOUTH IS: PROTECTING YOUR TEETH AND GUMS

"Oral care during treatment is extremely important," my dentist, Dr. Thomas Magnani, explained to me. "Chemotherapy kills rapidly growing tissues like cancer cells and also salivary glands. The lining of your mouth and stomach are also affected. If your salivary glands are not working properly, this can lead to tooth decay and painful mouth ulcers."

Here is a quick checklist of what you should review and consider with your dentist prior to treatment. The products listed are recommended by Dr. Magnani based on his experience treating patients with cancer.

PRIOR TO SURGERY OR TREATMENT

- Have your teeth cleaned and examined prior to treatment and take X-rays.

- Address any special dental work required, like filling a cavity.

- Have dental impressions made for fluoride trays. Sleeping with fluoride trays containing thin strips of Henry Schein Acclean fluoride gel nightly during and after treatment can help prevent tooth decay from chemo. If you cannot tolerate the trays overnight, try wearing them during the day for one hour. If you cannot afford dental trays, Dr. Magnani recommends applying Colgate PreviDent 5000 ("paint on teeth, swirl, and spit") or rinsing your mouth with Colgate Phos-Flur.

DURING TREATMENT

- Brush and floss daily to maintain optimum dental health.

- For sensitive teeth, avoid products with sodium lauryl sulfate or baking soda that can irritate the mouth. Better options are Biotene, Clōsys, ProEnamel, Sensodyne, Clōsys, and Tom's of Maine (natural). Use a soft-bristle toothbrush or an electric toothbrush like Arm & Hammer Spinbrush if you are too weak to manually brush.

- For dry mouth: Try Biotene dental rinse or spray (they also have a toothpaste), Colgate PreviDent 5000, or Clōsys dental rinse. Chew sugar-free gum like Orbit with Xylitol. Most lozenges include sugar or a sugar substitute and can accelerate tooth decay in cancer patients. Dr. Magnani recommends a synthetic saliva lozenge like SalivaSure from Scandinavian. Dr. Lacouture also notes that your doctor can prescribe oral medications that stimulate your glands to form saliva (with your medical oncologist's approval).

- For mouth sores, avoid alcohol-based mouthwashes. Rinse instead with a cup (eight ounces) of warm water and one teaspoon of salt. (Or ask your doctor for a prescription corticosteroid mouthwash or paste, adds Dr. Lacouture.)

- For fungal infections, have your dentist or doctor prescribe Nystatin, and for canker sores, a prescription rinse with Xylocaine (lidocaine).

- Avoid spicy or acidic foods that aggravate your mouth sores and avoid sugary foods that can cause tooth decay. If you crave citrus fruits (like I did), rinse after eating so the acids do not aggravate your mouth.

- If your mouth is sore and you have trouble chewing, drink your nutrition. Smoothies are a great option. Consider grinding up your meat and vegetables or drinking nutritious high-protein broths. And drink through a straw if you mouth and gums are sore.

- Your taste may be affected for some time. Things may taste rotten. Some have increased sensitivity. Keep a record of what foods do and do not taste good to you so your caregiver knows what you can tolerate.

"It is very important to stay nourished even if you have to puree your food. Your body is fighting disease. It does not have time to fight malnutrition," stresses Dr. Magnani.

MAKEUP

Makeup is a great way to boost your complexion and create a healthy glow. Before you start treatment, I suggest meeting with a skin care and makeup specialist to formulate a plan. You can go to your favorite makeup counter or splurge and have a makeup artist come to you. There are also complimentary services for women facing cancer. One of the best known is The American Cancer Society's Look Good Feel Better program. Workshops around the country are led by volunteer beauty professionals. One-on-one consultations are also available (www.lookgoodfeelbetter.org, 800-395-5665).

I took a five-step approach to my makeup routine:

- *Hydrate*: using a moisturizer for sensitive skin.

- *Protect*: using sunscreen for the face with an SPF 30.

- *Illuminate*: to brighten skin (I used Laura Mercier's skin illuminator that also provides a little coverage and an SPF 20).

- *Cover*: I strategically placed makeup base or concealer to cover any bumps during my second round of chemo.

- *Enhance*: complexion-lifting blush (cream), lipstick, and gloss.

Karol Moses Young, owner of I. C. Artistry (www.icartistry.com), is a Los Angeles-based professional makeup artist and breast cancer survivor. Here are some of her tips:

SKIN

- Use products that increase your skin's radiance, such as serums, sprays, or lotions designed for this purpose.

- A tinted moisturizer or light bronzer will help combat sallow skin.

- Cream blush will add glow and a pop of color in one step.

- Keep makeup as close to your natural skin tone as possible and don't overcompensate by applying it heavier or using a darker shade.

- BB (beauty balm) and CC (color correcting) creams are great options for an all-in-one moisturizer, complexion evener, and color. Some contain sunscreen. Choose one close to your natural skin tone.

- If your skin becomes discolored from radiation, a full-coverage foundation for face and body is the best way to go. Both MAC and Dermablend make nice full-coverage foundations that can be purchased over the counter. Two professional brands, RCMA and Joe Blasco, also work beautifully and won't transfer onto your clothing. These can be found online or in professional stores.

- Avoid applying makeup to any area of your skin that is irritated or infected.

EYES

- Use concealer or under-eye brightener to counter dark circles.

- While you still have your brows, purchase a pencil or brow powder and practice so you can match your natural shape and thickness.

- Purchase a set of false eyelashes and have someone teach you how to put them on.

- Use eyeliner that complements, not necessarily matches, your natural eye color. For example, taupe, brown, and grey complement blue eyes; purples and plums accent green eyes; and lucky brown eyes can use any of these colors. Make a nice bold line on top. Leave the bottom lash area clean or use a powder eye shadow with a brush to add a soft line under the bottom that will accent your eye shape.

LIPS

Many women I spoke with said lipstick was the one product they wore everywhere, even into the surgery room.

- Carry lip balm to combat dry lips.

- Avoid lipstick colors that are too nude. A pop of color will brighten your complexion.

- Choose a color that complements your skin tone. The more color you have in your complexion, the more intense lip color you can wear.

- Choosing matte or gloss is a matter of preference. You may want to try a creamy lipstick with a gloss on top.

SCENT AND SENSIBILITY

"I couldn't stand the smell of the air freshener in the lobby of my oncologist's office. I had to hold my breath walking into the building."

—Melanie, diagnosed 2008

Many cancer patients become sensitive to smells. In my case, my sense of smell grew stronger and remains that way today, which is great for working in wine and food, but wreaked havoc on my intimate life. For some reason, during my chemo treatments, I thought my husband smelled strange. Going to bed was a nightly mist-fest as I kept spraying him and my bedding with orange blossom water, a scent I found appealing and calming. Other patients tell me that lavender was calming for them. If you find a scent that appeals to you, or does not, tell people so you don't end up with a lot of smelly gifts (not a great idea anyway). This may be a good time to review your cleaning supplies and laundry detergent. The keywords are "gentle," "nontoxic," "natural," "no perfume," and "for sensitive skin." If you have a cleaning service, tell them that you are sensitive to chemicals and smells so they can use products that will not irritate you.

NOTES

1. Mario E. Lacouture, MD, "All Rashes Are Not Created Equal," *Dr. Lacouture's Skin Care Guide for People Living with Cancer* (Cold Spring Harbor, New York: Harborside Press, 2012), 11–51.

2. Lacouture, "A Rash by Any Other Name," *Dr. Lacouture's Skin Care Guide,* 24–37.

3. Lacouture, "Using Cosmetics to Look and Feel Better," *Dr. Lacouture's Skin Care Guide,* 210–12.

4. S. Delanian, R. Porcher, J. Rudent, and J. L. Lefaix, "Kinetics of Response to Long-Term Treatment Combining Pentoxifylline and Tocopherol in Patients with Superficial Radiation-Induced Fibrosis," *Journal of Clinical Oncology,* 2005, 23 (34), 8570–79, doi: 10.1200/JCO.2005.02.4729.

5. Lacouture, "Better Healing of Scars," *Dr. Lacouture's Skin Care Guide,* 150–54.

6. Lacouture, "Making Brittle Nails Better," *Dr. Lacouture's Skin Care Guide,* 92–94.

Lymphedema

ARM YOURSELF

CELLULITIS! ELEPHANTITIS! OH MY!

Just when I finally understood the purpose of a lymph node, I learned about my risk for lymphedema, an unsightly, unpredictable, and permanent side effect from breast surgery involving the removal of the lymph nodes during mastectomy or damage from radiation.

Lymphedema is an abnormal swelling of the arm or hand where a protein-rich fluid accumulates with inadequate drainage. As a result, the arm and/or hand swell up. Lymphedema can also occur in the breast, chest, and trunk areas. Swelling can be minimal ("when pressed by fingertips, the area indents and holds the indentation") to "elephantitis" ("swelling is irreversible and the limb(s) is/are very large").

"Oh, great!" I said to myself. "First, I lose my breasts. Then my hair falls out. My brain's on fire. My hands, feet, and joints are as tight as the Tin Man. And now I have to worry about my arm blowing up."

According to the pamphlet my hospital gave me in case I did get it, lymphedema occurs in roughly "6 to 30 percent" of patients who have a large number of lymph nodes removed. That's a pretty wide range. The greater number of lymph nodes removed, the higher the risk. Other risks include radiation, an infection in the arm or chest on the side of the surgery, weight gain, or a recurrence of breast cancer that blocks the flow of lymph fluid.

For more information on lymphedema, I reached out to the National

177

Lymphedema Network (NLN), a not-for-profit organization that provides education and guidance on the subject of lymphedema (www.lymphnet .org). I spoke with Robin Miller, a survivor living with lymphedema who works at NLN.

"While it is hard to predict who will get lymphedema, the NLN does recommend that all breast cancer patients undergo prescreening prior to surgery since early identification will help improve patients' outcomes." Robin suggests that prior to surgery you see a certified lymphatic therapist (CLT) who can measure both of your arms. "This will serve as a baseline measurement. If you notice some swelling or changes in your hand or arm, your therapist can go back and look at the measurements and compare." NLN also recommends having your height, weight, and body mass index (BMI) taken since increases in weight and BMI can impact lymphedema. Once you have the information recorded you can use this as a barometer to measure against.

Lymphedema is irreversible. But it is manageable. The sooner you treat lymphedema, the better chance you'll have to keep it under control. "For me, lymphedema was much worse than the cancer because it is a permanent condition. But it is a condition many doctors do not want to discuss," Robin told me.

Robin did point out that you should never forgo any treatment out of fear of coming down with lymphedema. "Conventional cancer therapy comes first. You need to kill the cancer. You can live with lymphedema, but you cannot live with cancer."

She also suggested getting fitted for a special lymphedema compression sleeve for your arm and hand piece to keep the lymph fluid moving and alleviate swelling. "The two work together because you don't want fluid from the compression garment on your arm to be forced into your hand." Robin advises having a CLT properly fit you for both arm and hand garments so that they don't create a tourniquet effect and cut off circulation of the fluid.

WAYS TO MINIMIZE THE RISK OF GETTING LYMPHEDEMA

- Make sure your blood is drawn from the arm where the lymph nodes were not removed. This also goes for taking your blood pressure.

- Avoid cuts, scrapes, or any breaks on the skin that could lead to infection.

- Avoid getting sunburned; use a high-SPF (minimum 30), UVA and UVB protective sunscreen.

- Wear insect repellent to avoid stings and bites to the arm or hand.

- Wear daily moisturizer to protect the skin.

- Avoid tight jewelry or clothing on the fingers or arms (e.g., sleeves with elastic bands).

- Don't use heating pads on your affected arm or shoulder.

- Wear gloves for gardening, cleaning, or washing dishes (a great excuse to do none of these!).

- If you have manicures, don't have your cuticles cut.

- Avoid gaining weight.

- Don't lift anything too heavy (over ten pounds) without discussing with your doctor.

- If you get a massage, tell the masseuse which side is at risk so he or she will be less vigorous in that area.

- A traumatic injury can trigger lymphedema.

WARNING SIGNS

- Heaviness, aching, swelling, or pain on the arm, hand, or chest.

- Tightness and/or persistent ache of the arm, hand, or chest.

- Weakness in the arm.

- Red and blotchy skin, itching, or discoloration in the affected area.

MANAGING LYMPHEDEMA

If you show symptoms of lymphedema, notify your breast surgeon and request a referral for a certified lymphedema therapist who can work with you and provide guidelines and exercises to follow. Here are some more guidelines from the National Lymphedema Network:

- Exercise and move the arms. Your therapist will give you specific movements.

- Wear a lymphedema compression garment on your arm (not just any compression bandage). Robin notes that an arm compression sleeve is not enough. "Make sure to wear a hand piece with your arm sleeve. This is important because otherwise the fluid could be forced into the hand."

- Have a lymphatic drainage massage.

- Use an electric shaver to remove underarm hair. Do not use a razor or wax.

- If you are taking long airplane flights, discuss with your therapist whether you should purchase a special graduated compression lymphedema garment to counter changes in cabin pressure. This includes both a lymphedema sleeve and hand piece.

- Avoid repetitive motions with the affected arm. Give your arm a rest.

- Avoid sleeping on the affected side or arm.

- Don't carry large bags on the affected arm.

- Elevate the affected arm or hand or prop it on pillows to help reduce swelling.

- Drink lemon water to help clean out the lymphatic system, which helps reduce swelling.

- Avoid intake of too much sodium, which can lead to swelling.

- If you are traveling overseas, ask your doctor for a prescription for prophylactic antibiotics in case you incur infection.

- You can also have your doctor prescribe a lymph pump, but make sure your health insurance covers it and that you have the correct wording on your written prescription.

Lymphedema can also increase the risk of infection. If you notice any pain, redness, warmth, or increased swelling in your arm or chest area, contact your doctor. Cellulitis, a bacterial skin infection, is also a risk because the infection can spread in your body. One thing I learned as a cancer patient was not take any ache, pain, swelling, or rash lightly . . . ever!

RISK REDUCTION

I had the opportunity to meet with Dr. Sheldon Feldman, chief of breast surgery at Columbia University Medical Center, and he explained what it means to have a lymphatic-venous bypass microsurgery performed at the time of lymph node dissection during mastectomy. "We can, in effect, reconnect the lymphatic vessels to the veins, thus reducing the risk of lymphedema. We have performed two successful bypasses at the breast center," said Dr. Feldman. "Patients undergo baseline measurements and scans of both arms prior to surgery and they are checked every six months. This type of surgery may be beneficial for women with a high number of lymph nodes removed during surgery and for those who will also undergo radiation."

Staying Fearless
& Fabulous Out
& About

18

"Do not let cancer confine you. You are not your illness. Keeping active and involved will help prevent you from falling into a pit of self pity."

—*Melanie*, diagnosed 2009

PEOPLE SEEMED SHOCKED WHEN I TOLD THEM I HAD business meetings. "You mean you are still working?" someone would ask. I had to make a living, so not working was not an option. I learned to manage my schedule carefully and book outside appointments in the late morning, when I had more energy, and never right after chemotherapy or late in the day.

One of the things that will be important to you is to try and have as normal a life as possible. Do not become a cancer cave dweller. Go visit a friend. See an upbeat movie. Have dinner out. Go window-shopping. Stay active and stay busy. Every time I felt down in the dumps, I would take a walk and soak in the world around me. I would schedule lunch with a friend. The key is not to lie around feeling sorry for yourself.

Now, your oncologist will tell you to avoid public areas where you could contract germs since your resistance is low, and he's right. This may not be the best time to go to a football game or a crowded mall—anywhere people are packing in. Here are some tips to staying healthy when you venture out:

- Carry and use hand sanitizers and have packets of tissue or baby wipes on hand.
- Wear comfortable, sturdy shoes.
- Always wear sunscreen. And pack a hat for rain, cold, or to shield you from the sun.
- Carry lip balm and throat lozenges for dry mouth.
- Bring medication for nausea just in case.
- Bring a disposable paper bag (like you find on airlines) in case you become nauseated.
- Bring a toothbrush toothpaste, and breath mints in case you become nauseated.
- Carry an umbrella in case of a surprise shower; a wet wig is not a good thing!
- Bring a bottle of water.
- Pack a spare pair of underpants (accidents may happen).
- Carry a list of the medications you are taking and the names and phone numbers of your caregiver and doctors and the hospital where you are treated in case you become dizzy or faint.
- Wear a medical alert bracelet on your affected arm or carry a medical ID card so no one tries to take your blood pressure or blood from that arm if you are unconscious.
- Dress appropriately for the weather but also layer in case you get hot flashes.
- If your resistance is really off, wear a surgical mask, and if you are unsteady on your feet, carry a walking stick.

FEARLESS, FABULOUS, AND STYLISH

As soon as you can disrobe from the hospital gowns, do it! I found that creating my "look" postmastectomy and during treatment was a way to feel good about myself. My cancer mentor, Melanie, gave me some soft cotton tank tops with side snaps to wear after my drains were removed. Whether you are undergoing chemotherapy or radiation or just surgery, it's important to have soft, breathable clothing next to your skin.

After a mastectomy, large shirts, dresses with front buttons, smock tops, cardigans, and loose peasant tops can disguise drains. I wound long scarves in every kind of material around my neck and draped them over my chest. During chemotherapy I avoided wearing a lot of dull black, brown, gray, or neutral tones close to my face. Turtlenecks were unbearable (and still are). They felt too constricting around my neck and made me feel uncomfortably hot. Soft draped or wrap tops in complexion-enhancing tones and colorful scarves looked good and were easy to wear.

I wore great hats and large sunglasses to protect my face and cover my browless, lashless eyes. My treatment took place during the winter, so wearing slouchy hats and cashmere or fleece caps was easy. During the summer, sun hats with wide brims, cowboy hats, and fedoras look nice and shield the scalp and skin. There are even baseball caps with synthetic ponytails attached to them for an athletic look.

Doing my research, I found very few fashion lines dedicated to post-mastectomy patients or women who do not reconstruct. Someone who worked in the clothing industry told me it was too small of a market. I have to disagree based on feedback from survivors and the statistics on women who do not reconstruct. Here are two fashion lines I recommend for women postmastectomy.

THE ALLORO COLLECTION

The night before her own double mastectomy in 2011, Laurel Kamen, a former executive for American Express, envisioned creating a line of apparel for women who undergo mastectomies. She recruited longtime friend Christine Irvin, an artist and Wall Street veteran, and Laurel's cousin Roedean Landeaux, a New York City-based fashion designer, to realize her dream. The result is the Alloro Collection, a stylish, beautifully tailored line of clothing that would look great on anyone. The initial fifteen-piece collection features soft, shapely materials with tailored folds and drapes in all the right places, flattering and practical necklines, and soft jackets with hidden pockets for drains. The colors include complexion-brightening jewel tones as well as classic blacks and creams. Lightweight hats, scarves, and necklaces accessorize the clothes. The line is currently available through special trunk shows and online (www.alloro-collection.com; Twitter: @recapturejoy).

CHIKARA DESIGN

Chikara means "power and strength" in Japanese. And this line makes a powerful fashion statement for women with breast cancer who want to look stylish. Designed by Hilary Boyajian, Chikara offers design details such as raglan, dolman and kimono sleeves, asymmetrical necklines, draped tops, front closure wraps, and cardigans, all of which are designed to conceal drains, ports, swelling, and scars and to help women who have limited mobility (www.chikaradesign.com).

Survivor Wisdom

Dress the part you want to look. Apply lipstick to brighten your face, put on some fun earrings and a great pair of sunglasses, and wrap a colorful scarf or cape around you when you step outside.

Reality Check: There will be days when you really do not want to go out. But get up. If you feel the need to be housebound, connect with friends online. Join a community (it does not necessarily have to be a cancer community). Research a new subject. Find inspiration. It's important for cancer patients to stay connected in a positive way.

Positive Side Effects

19

"My 'aha!' moment was realizing the entire experience wasn't as bad as I thought it would be. How nice it was to get all the loving attention. . . . Today, my experience with cancer allows me to feel emboldened in the face of everyday challenges, and I have a keener sense of absurdity and fleeting existence."

—*Peaches*, diagnosed 2005

HOW I LOOKED TEN YEARS YOUNGER

"You look amazing, Melanie! Did you have a little work done?" asked someone at an event after I had recently finished my third round of chemo.

A great side effect from the treatment for me was getting in better shape and learning to take better care of myself inside and out. I was more disciplined than I had been before my cancer diagnosis, and it showed. While I did not intend to lose weight, it happened because of my more conscientious diet and exercise plan. Despite the chemicals that were being pumped into my body every two to three weeks, the exercise program was making my skin glow and my body become lean and firm. And I had great hair thanks to my wig.

Even after treatment was over, I remained committed, and my new regimen was pretty much no meat, less sweet, more green, more lean protein, whole grains, and no processed foods. I maintained a steady exercise program. This was a pretty huge about-face for someone whose professional life has centered on dining at some of the best restaurants in the country. I went from living to eat well, to eating well to live. Most women I spoke with said breast cancer taught them the importance of healthy eating and weight management. I still enjoy food, and I am still a choosy eater. I choose to eat healthy, fresh, wholesome food that tastes good.

ESTABLISH A CANCER KITTY

The financial challenge of paying for cancer treatment doesn't help the stress factor. Every time you turn around there's another bill to pay, and my bank account shrank as months wore on and it was harder for me spend the time pitching new business. But I looked for the silver living and made a list of all the ways I was also saving money. I figured out how much money I was *not* spending on haircuts and color, mani-pedis, bikini waxes, and going out for coffee and cocktails or restaurant meals. I established a "Cancer Kitty" and put a small amount away each month to do something special to celebrate the end of treatment with my husband.

SECTION 4

Be Fearless and Fabulous after Treatment

"My best 'aha!' moment was this: 'My contribution to the world is not related to how long I live. I thought about Jesus and how He died when he was in His early thirties.'"

—*Nancy*, diagnosed 2011

Emotional Rescue

"Don't underestimate the psychological impact of breast cancer. Allow time for restoring balance after your treatment."

—*Nancy, diagnosed 2011*

THE NATIONAL CANCER INSTITUTE AND NATIONAL COALITION for Cancer Survivorship both say that an individual is considered a cancer survivor from the time of diagnosis, through the balance of his or her life. But there is always a risk of recurrence, and my breast surgeon told me I would need to be checked for ten years. I think "survivorship" is something you define on your own terms. For me it was toward the end of 2011 when I finally opened up about my cancer and decided to change some things in my life that I felt were still weighing me down. It's when I really got things off my chest.

As I write this book, I am closing in on four years since my diagnosis in 2009. Each year has taught me lot about survivorship, yet I will always feel there is more to learn. Like a soldier returning from a tour of duty, easing back into civilian life after cancer treatment takes time. For some it can take years. Be prepared for a mixed bag of emotions and realize it is a form of strength, not weakness, if you choose to see professional help to address lingering sadness, anxiety, or other fear.

YOU MAY GO THROUGH DOCTOR WITHDRAWAL

When I walked out of my last chemo treatment with my friends Melanie and Susan, I could hear the soundtrack to the movie *Rocky* in my head. I felt like a marathon runner who had crossed the finish line! We celebrated over a light lunch and ripped off the hospital wristband in victory. But a number of women told me they experienced "doctor withdrawal." After months of listening to doctors on a regular basis, you are eased into biannual and eventually annual visits with your surgeons and oncologists. Like Elsa, the lion in the film *Born Free*, you are sent back into the wild and trusted to cope on your own.

EVERY CHECKUP BECOMES A CHECKPOINT FOR SURVIVORSHIP

"I was given a gold bracelet with an angel pendant. After each annual checkup, I add a charm."

—Stefania, diagnosed 2009

During your checkups, the doctors will ask how you are doing, examine your chest wall and muscles, and take blood. They may order additional tests such as a bone density scan. Try not to focus on the possibility of recurrence. Instead think of each checkup as an important marker on your road to continued good health.

YOUR CANCER-VERSARY: A DATE THAT WILL GO DOWN IN YOUR HISTORY

August 9, 2009, was a day that changed my life. Not *the only* day, but *a significant* day in a life of a number of milestones, some happy, some sad. A cancer-versary is not a date I want to mark in my life, but neither is September 11, 2001, when I watched the World Trade Center towers fall before my eyes. I was living in New York City on both days and had the same horrible, hopeless feeling that my world would never be the same. And when each date rolls around every year, I continue to pause and reflect on how precious and momentary life really is. Both events taught me in the words of an unknown Canadian poet, "Life is not about how many breaths you take, but about how many moments take your breath away."

I JUST GOT MY LIFE BACK. WHY AM I HAVING PANIC ATTACKS?

You just went through a heck of a lot. It's perfectly normal to have bouts of fear, anger, and emotion as you ease back into life. And how everyone handles it is different.

"I tell my patients it can take six months to feel better and to give themselves a full year to acclimate," says clinical psychologist Dr. Carla Marie Greco. "You have been through a physical and emotional trauma. Many women don't realize how difficult this can be on their emotions. What you are looking at is a scar on your psyche as much as your body. And don't let the word *scar* scare you. Remember this quote: 'Scars are part of the treasure map that makes you who you are.'"

FOLLOW YOUR GUT, BUT DON'T STARE AT YOUR NAVEL

"Illness can become an opportunity to go deeper into your life and discover what really counts."

—Stefania, diagnosed 2009

It can take some time for the entire experience to sink in. I was so busy going through cancer, running my business, dealing with the fallout of my father's death, and just trying to stay healthy that it took a good year and a half to sit down and reflect on "What the heck did I just go through?" After undergoing a period of post-traumatic stress syndrome, I acknowledged that I needed to "dial down" a bit.

"Having cancer gave me the courage to pursue a path that is more important to me."

—Didi, diagnosed 1988

BE TRUE TO YOURSELF AND FOLLOW YOUR INSTINCT

If something doesn't feel right emotionally, seek help. Don't lose yourself in trying to sort it out alone. Seek professional guidance.

BE INCOMPARABLE

Many women told me they "no longer sweat the small stuff." Others told me that the experience gave them a new impetus to change their careers or get involved and make a difference. Some become advocates for the fight against breast cancer; others go out and raise money for good causes. Many breast cancer survivors write blogs and books, create products, and start websites and nonprofits to help other cancer fighters through their journeys. Many cancer patients say they gain more patience; others become more impatient and start checking items off bucket lists. Doing my research for this book, I found a whole community of "cancer-preneurs" and cancer citizens doing truly impressive things to make a difference. This is a wonderful calling for those who do it, but it is not an obligation after surviving cancer. Do not—I repeat, do not!—compare how you are living your life after cancer to how others are living theirs.

CHANGE IS WHAT YOU WANT, NOT WHAT OTHERS WANT FOR YOU

Cancer is a game changer, and everyone I spoke with underwent a personal transformation. Some women change their lives, their looks, their careers, and their partners. Other women just want to go home and embrace the life they had before cancer with more intention and purpose. Don't let family members convince you to make a change or "move beyond your cancer and get a new life." They didn't go through cancer; you did. You spent at least a year following doctors' orders; now follow your own rules on how you want to live, who you want to be, and what you want to do next.

WELL . . . THERE ARE SOME RULES

There is no right or wrong direction in how you decide to live your life after surviving cancer. But there are some rules to follow:

- Take better care of yourself through diet, exercise, decent sleep, and stress management. You only have one body and one mind; take care of them.

- Be rigorous about your health care and keep regular doctors' appointments.

- Watch out for emotional triggers that set you off. Learn what they are and how to deal with them.

- Realize that you were not the only person affected by cancer. Your spouse, partner, children, family, and other loved ones were also impacted in a big way. Realize that they are recovering with you.

- You may have a different relationship to food, sex, and day-to-day situations and people. Be sensitive to changes and seek professional help if anything becomes an emotional roadblock.

"Having cancer means it is easy to say no to things that you do not want to do. Use this to your advantage to clear out unwanted obligations and create more space in your life just to be."

—Nancy, diagnosed 2011

I May No Longer Sweat the Small Stuff, But What About the Hot Flashes and Night Sweats?

Between the menopause and aromatese inhibitor medication, my body swings between hot and moist or shivering. Almost nightly, I toss off the covers around 4:00 a.m. in a hot sweat that is followed by a bout of chills from the dampness on my sheets. I don't think I will ever be able to wear a turtleneck or wool top without wanting to yank it off. Just writing this section is getting me clammy.

Here are some tips for dealing with your body heat:

- Be a lady and carry elegant hand fans.

- Carry wet naps or spray cologne.

- Avoid hot caffeinated drinks, spicy foods, hot soups or stews, and red wine.

- Avoid saunas and steam rooms.

- Wear layers so you can remove clothes as your body heats up. I like to wear a sturdy camisole or tank top with a light jacket, sweater, or wrap shirt over it.

- Avoid constrictive clothes. This includes body shapers, tight jeans, turtlenecks, and any materials that don't breathe.

- Moisten bandanas, sports head bands, or wristbands with Sea Breeze astringent for sensitive skin or a light cologne and tie them around your neck and wrists.

- Sleep with one leg outside the sheets. This always seems to work for me.

Diet & Nutrition Smarts

AFTER TREATMENT ENDS

ONCE YOU HAVE FINISHED TREATMENT, MAINTAINING A balanced diet is important for your return to optimum health. Diet is also an important factor in reducing the risk of recurrence. To review managing your diet after treatment, I turned to Holly Mills, MS, RD, CDN, CSO, CDE,* who in 2011 created a nutrition and weight management group for breast cancer survivors. Holly is also the cofounder of FreshView Nutrition with Megan Fendt and Jessica Miller, both RD, CDN and CDE.* The company offers counseling for individuals with a diagnosis of cancer, diabetes, or cardiac or renal disease, as well as education on nutrition during pregnancy, pediatric nutrition, and the management of food allergies (www.freshviewnutrition.com).

Holly recommends working with a registered dietitian for six months to a year after treatment in order to establish accountability and support and for help adopting healthy eating habits and maintaining weight. Here is what she shared with me:

"This is the time when patients want to make changes. I work with them on addressing healthy eating at home, healthy dining out, small portions and behavior modification, and other activities to manage diet.

---

* (MS) master of science, (RD) registered dietitian, (CDN) certified dietitian-nutritionist, (CSO) certified specialist in oncology, (CDE) certified diabetes educator

The goal is to get on a regimen that is right for you. It needs to be a lifestyle change for the rest of your life.

"A lot of women are getting back to their normal lives, and they tell me that there is a lot of stress involved in doing so. In that environment you don't always make the best choices. It may be a difficult time to deal with this. Usually stress is the biggest challenge to having a healthy lifestyle. I try to help patients identify what is triggering their stress. I have them log their moods and behavior and what may be triggering changes. During one of my group sessions I have a social worker come in to help teach women how to manage their stress through breathing techniques, meditation, and other stress reduction activities."

WEIGHT MANAGEMENT

Many women report gaining weight from treatment. Weight gain may be caused by many factors: medications, stress eating, inactivity, and hormonal fluctuations, among others. Almost every breast cancer survivor I contacted told me they were working hard to maintain a healthy weight by changing their diet after treatment.

Holly continues: "When I meet with patients in the middle of treatment, I usually tell them to focus on weight maintenance. However, I will review their diets and level of physical activity. A lot of people don't realize they may gain weight, so I work with them on appropriate techniques that they can start during treatment, such as making healthier food choices and eating smaller portions. I encourage patients to see me for weight loss recommendations after their treatment is over and not during. During treatment I do not promote a lot of lifestyle changes. However, I advocate continuing a relationship with an RD after treatment has ended to begin weight management counseling, since being overweight is a risk factor for recurrence," said Holly.

DIET AND ESTROGEN

I asked Holly: "If your cancer is estrogen receptor-positive, what foods should you avoid? What foods are essential? What if you are estrogen receptor-negative?

Her response: "In terms of diet, there is not a lot of evidence or enough good science about this topic. However, studies have shown that carotenoids, micronutrients in fruits and vegetables, may reduce breast cancer risk. For several carotenoids, associations appeared stronger for estrogen receptor-negative tumors.[1]

Research on flaxseed has found that it may be effective in inhibiting estrogen. Animal studies have shown that flaxseed, lignans, and flaxseed oil decrease several different growth factors, and they slow tumor growth and the ability to spread both estrogen receptor-positive and estrogen receptor-negative breast cancer. In addition, flaxseed oil is high in alpha-linolenic acid, an omega-3 fatty acid found to boost energy and have positive effects against cancer.[2]

DO I HAVE TO GIVE UP SOY SAUCE AND EDAMAME FOREVER?

Holly's response: "Determining whether soy is safe for breast cancer survivors has been a big topic of conversation and research for the past few years. Previous concerns with soy and increased breast cancer risk stem from the isoflavones in soy foods, a group of compounds that in some ways mimic the action of estrogen. High blood levels of estrogen are linked to increased breast cancer risk. These concerns were enforced by rodent studies that suggested certain isoflavones led to breast cancer cell growth. Scientists now know that rodents and most other laboratory animals metabolize soy isoflavones differently than humans. And soy consumption does not lead to increased estrogen levels in humans."

"According to recent studies performed, moderate consumption of soy-rich foods does not increase a breast cancer survivor's risk of recurrence. A moderate amount of soy is one to three standard servings daily of whole soy foods such as tofu, soy milk, and edamame."[3]

"Some preliminary human studies suggest that soy foods may be most protective among breast cancer survivors who are taking Tamoxifen, but this research is ongoing. There are limited or no data to support the use of supplements containing isolated soy phytochemicals for reducing cancer risk."

"There is a lot of information out there, and it can be confusing and scary for some. It's important to look at the science behind the claim and the type of study conducted. Was the study done in a laboratory with animal testing or human testing?' I encourage patients to visit reputable websites like those of the American Institute for Cancer Research and the American Cancer Society for the latest information on research conducted on cancer, diet, and physical activity."

THE HORMONES ARE MAKING ME CRAZY! ARE THERE ANY "MOOD FOODS" TO HELP?

Holly responds, "Researchers have studied the relationship between omega-3 fatty acids and mood disorders like depression. Some studies have found that subjects who consumed adequate amounts of omega-3 fatty acids daily lowered their depressive symptoms. However, consumption of foods high in omega-3 fatty acids should not be used as a home remedy for depression. Individuals at risk for depression should speak to a physician about treatment options. In general, I try to encourage my patients to avoid skipping meals. Food is your body's fuel. If you go for an extended period of time without food your blood sugar can drop. Some of the symptoms related to low blood sugar include fatigue, irritability, and headaches."

ARE THERE "TRIGGER FOODS" I SHOULD AVOID?

Holly responds, "Not really. Many patients ask me if there are foods to avoid for the management of menopausal symptoms like hot flashes. Some of the foods and beverages that may trigger hot flashes include spicy foods, caffeinated beverages, and alcohol.

"To see what foods are triggering symptoms, I recommend keeping a diary with a list of the foods you eat and related symptoms for at least one week. Under the care of an RD or physician, you can try to eliminate the foods or food groups you believe are related to your symptoms for two weeks. If your symptoms have not improved in two weeks, stop the elimination diet and talk with your health care practitioner about whether or not to try it again."

WHAT ABOUT TAKING VITAMINS AND SUPPLEMENTS?

Holly responds, "I do not recommend vitamins or mineral supplements as a substitute for eating fruits and vegetables. I recommend 'food first,' as food is the best source of vitamins and minerals. Many healthful compounds are found in vegetables and fruits, and it is likely that these compounds work synergistically to exert their beneficial effect.

"Vitamins and supplements should be used as needed if you have a deficiency. Some medications or treatments for breast cancer may require taking a calcium plus vitamin D supplement to counter bone loss. Your doctor should conduct blood work first and then recommend what you need."

TRACK YOUR PROGRESS

Holly also recommends keeping a food diary to track what you eat. "You can't change what you don't know. For those patients who are unable to keep a diary on a regular basis, I encourage them to try and do it a few days out of the week. This will give them some idea of their usual caloric intake. These days there are a number of smart phone and iPad apps that provide great resources to calculate energy needs and energy expenditure. On some you can even run reports on your micronutrient intake as well."

Two free diet and nutrition management apps that Holly recommends are the USDA's ChooseMyPlate SuperTracker (www.choosemyplate.gov/supertracker-tools/supertracker.html) and Lose It! (www.loseit.com).

NOTES

1. A. Heather Eliassen, et al., "Carotenoids and Risk of Breast Cancer," Oxford Journals, *Journal of The National Cancer Institute*, 2012, 104 (24), 1905–16.

2. American Cancer Society, "Flaxseed," http://www.cancer.org/treatment/treatmentsandsideeffects/complementaryandalternativemedicine/herbsvitaminsandminerals/flaxseed.

3. American Institute for Cancer Research, "Soy Is Safe for Breast Cancer Survivors," AICR's Foods That Fight Cancer, November 2012, http://www.aicr.org/press/press-releases/soy-safe-breast-cancer-survivors.html. Accessed June 27, 2013.

Post-Treatment

GYNECOLOGICAL CARE AND OTHER TESTS

YOUR OB-GYN NEEDS TO BE APPRISED OF YOUR DIAGNOSIS and treatment every step of the way. Post-treatment, you should meet with her to review your follow-up and long-term care and what tests you need. Here are some questions I asked my OB-GYN, Dr. Melanie Marin:

IF YOU HAD BREAST CANCER, DO YOU STILL NEED TO HAVE AN ANNUAL MAMMOGRAM?

Dr. Marin responds, "For survivors who have had a lumpectomy or single mastectomy, you will continue to have mammograms every six months and should conduct monthly breast self-examinations. If you have had a mastectomy, with or without reconstruction, your breast surgeon or your OB-GYN will need to examine your chest wall, scar tissue, and surrounding areas every six to twelve months at your breast surgeon's discretion."

WHAT OTHER TESTS DO I NEED?

Dr. Marin responds, "Post-treatment tests will depend on the type of treatment you had, if you are pre- or postmenopausal and if you tested positive for either of the BRCA gene mutations for cancer."

TESTS YOU SHOULD DISCUSS WITH YOUR
HEALTH CARE PROVIDER

- *Pap smear and HPV* testing will help detect cervical cancer. If you are between the ages of 30 and 65 years, you will need to be tested every five years if your pap test and HPV tests are both normal. If your Pap test and/or HPV tests are *not* normal, you will need to have more frequent evaluations. You *always* need to be tested for cervical cancer, even if you have had the HPV vaccine.

- *Pelvic Exam*: Requirements will depend on factors such as whether or not you still have your uterus, ovaries, or fallopian tubes.

IF YOU STILL HAVE YOUR OVARIES,
FALLOPIAN TUBES, AND UTERUS

You will continue to have an annual pelvic exam. However, if you have tested positive for either the BRCA1 or BRCA2 gene mutation and elect not to have surgery to remove the ovaries and fallopian tubes, you will need to have a vaginal ultrasound and CA-125 blood test every six months to check for elevated levels of protein. These tests are the two ways to screen for ovarian cancer, which usually goes undetected until symptoms start to appear.

Removal of ovaries and fallopian tubes

"You should know that none of the screening tests for ovarian cancer are very good. That is why we strongly recommend removal of the fallopian tubes and ovaries for those who carry the BRCA1 and BRCA2 gene mutation," said Dr. Marin. "If you are over the age of forty and finished with childbearing and test positive for either BRCA gene mutation, you should have a *bilateral salpingo-oophorectomy* (BSO), a surgical procedure to remove your fallopian tubes and ovaries. This not only reduces the risk of ovarian cancer, but it also significantly reduces the risk of recurrent breast cancer." Once you have had your ovaries and fallopian tubes removed, you will need to have a routine pelvic exam every two years provided you still have your uterus. If you had a hysterectomy, you no longer need to have a pelvic exam.

- *Colonoscopy*: You should plan to have a colonoscopy to screen for colon cancer every ten years unless you have an overriding condition that may require you to be tested more frequently.

- *Bone density test*: Schedule one every two to five years, depending on the results and your risk factors. This is especially important if you are taking aromatese inhibitors, which can weaken the bones and lead to osteoporosis and the risk of bone fractures, back pain, and weakening of the vertebrae.

- *Blood test*: Your oncologist will arrange a blood test for you at each visit.

- *Urine test*: These check for any signs of infection or blood in the urine, which could be signs of bladder cancer.

- *Blood pressure*: taken at each visit

- *Skin check*: Your dermatologist should thoroughly check your skin for cancers annually. This is especially important if you have fair skin, tanned or burned frequently when you were younger (or still do), or if you tested positive for either the BRCA1 or BRCA2 gene mutation.

MORE ON GENETIC TESTING

Dr. Marin stresses the importance of undergoing genetic testing for the BRCA1 or BRCA2 gene mutation for any woman who is diagnosed with breast cancer at a young age, has a family history of breast, prostate, ovarian, skin, or pancreatic cancers, or whose heritage is Ashkenazi Jewish.

She says, "Under any of these circumstances, the likelihood of having either gene mutation is statistically greater and means you may have a higher risk for these kinds of cancer. Ovarian cancer is almost never detected early, even with the best screening available, so if you test positive and know it, you can take steps to save your life by having your fallopian tubes and ovaries surgically removed. If you still have your breasts and test positive, you will also want to have MRIs in addition to mammograms and breast ultrasounds, or you may choose to have a prophylactic mastectomy with reconstruction." In May 2013 the topic of BRCA testing and choosing prophylactic surgery received international attention after the actress Angelina Jolie wrote an op-ed piece in the *New York Times* documenting her choice to undergo the procedure after testing positive for the BRCA1 mutation.

I applaud Ms. Jolie for sharing her personal decision because it sent a message to all women to be aware of their bodies and make informed, confident decisions about their health management.

The test for me involved a doctor taking blood on which the lab will run tests. So it is pretty painless. But what *is* painful for some women is making the decision to undergo genetic testing. A negative test will alleviate fears that the cancer is genetic. A positive test means you *are statistically* at a higher risk for the other cancers and for passing the gene to your children. It also means you may want to share the information with your close blood relatives in case they want to undergo testing.

My medical oncologist, Dr. Maria Theodoulou, also pointed out that "testing negative for BRCA1 and BRCA2 does not eliminate a hereditary risk for malignancy. There are other mutations that may be of concern, depending on family and personal history. It is important to meet with a clinical geneticist for complete evaluation."

The additional pain comes in deciding how to digest and address a positive test result.

If you have not undergone a mastectomy, would you consider having a prophylactic double mastectomy? If you still have your ovaries, do you have an oophorectomy to prevent ovarian cancer and decrease your risk of recurrent breast cancer? What if you still want to have children? You should always be vigilant about wearing a broad-spectrum high SPF sunscreen and undergoing annual skin cancer examinations to reduce the risk of melanoma.

But what the heck do you do about pancreatic cancer, which is usually asymptomatic?

Your health insurance provider cannot discriminate against you if you test positive for the BRCA mutation; it is against federal law. Dr. Marin informed me that if your health insurance provider is made aware that you tested positive for this mutation, the provider can help with obtaining coverage for important monitoring tests that may not routinely be covered, such as more frequent breast MRIs, and ovary and blood tests.

If you undergo genetic testing, hopefully it will bring you more peace of mind. I took the test, and it came back positive for BRCA2. Knowing the risk for ovarian cancer, I felt no pain choosing to have an oophorectomy, which was a laproscopic surgery that left no scars. It took a load of worry off my chest.

BRCA1 and BRCA2 testing has been an expensive test and not always covered by health insurance unless there was a significant risk such as family history or, in my case, I already had breast cancer and wanted to find out what my other cancer risks might be. However, in June 2013 the US Supreme Court ruled that naturally occurring human genes could not be patented. This landmark decision means that BRCA1 and BRCA2 genetic testing will become more accessible and affordable for women and opens the doors for more scientific research.

WHAT IF I WANT TO HAVE CHILDREN?

Women of childbearing age who are diagnosed with breast cancer face the additional agony of not knowing if they will ever be able to conceive after treatment. Some chemotherapy and targeted endocrine treatments will result in temporary loss of your periods or full-blown menopause. Others, like radiation treatment (alone and not in conjunction with chemotherapy), do not affect fertility.

For women who hope to have children, the issue of fertility and breast cancer treatment needs to be addressed at the start of the journey. You should speak with your OB-GYN, your surgeon, and possibly a fertility specialist once you have been diagnosed and ideally before your surgery or treatment. This allows you time to have all your questions answered and to weigh your options once your course of treatment is confirmed. Here are some things you should be prepared to ask:

- How will conceiving a child affect my long-term health and risk for recurrence?

- If I become pregnant, what potential risk(s) are there to my fetus?

- Which cancer treatments run the risk of my becoming infertile?

- Which treatments will still allow me to become pregnant and are they a good option for my condition?

- If I am able to conceive after treatment, how long should I wait to become pregnant?

- What birth control methods are safe for me to use after treatment?

- What fertility preservation options do I have (such as storing and freezing embryos or my unfertilized eggs)?

- If I can freeze and store my eggs or embryos, what is the process and at what stage in surgeries and treatment should that take place?

- How long will they remain fertile? This is important if you intend to delay having children.

- What other fertility treatment options do I have?

- If my treatment temporarily shuts down my ovaries, are there medications or supplements I can take afterward to increase my fertility?

- Will I be able to breastfeed my baby?

For more information on this sensitive issue, check out Breastcancer.org: Fertility and Pregnancy Issues During and After Breast Cancer (www.breastcancer.org/tips/fert_pregnancy).

Intimacy

"If my sex life was a book, it would be Fifty Shades of Gray Hair."
—*Melanie*, diagnosed 2009

ACCORDING TO THE *JOURNAL OF SEXUAL MEDICINE*, SEVEN IN ten breast cancer survivors experience sexual problems in the two years after their diagnoses (September 2012).

Chemotherapy-induced menopause, body image issues, the emotional fallout of getting through treatment, having hormones in flux, and just the seismic adjustment to a life after cancer are just some of the factors that result in a lapsed libido.

They say getting back into sex is like hopping on a bicycle; once you know how to do it, you can start up again easily. A man said that. And he probably didn't have cancer. Easing back into intimacy and sex takes time and effort after treatment.

LIVING LIBIDO LOCO (MOTHER, YOU CAN SKIP THIS SECTION!)

No one really likes to discuss their sex life. So, I am really getting it off my chest and discussing my own experience. Sex was the last thing on my mind during cancer treatment. According to my red-blooded husband, during those months of abstinence, "Sex was just a number in Latin."

Let's face it: chemotherapy does not mix well with sexual chemistry. But you still can be intimate in a warm fuzzy manner, and nothing beats a soft touch by a gentle person.

I always loved having my back caressed, but more so after my mastectomy. My nerve endings seem to have rearranged from between my legs to between my shoulders!

Here is a quick checklist for getting reacquainted with your sexual self:

Communicate: Tell your partner—in a nice way—what feels good to you and what does not. If he still does not get it, then demonstrate.

Lubricate: Use unscented water-soluble vaginal lubricants (like Astroglide, KY Jelly, and Replens) to replenish delicate tissues. Another person suggested using olive oil as a lubricant, and there are numerous mentions of this online, but my sex-pert for this book, Barbara Musser, says to stick with water-based lubricants designed for the vagina and keep olive oil to your pasta and salads. Oils are hard to remove from the vagina.

Dilate: Exercise to keep the blood flow moving. There are special devices you can purchase to help manually stretch the vaginal tissue so it can dilate easier.

Stimulate: This could include a heady (excuse the double entendre) dose of foreplay or self-stimulation.

Also, prepare the stage. Here are some ways to set the boudoir mood:

- If you don't want to sleep in the nude, wear beautiful camisoles, sexy T-shirts, or sarongs.

- Put all electronics and anything with flashing lights in another room if you want more sexual electricity between the sheets.

- Keep the temperature in the room cool. This helps with night sweats.

- Declutter. Put away clothes or piles of stuff lying around.

- Install softer lightbulbs or light candles.

AN EXPERT WEIGHS IN

I asked breast cancer survivor and sex educator-coach Barbara Musser, author of *Sexy After Cancer: Meeting Your Inner Aphrodite on the*

Breast Cancer Journey, to share her insights. Barbara leads workshops and retreats in California to help cancer patients and couples rekindle their sexual selves after treatment. Here is what she shared with me:

"With many forms of breast cancer treatment your estrogen is suppressed and your oxytocin, or your feel-good hormones, go out of balance. Body dryness and poor self-image are other factors. Many women who undergo chemotherapy may be thrown into menopause or are already underway and experience mood swings, hot flashes, night sweats, fatigue, and weight gain, which wear on your feelings of desire. Younger women face other issues. Some are single and dating. Others hoped to start families and face chemotherapy-induced menopause or decreased hormone production from drugs like tamoxifen. Some women have their ovaries removed. And there is the fear of recurrence.

"Different cultures and religions have stronger views about a woman's sexuality, and that can be hard for a woman who suddenly sees herself as less womanly or desirable. My gift is to help open the doors for them to feel better about themselves. We all want to be loved and accepted for who we are."

SEXERCISE AND SEX-ESSORIZE!—GETTING BACK INTO SEXUAL SHAPE

Barbara stresses the importance of "exercising" your sexual self: "The reason the vaginal tissue dries up is because there is inadequate blood and lymphatic flow. After treatment and hormone therapies, the genital tissue is delicate and thin. It can tear easily, which can lead to bleeding and discomfort. It is important to get your genitals back in shape. You need to ease into it slowly."

Kegel exercises can help strengthen your pelvic floor muscles and also help with urinary incontinence (which may dampen sexual heat). Barbara advises that proper technique is important: "Contract the pelvic muscles slowly and hold (imagine you are pulling your internal muscles up to your belly button, like an elevator going up) and then slowly and fully relax the muscles (lowering the elevator). Lift, lower, release, relax, and then repeat. And breathe deeply!"

"In terms of easing back into sexuality, I think it is important to do a lot of exploration of your body. If your breasts are removed and you received a lot pleasure from them, tell your partner how it feels now when your breasts are touched," says Barbara. "Also, if you have not had sex for some time, you may not want to jump right into intercourse. Take it slowly and try other things that give you both pleasure."

Barbara will take her clients shopping at Good Vibrations to discuss different toys and how they work. "I have had clients write me after one of my retreats to say I changed their lives."

In addition to her own practice, Sexy Cancer Survivor (www.sexy-cancersurvivor.com), and her book, Barbara's website also recommends the following resources:

A Woman's Touch (www.a-woman's-touch.com): This is a Madison, Wisconsin-based sexuality boutique and website dedicated to sexual health. They sell a vaginal renewal kit.

Good Clean Love (www.goodcleanlove.com): Founded by "lovologist" Wendy Strgar, Good Clean Love offers a line of organic lubricants.

Good Vibrations (www.goodvibrations.com): This company with locations in Boston and San Francisco offers a great selection of sex accessories and toys and has a sexologist on staff to answer questions

LEARNING TO LOVE YOUR BODY

"Learn not to expect perfection."

—Didi, diagnosed 1988

Barbara notes that one thing that happens with a lot of people during treatment is they disassociate with their bodies because treatment is so traumatic. "Many doctors treat us as if we are the body part and not the whole person. I am an advocate of whole body-mind-spirit integration. You need to bring back awareness to your body and to the places that feel pleasurable to you. One of the things that happens with cancer is there is heartbreak. When our hearts are broken open there is pain, but there is also an opportunity to experience much deeper love. You realize how precious life is and that it is not a dress rehearsal."

Barbara points out that it is important to become comfortable in your new body. This can take time because your body has undergone a transformation and, for women who have had mastectomies, a pretty major one. Taking care of your body through diet, exercise, and proper skin care will make a big difference.

"The big moment is when you can be comfortable looking at your naked body. Stand in front of the mirror and look at yourself and say 'I love you.' Most of us don't really look at ourselves in the mirror unless we are checking our makeup or if we have spinach in our teeth," says Barbara.

It took time for me to be comfortable with my new body. The first thing I did was toss out all my old lingerie and bought beautiful new bras, underwear, and camisoles. If you really feel emboldened, have professional boudoir photos taken of your new self. I did a few years after my treatment as an anniversary gift for my husband, and it was a big emotional step forward for me to throw off any remaining negative body issues.

LEARNING TO CONNECT

Single women at any age face the challenge of when to start dating again and when to share their cancer story. "There is no cookie cutter approach," said Barbara. "If you are thinking about it, you are ready. Some people lay their cards on the table and some play it closer to their vest. It is important to honor your style and be flexible. And it may change from week to week. But be honest about it. You don't want to go into a relationship without revealing this important part of yourself."

LEARNING TO DISCONNECT

Some cancer survivors say the experience gave them the courage to walk away from bad relationships. One woman told me her husband served her with divorce papers. Another said her husband treated her like "damaged goods" and she said, "I've had enough!"

PARTING SHOTS: AN URBAN LEGEND

In 2003 some reputable news media outlets reported on a study from North Carolina State University citing that women who performed the act of fellatio and swallowed semen at least two times a week may reduce their risk of breast cancer by 40 percent! It turns out the study was a hoax by a male (of course!) student at the college who was just blowing smoke and managed to pull off a great publicity stunt. The story is still circulating on the web, though it is refuted by the American Cancer Society.[1] For the record, I checked with my dentist, Dr. Thomas Magnani, when discussing oral care. Fellatio during treatment is okay if you can stomach it.

NOTE

1. American Cancer Society, "Fellatio and Breast Cancer," http://www.cancer.org/aboutus/howwehelpyou/fellatio-and-breast-cancer. Accessed June 27, 2013.

Making Cancer a Positive "Life Sentence"

"Breast cancer helped to put me on a path to better health and well-being. In some ways, I think cancer may have saved my life."

—*Nancy L.*, diagnosed 2011)

NO MATTER HOW ROUGH IT MAY BE, *DO NOT* VIEW CANCER as a death sentence. View it as a life sentence: You can and should make choices about how you want to live. We all have a limited life span on this earth, and most of us are too busy to dwell on this. The cancer diagnosis reminded me how valuable every day is and to divest myself of anything weighing me down.

I learned that spending time is more important than spending money. Time becomes a universal currency that you no longer want to waste and you want to spend more wisely.

Money is what you earn to pay the bills and invest in your and your loved ones' happiness and well-being, but it is not a cure for anything. Spending time with family and friends is more important than anything else.

I started by following all the commandments in this book. When my cancer journey started, I felt overloaded and overwhelmed—not just from the diagnosis, but from other things like my crazy workload and day-to-day pressures. So I took each day and each task in small steps to avoid being overwhelmed. I made a goal of throwing out something every day. By eliminating anything that cluttered my space or upset me emotionally, I felt more balanced and less encumbered. I cleaned out drawers and closets and gave away old clothes. I loaded files I needed to keep onto my computer to have less paper and tossed out anything that was just taking up space. I made lists of my bank, airline, and credit card accounts, and my insurance and mortgage documents to keep in one computer file. I figured that if anything happens to me in the future, at least my husband would be able to locate critical information with ease.

Managing stress continues to be a challenge but has improved over time as I learn to strike a balance between a personal and professional life, city and country, and obligations and inspiration. I never fear recurrence of my cancer, but my heart skips a beat when a friend or colleague calls me crying because she received her diagnosis. And I make sure I am there for her if she needs a mentor to offer advice and cheer her up.

I still adhere to my "Holy Trinity" of hydration, exercise, and a healthier diet despite the challenges of working in the wine and food industry. I try to focus on *mindful moderation* and more *conscious consumption*, which means higher quality food and drink in smaller amounts so I can stay healthy without giving up the pleasure of the palate. And when I find myself slipping (it happens!) and I break the Holy Trinity, I look up and give a silent blessing and wink to JC. No, not Jesus Christ . . . Julia Child, a breast cancer survivor who ate and drank what she wanted and lived to the ripe old age of 92!

The ten takeaways I learned from cancer are no different than those we should live by when we are healthy. It took a health scare to put it all back into perspective:

- Be physically active.
- Maintain a healthy body weight.
- Make smart food choices.
- Lower alcohol intake.
- Use sunscreen daily.
- Reduce/manage stress.
- Get enough sleep.
- Don't smoke or use recreational drugs.

- Be vigilant about your health care, including annual exams, screenings, and vaccinations.
- Focus on positive energy and make quality time for yourself and loved ones.

Survivor Wisdom

Being diagnosed with cancer can make you feel vulnerable. But surviving cancer will make you feel invincible. At some point you come to terms with the fact that cancer is or was a defining moment in your life. I hope it is the moment when you learn the value of living a healthy life and you realize that some of the things that stressed you out really do not matter.

Looking back at my "Year of Living Surgically and Chemically," I view it as a nasty bump in the road of life that taught me I needed to kick my own tires and make some adjustments. I no longer have anger about it; I gained acceptance long ago and embrace my new body and my special breast tattoos. My passions are still the same; I just pursue them with more effort rather than put them aside for things that used to seem so important and no longer do. For all that I lost from cancer—two breasts, now replaced; some hair, now returned; some time, now regained; and some physical and emotional weight that I shouldn't have been carrying in the first place and don't plan to allow back—I've gained clarity, perspective, and purpose. The road ahead will always have dangerous curves and bumps but I have learned better skills to maneuver them and plan to enjoy the ride with even more spirit. I hope this book does the same for you!

May there always be tradewinds behind you
Rainbows over your head
And Aloha all around you.

—KAUAI BLESSING

Resources

GENERAL INFORMATION FOR PATIENTS, SURVIVORS, CAREGIVERS, AND HEALTH PROFESSIONALS

American Cancer Society (ACS): www.cancer.org
(800) ACS-2345 (227-2345); Twitter: @AmericanCancer

The American Cancer Society is a nationwide community-based voluntary health organization dedicated to eliminating cancer as a major health problem. The ACS has 12 geographic divisions and more than 900 local offices nationwide and a presence in more than 5100 communities. Here are some helpful links on this website:

- Americans with Disabilities Act: http://www.cancer.org/treatment/findingandpayingfortreatment/understandingfinancialandlegalmatters/americans-with-disabilities-act

- Side Effects: http://www.cancer.org/treatment/treatmentsand sideeffects/physicalsideeffects/index

American Institute for Cancer Research (AICR), www.aicr.org
(800) 843-8114; Twitter: @aicrtweets

This was the first organization to focus research on the link between diet and cancer and to translate the results into practical information for the public. The AICR funds cutting-edge research to give people practical tools and information to help them prevent and survive cancer.

National Cancer Institute (NCI): www.cancer.gov
(800) 4-CANCER (422-6237); Twitter: @theNCI

The National Cancer Institute is part of the National Institutes of Health (NIH), one of eleven agencies within the federal government's Department of Health and Human Services (HHS). The NCI coordinates the National Cancer Program, which conducts and supports research, training, health information dissemination, and other programs with respect to the cause, diagnosis, prevention, and treatment of cancer, rehabilitation from cancer, and the continuing care of cancer patients and the families of cancer patients. These are some of the many helpful links:

- Finding a doctor: http://www.cancer.gov/cancertopics/factsheet/Therapy/doctor-facility

- Coping and emotional care during treatment: http://www.cancer.gov/cancertopics/coping#Emotional+Concerns

- Life after treatment: http://www.cancer.gov/cancertopics/coping/life-after-treatment

National Comprehensive Cancer Network (NCCN): www.nccn.org

A not-for-profit alliance of twenty-three of the world's leading cancer centers, NCCN is dedicated to improving the quality and effectiveness of care provided to patients with cancer. Here is the NCCN breast cancer link for patients: www.nccn.org/patients/patient_guidelines/breast/index.html

ONCOLOGY (IN ADDITION TO ABOVE)

The American Society of Clinical Oncology (ASCO), www.oncology.com

The ASCO's site for people living with cancer: www.chemotherapy.com. This is a good resource for answering your questions about chemotherapy.

BREAST CANCER EDUCATION INFORMATION, RESEARCH, AND RESOURCES

The Breast Cancer Research Foundation (BCRF): www.bcrfcure.org
(866)-FIND-A-CURE (346-3228); Twitter: @BCRFcure

Founded by the late Evelyn H. Lauder, BCRF's mission is to achieve prevention and a cure for breast cancer by funding innovative clinical and translational research at leading medical centers around the world and by raising public awareness of breast health.

Breastcancer.org

Twitter: @Breastcancer.org

Provides complete and up-to-date information about breast cancer to help patients and loved ones make informed decisions.

Susan G. Komen For the Cure: ww5.komen.org

(877) GO-KOMEN (465-6636); Twitter: @KomenfortheCure

Susan G. Komen for the Cure has raised more than $2 billion to support grants to fund research, advocacy, and patient support programs in more than fifty countries. The Susan G. Komen Race for the Cure Series is one of the largest and most successful grassroots run/walk programs, attracting more than 1.6 million participants in more than 150 locations around the world, including 120 chapters in the United States.

Dr. Susan Love Research Foundation: www.dslrf.org

(866) 569-0388; Twitter: @actwlove. Army of Women: www.armyofwomen .org; Twitter: @ArmyofWomen

The Dr. Susan Love Research Foundation's Army of Women program, supported by a grant from the Avon Foundation for Women, affords women with or without breast cancer the opportunity to voluntarily participate in research studies to help eradicate the disease.

Reading: *Dr. Susan Love's Breast Cancer Book* by Dr. Susan M. Love, MD (A Merloyd Lawrence Book) (Boston: Da Capo Press, 2010)

MAGAZINES

MAMM: www.MAMM.com

(977) 668-1800

MAMM is a magazine devoted to meeting the needs of women diagnosed with breast and reproductive cancers.

COUNSELING, ASSISTANCE, EDUCATION, AND RESOURCES

CancerCare: www.cancercare.org

(800) 813- HOPE (813-4673); Twitter: @CancerCare

Cancer*Care* is a national nonprofit organization serving all fifty states that is dedicated to helping people cope with and manage the emotional and practical challenges of a cancer diagnosis. Cancer*Care* provides free professional counseling and educational programs, practical help, and financial assistance.

Cancer Support Community: www.cancersupportcommunity.org
(888) 793-9355; Twitter: @CancerSupportCm

This is an international nonprofit network dedicated to providing support, education, and hope to people affected by cancer. Use it to find local counseling or support groups and workshops, create your own webpage, or download a free booklet, "Frankly Speaking About Cancer."

Living Beyond Breast Cancer (LBBC): www.lbbc.org
(888) 753-(LBBC) 753-5222; Twitter: @LivingBeyondBC

Living Beyond Breast Cancer (LBBC) provides support, education, and resources to women with cancer to empower them to have the best quality of life. LBBC offers several workshops, forums, an annual conference, and free publications covering a range of topics. LBBC works in collaboration with the Young Survivors Coalition (YSC) (www.c4yw.org).

PEER SUPPORT AND COMMUNITIES

SHARE (Self-Help for Women with Breast or Ovarian Cancer)
www.sharecancersupport.org, Helpline: (866)891-2392; Twitter: @SHAREing

SHARE's mission is to create and sustain a supportive network and community of women affected by breast or ovarian cancer. SHARE provides free telephone support, support groups, webinars, and educational workshops in English and ten other languages for women and men of all ages and ethnicities. Based in New York City, SHARE is comprised of survivors who can help you face the emotional and practical issues of cancer. All services are offered in both English and Spanish.

Breast Friends: www.breastfriends.com
(888) 386-8048; Twitter: @BreastFriends

Breast Friends is dedicated to improving the quality of life for female cancer patients through support, a volunteer mentor-patient connection, programs, workshops, and resources.

Imerman Angels: www.imermanangels.org
(877) 274-5529; Twitter: @ImermanAngels

Imerman Angels carefully matches a person touched by cancer with someone who has fought and survived the same type of cancer (A Mentor Angel). The service is free and available to anyone touched by any type of cancer, at any cancer stage level, at any age, living anywhere in the world.

Pink-Link: www.pink-link.org

Founded by breast cancer survivor Victoria Tashman in 2005, Pink-Link is a free online breast cancer support network that provides an intimate link between mentor and patient through its extensive database. The website also has an online store featuring postmastectomy and chemotherapy apparel

Young Survival Coalition (YSC): www.youngsurvival.org
(877) 972-1011; Twitter: @YSCBUZZ

YSC is a national not-for-profit network that offers resources, workshops, connections, and outreach to provide hope, encouragement, and empowerment to young women diagnosed with breast cancer. YSC hosts an annual C4YW national conference in collaboration with Living Beyond Breast Cancer (LBBC) that is exclusively dedicated to the unique needs of young women affected by breast cancer.

Sisters Network Inc.: www.sistersnetworkinc.org
(866) 781-1808; Twitter: @sistersnetwork

Sisters Network Inc. is committed to increasing local and national attention to the devastating impact that breast cancer has in the African American community. Programs include advocacy, education, and financial assistance.

Sharsheret: www.sharsheret.org
(866) 474-2774; Twitter: @Sharsheret

Sharsheret links young Jewish women who are fighting breast cancer and includes information on managing cosmetic side effects through its Best Face Forward initiative.

National LGBT Cancer Network: www.cancer-network.org
(212) 675-2633; Twitter: @cancerLGBT

The National LGBT Network is dedicated to improving the lives of LGBT people with cancer and those at risk.

Pregnant with Cancer Network (PWCN): www.pregnantwithcancer.org
(800) 743-4471; Twitter: @HopeforTwoPWCN

PWCN offers free support for women diagnosed with cancer while pregnant and connects women who are currently pregnant and have cancer with other women who have experienced a similar cancer diagnosis.

American Cancer Society Asian Initiatives: http://www.cancer.org/myacs/eastern/programsandservices/asian-initiatives

This website provides resources and education for Asian Americans diagnosed with cancer.

Asian & Pacific Islander American Health Forum (APINCSN): www.apiahf.org
Twitter: @apiahf

APINCSN is a network of cancer survivors, families, health care providers, researchers, and advocates that provides information and resources for Asian Americans, Native Hawaiians, and Pacific Islanders.

Men Against Breast Cancer: www.menagainstbreastcancer.org
(866) 547-MABC (547-6222); Twitter: @MABCcares

MABC provides support services that educate and empower men to be effective caregivers when cancer strikes.

COMMUNITIES (AMONG MANY)

I Had Cancer: www.IHadCancer.com
Twitter: @IHadCancer

Started by breast cancer survivor Mailet Lopez, I Had Cancer is an online community of cancer fighters, survivors, and caregivers who can connect and share their stories.

My BC Team: www.mybcteam.com
Twitter: @MYBCTeam

My BC Team is a social network where women with breast cancer connect, share stories, and exchange insights.

Breast Cancer My Story: www.breastcancermystory.org
Twitter: @BCCancerMyStory

Founded by survivor Britta Wilk McKenna. Breast Cancer My Story provides online companionship and relevant information for all those affected by breast cancer.

FINANCIAL ASSISTANCE AND RESOURCES

Cancer*Care*. See above.

Corporate Angel Network: www.corpangelnetwork.org
(866) 328-1313

Corporate Angel Network's sole mission is to help cancer patients access the best possible treatment for their specific type of cancer by arranging free travel to treatment across the country using empty seats on corporate jets.

My Hope Chest: www.MyHopeChest.org
(727) 488-0320; Twitter: @MyHopeChest

Created by Las Vegas performer and breast cancer survivor Alisa Savoretti ("The Lop-Sided Showgirl"), My Hope Chest is a national breast reconstruction organization working to help uninsured and under insured women heal completely. The organization provides financial assistance for women who cannot afford reconstruction.

HEALTH INSURANCE INFORMATION

US Department of Health & Human Services: www.healthcare.gov
Twitter: @HealthCareGov

A website of the US Department of Health & Human Services addressing health insurance topics, health care law, prevention, wellness, and comparing providers.

PATIENT ADVOCACY

Patient Advocate Foundation (PAF): www.patientadvocate.org
(800) 532-5274

Patient Advocate Foundation's Patient Services provides patients with arbitration, mediation, and negotiation to settle issues with access to care, medical debt, and job retention issues related to their illness. The PAF website includes *Your Guide to the Appeals Process* to help patients who are having problems getting their health insurance companies to pay for diagnostic tests, lab work, or treatment.

Patient Advocate Foundation Co-pay Relief Program: www.co-pays.org
866-512-3861

This organization provides direct financial assistance to qualified patients, assisting them with prescription drug co-payments required by their insurance. CRP call counselors work directly with the patient as well as with the care provider to obtain necessary medical, insurance, and income information to advance the application in an expeditious manner.

NeedyMeds: www.needymeds.org
Helpline: (800) 503-6897; Twitter @NeedyMeds

This is a resource clearinghouse to help people in need find assistance programs to help them afford their medications and health care-related costs.

WORKPLACE RESOURCES

Cancer and Careers: www.cancerandcareers.org
Twitter: @CancerAndCareer

Cancer and Careers empowers and educates people with cancer to thrive in their work place by providing expert advice, interactive tools, and educational workshops. They also offer helpful free booklets: "Living and Working with Cancer" and "The Most Important Resources for Working Women with Cancer."

NATUROPATHIC ONCOLOGY

Lise Alschuler, ND, FABNO: www.drlise.net and www.fivetothrive.com
Twitter: @FivetoThrive

SOURCES FOR LOCATING NATUROPATHIC ONCOLOGISTS

American Association of Naturopathic Physicians: www.naturopathic.org
Twitter: @AANP

Oncology Association of Naturopathic Physicians: www.oncanp.org
Twitter: @OncANP

MOVEMENT AND FITNESS PROGRAMS FOR BREAST CANCER SURVIVORS

Moving For Life: www.movingforlife.org
(212) 414-2921, info@movingforlife.org

Dr. Martha Eddy, CMA, RSMT, a Certified Movement Analyst and a Registered Somatic Movement Therapist, founded this nonprofit organization that provides aerobic exercise classes incorporating specific movements that she designed to help with different physical and emotional side effects from cancer treatment. The organization has certified instructors around the country and a "Dance For Recovery" DVD.

New England Physical Care (Norwalk, CT): www.nephysical.com
(203) 838-9822

Brian Nathanson, DC, specializes in working with women who have undergone mastectomies and reconstruction to help them regain strength and mobility and alleviate post-surgery discomfort.

LYMPHEDEMA

The National Lymphedema Network (NLN): www.lymphnet.org
(415) 908-3681

NLN provides education and guidance to lymphedema patients, health care professionals, and the general public by disseminating information on management of primary and secondary lymphedema and related disorders, and education in risk reduction practices.

Lymphedivas: www.lymphedivas.com
(866)-411-DIVA (411-3482); Twitter: @LympheDIVAS

Offers a collection of medically correct fashion choices for women with lymphedema, as well as helpful education and resources on the subject.

NUTRITION RESOURCES AND MANAGEMENT

The Academy of Nutrition and Dietetics: www.eatright.org
(800) 877-1600; Twitter: @EatRight

The Academy is the world's largest organization of food and nutrition professionals and is committed to improving the nation's health and advancing the profession of dietetics through research, education, and advocacy.

CancerNet (National Cancer Institute): www.cancernet.nci.nih.gov

This resource provides nutritional information for people with cancer and for health care professionals, and includes information on assessment, management, and the effects of cancer therapies.

International Food Information Council (IFIC): www.ific.us
(202) 296-6540; Twitter: @FoodInsight, www.foodinsight.org

A nonprofit, nonpartisan organization established to effectively communicate science-based information about food safety and nutrition to health professionals, government officials, educators, journalists, and consumers. The International Food Information Council Foundation's website provides the latest food safety, nutrition, and health information.

USDA Center for Nutrition Policy and Promotion: www.cnpp.usda.gov and www.choosemyplate.gov
(888) 779-7264; Twitter: @MyPlate

Provides information on nutrition policies and guidelines for professional and consumer use and printable materials such as the food guide pyramid and dietary guidelines.

NUTRITION: MEAL SERVICES AND COUNSELING

Meals to Heal: www.meals-to-heal.com
(888) 721-1041; Twitter: @meals2heal

For patients and caregivers with little time or energy to prepare meals, this service will do it for you. Meals-to-Heal provides fresh, nutritious meals customized to a cancer patient's specific needs and delivered right to your door. The website has great information, a helpful blog, and a list of nutrition and resources. Delivery is offered in the continental United States.

Locally there many other meal delivery options that are free or low cost if you need assistance. For information on local programs that may be available in your area, visit:

- CancerCare (www.cancercare.org, (800) 813-HOPE (4673))
- Cancer Support Community (www.cancersupportcommunity.org; Twitter: @cancersupportcommunity)
- Meals on Wheels Association of America (www.mowaa.org/findameal)

Freshview Nutrition LLC (New York, NY): www.freshviewnutrition.com
(888) 939-VIEW

This company provides a wide range of nutrition consulting and services, including one-on-one counseling and educational workshops with experts in oncology nutrition, weight management, diabetes management, and nutrition during pregnancy.

FOOD AND BEVERAGE BOOKS

The Cancer-Fighting Kitchen: Nourishing, Big-Flavor Recipes for Cancer Treatment and Recovery by Rebecca Katz with Mat Edelson (Celestial Arts, 2009). I used this book during and post-treatment.

Preggatinis: Mixology for the Mom-to-Be by Natalie Bovis, "The Liquid Muse," is filled with creative and healthy nonalcoholic cocktails (Globe Pequot Press, 2009).

OTHER NUTRITION RESOURCES

Memorial Sloan-Kettering "About Herbs, Botanicals & Other Products: www.mskcc.org/cancer-care/integrative-medicine/about-herbs-botanicals -other-products

American Cancer Society: www.cancer.org/acs/groups/cid/documents/web content/002577-pdf

American Institute for Cancer Research: www.aicr.org/foods-that-fight -cancer

SKIN CARE/HAIR/BEAUTY CARE

American Academy of Dermatology (AAD): www.aad.org
Twitter: @AADskin

This is a great resource for finding a board-certified dermatologist in your area.

Cosmetic Ingredient Review: www.cosmeticsinfo.org

Cosmetic Ingredient Review is a resource for scientific information on the ingredients most commonly used in cosmetics and personal care products.

Look Good Feel Better (LGFB): www.lookgoodfeelbetter.org
(800) 395 LOOK; Twitter: @LGFB

This is a free nationwide program helping with appearance-related side effects from cancer treatment to help improve patients' self-images.

Lindi Skin: www.lindiskin.com
(800) 380-4704; Twitter: @LINDISKIN

A line of skin care products formulated to help alleviate the side effects of cancer treatment.

Lashes-of-Love: www.lashes-of-love.org
Twitter: @Lashes_of_Love

Lashes-of-Love provides replacement eyelashes, eyebrow restoration, skin care advice, and facial treatment to cancer patients. Check their website for services around the United States.

Tender Loving Care (TLC): www.tlcdirect.org
(800) 850-9445

Tender Loving Care is a nonprofit website and catalog of the American Cancer Society that features wigs, head coverings, mastectomy products, and other apparel and accessories for cancer patients.

Paula Young: www.paulayoung.com
(800) 364-9060; Twitter: @PaulaYoungWigs

Paula Young offers a large selection of wigs and hairpieces online and by catalog.

The Wig Exchange: www.thewigexchange.org
(914) 412-4884; Twitter: @TheWigExchange

Based in Westchester County, New York, The Wig Exchange is a nonprofit organization that provides high quality recycled wigs and practical tips for managing cancer-related hair loss for women undergoing cancer treatment. According to cofounder Sandy Samberg, The Wig Exchange is working on a manual to help similar grassroots initiatives get started around the United States.

REFERENCE BOOKS FOR SKIN/NAIL/DENTAL/HAIR CARE

Dr. Lacouture's Skin Care Guide for People Living with Cancer by Mario E. Lacouture, MD, board-certified dermatologist and Associate Member at Memorial Sloan-Kettering (Harborside Press, 2012).

Beauty Pearls for Chemo Girls by Marybeth Maida and Debbie Kiederer (Citadel Press, 2009)

PROSTHESES, MASTECTOMY FASHION, POSTOPERATIVE APPAREL

Amoena: www.amoena.us
(800) 926-6362; Twitter: @AmoenaUSA

Amoena is a major manufacturer of breast prostheses and mastectomy bras—their website offers a helpful store locator.

BFFL Co Best Friends For Life: www.bfflco.com
(855) BFFL-BAG (233-5224) Twitter: @bfflco

Conceived by radiation oncologist Dr. Elizabeth Chabner Thompson, BFFL Co offers a fashionable and practical line of products for women undergoing mastectomy or radiation, including comfortable bras specifically designed for post-surgery and radiation, the Axilla-Pilla, and the Breast BFFLBag, which is filled with helpful gifts, among other products. The website has a very informative blog.

Underneath It All, New York City: www.underneathitallnyc.com, (212) 779-2517

Run by breast cancer survivors, this elegant atelier on New York's Fifth Avenue supplies a range of breast prostheses, bras, lingerie, headpieces, wigs, and bathing suits dispensed with caring and experienced advice from certified fitters.

Alloro Collection: www.allorocollection.com
Twitter: @recapturejoy

Conceived by breast cancer survivor Laurel Kamen, The Alloro Collection is a line of fashionable apparel specifically designed for women who have experienced breast cancer. The designs address the changes in contour, comfort, and appearance of a woman's body without sacrificing style.

Chikara Design: www.chikaradesign.com

Created by New York fashion designer Hilary Boyajian, Chikara offers a chic line of clothing for women who have had a partial or full mastectomy and incorporates a beautiful mix of symmetry and asymmetry to enhance a woman's new body.

Land's End: www.landsend.com
(800) 963-4816; Twitter: @LandsEnd

This retailer offers a line of mastectomy swimsuits.

Nordstrom: www.shop.nordstrom.com/c/prosthesis-program
(888) 282-6060; Twitter: @Nordstrom

Nordstrom offers an in-store prostheses program with certified fitters and a selection of prostheses, mastectomy bras, and lingerie.

COPING AND COACHING

American Psychological Association (APA): www.apa.org
(800) 374-2721; Twitter: @APA

The APA is the largest scientific and professional organization representing psychology in the United States and a great resource for finding a certified practicing psychologist. The APA Help Center is an online consumer resource with articles and information related to psychological issues and emotional well-being.

The National Association of Professional Cancer Coaches (NAPCC): www. cancerwipeout.org
(855) 560-8344; Twitter: @cancerwipeout

An excellent source for finding professionally trained cancer coaches and cancer recovery workshops.

Moms Facing Cancer: www.momsfacingcancer.com
(970) 420-9300

Kerri J. Geary, MA, CPCC, is a three-time cancer survivor and certified professional cancer coach who helps guide women through the maze of decisions, changes, and emotional upsets brought about by a cancer diagnosis. You can download her free guide, "Facing a Cancer Diagnosis: Kerri's Top Twelve Hard-Earned Transformation Tips" on her website.

Carla Marie Greco, PhD: www.drcarlagreco.com
(707) 236-0012

Dr. Greco is a clinical psychologist based in Northern California and the author of *The Fear Handbook*.

Sexy After Cancer: www.sexyaftercancer.com
Twitter: @sexyaftercancer

Sex educator-counselor and breast cancer survivor Barbara Musser provides counseling, workshops, and retreats to help address and manage the emotional, spiritual, and sexual effects of cancer. Her book is *Sexy After Cancer: Meeting Your Inner Aphrodite on the Breast Cancer Journey*.

ORGANIZERS/TIME SAVERS

Cancer Fairy Godmother: www.cancerfairygodmothmother.com

This resource helps you find local and national resources and support groups in your area.

Ready for Recovery Cancer Planners: www.cancerplanners.com
Twitter: @CancerPlanners

Created by breast cancer survivor Julie Grimm, Ready for Recovery offers cancer planners and organizers for patients and caregivers.

CaringBridge: www.caringbridge.org
(651) 789-2300 (Customer Care); Twitter: @CaringBridge

A free online site where patients and caregivers can post and manage updates and news for their loved ones in a safe, personal space. The CaringBridge SupportPlanner helps families and friends coordinate care and tasks.

The Patient/Partner Project: www.thepatientpartnerproject.org

The Patient/Partner Project is a free service that allows you to post private updates about your treatment and condition on this website, and then notifies everyone on your private list so that they can read them.

Lotsa Helping Hands: www.lotsahelpinghands.com
Twitter: @LotsaHelping

Lotsa Helping Hands is a free online community service that brings caregivers and volunteers together to provide helpful support during times of need.

CREATIVE INSPIRATION

Beating Cancer in Heels
Twitter: @cancerinheels

Diagnosed with breast cancer at age 26 in 2009, fashionista Marlena Ortiz started a nonprofit to empower young women facing a diagnosis with the message, "Kick up your heels and embrace your femininity and personal style."

Cancer Club: www.CancerClub.com
Twitter: @c_clifford

Founded by best-selling author, speaker, and breast cancer survivor Christine Clifford, Cancer Club markets humorous and helpful products for people with cancer, including books and DVDs. Christine's cancer books include *Laugh Til It Heals* and *Not Now . . . I'm Having a No Hair Day*, among others.

The Grace Project: www.thegraceproject.net

Charise Isis is a professional photographer who has created a series of portraits of women of all ages who have experienced mastectomies. The Grace Project celebrates beauty, courage, grace, and positive self-image.

The SCAR Project: www.thescarproject.org
davidjayphotography@yahoo.com

The SCAR project is a series of large-scale portraits of young breast cancer survivors shot by fashion photographer David

SKY and LIVI: www.skyandlivi.com
(800) 809-6882; Twitter: @SKYandLIVI

SKY and LIVI empowers women battling cancer by transforming their hair loss from chemotherapy treatment into their very own personal, lab-grown diamonds set in exclusive jewelry designs.